The Familiar Dark

Also by Montana Carr

Beyond the Scent of Sugar: A Memoir by Billie River

Marti Starova Erotic Thrillers

Drowning in Broad Daylight (Book 1)
Shadow Work (Book 2)
Rain-Soaked (Book 3)
Almost (Book 4)

The Familiar Dark

A Marti Starova Erotic Thriller Book 5

Montana Carr

Northshore Noir Press

This is a work of fiction. All names, characters and incidents are the product of the author's imagination. Any resemblance to real persons, living or dead, is entirely coincidental.

THE FAMILIAR DARK. A Marti Starova Erotic Thriller Book 5. Copyright © 2025 by Montana Carr. All rights reserved.

Northshore Noir Press and the Northshore Noir logo are copyright and used with permission.

Northshore Noir upholds the principles of free expression and recognizes the significance of copyright protection. All rights reserved. No part of this publication may be reproduced, distributed, or transmitted in any form or by any means without the prior written permission of the Publisher, except for brief quotations incorporated into critical articles or reviews. Your adherence to and respect for the author's rights are sincerely appreciated.

Northshore Noir Press
Toronto, Canada
www.northshorenoir.com

ISBN: 978-1-998648-17-7

eBook ISBN: 978-1-998648-18-4

For more information visit: northshorenoir.com

Contents

Chapter 1	1
Chapter 2	14
Chapter 3	25
Chapter 4	32
Chapter 5	44
Chapter 6	54
Chapter 7	64
Chapter 8	74
Chapter 9	86
Chapter 10	96
Chapter 11	111
Chapter 12	122

Chapter 13	128
Chapter 14	138
Chapter 15	151
Chapter 16	157
Chapter 17	167
Chapter 18	173
Chapter 19	179
Chapter 20	185
Chapter 21	194
Chapter 22	200
Chapter 23	211
Chapter 24	219
Chapter 25	227
Chapter 26	234
Chapter 27	245
Chapter 28	254
Chapter 29	262
Chapter 30	271
Chapter 31	282
Chapter 32	294

Chapter 33	306
Chapter 34	312
Chapter 35	320
Chapter 36	330
Chapter 37	343
Chapter 38	355
Chapter 39	366
Chapter 40	374
Chapter 41	381
Chapter 42	391
Chapter 43	397
Chapter 44	405
Chapter 45	411
More Marti Starova	421

Chapter 1

"Who the fuck are you?"

Marti groaned, squinting at the tiny intruder hovering by her bed. Four, maybe five years old. Blond. Freckled. Staring at her like she was some zoo animal that might start throwing shit at any moment. And since she was Marti Starova, she just might.

"I said, who the fuck are you?" She pressed a hand to her temple. The headache pulsed behind her eyes while her shoulder and leg screamed in protest when she tried to sit up. Fantastic. Just fantastic.

"Aiden!" A whisper-shout from across the room. "Aiden! Leave her alone. She's sleeping."

"She's not sleeping," the kid—Aiden—observed blandly. "She's swearing."

Lori snorted, disguising it as a cough while she crossed the room and grabbed the kid by the shoulders. "Aiden, out," she said, steering him toward the door. "Go on, scoot your butt."

Marti flopped onto her back with a groan and stared at Lori through barely cracked eyelids. "Who the fuck was that?"

"Stop swearing." Lori leaned against the doorframe, arms crossed in that way that meant she wasn't actually mad but wouldn't mind making Marti suffer anyway. "That was my nephew. His mom, my sister, got called into work last minute, so I'm stuck with them for the day."

"Them?" Marti repeated, dread pooling in her gut.

Lori's ips curled into the exact smirk Marti knew was coming: the one that meant she'd been waiting for this precise moment of suffering. "Yes, them," she said cheerfully. "Aiden, Douglas, and Franny." She pushed off the doorframe, stepping closer, and pointed toward the hallway with her thumb. "I'm making breakfast if you feel like joining civilization."

"Toast?"

"I didn't say I was making your breakfast." She reached over and tucked a stray piece of hair behind Marti's ear. Too soft, too careful. Then turned and left before Marti could come up with something appropriately shitty to say about it.

Lori Harring was by far the best secretary she'd ever had.

Marti sighed and forced herself upright. "Fuck!" Her leg seized, the muscles contracting around the BioGen scaffold that barely held them together. She hated kids almost as much as hospitals. But not quite. After two weeks rotting away in one of those sterile hellholes, she'd spent every minute since itching to be anywhere else. So here she was, stuck recovering under someone else's roof.

Her fingers found the bottle of Fentafill on the nightstand. One pill down, she grabbed her cane and limped toward the bathroom, each step a reminder of how close she'd come to dying.

Three weeks ago, she'd ended the Andreas Katsaros case. Not that it had done her any favors. Cliff Kogoya had put a blade into Andreas thinking he was taking Marti off the board. Payback for Charlie Gomes murdering his daughter while on the run. Charlie, the same Charlie that Marti took the head for escaping. The same Charlie who'd torn the heart from Cliff's kid. Literally torn it out. Cliff had earned that much mercy when she gave him a choice: feds or a grave. And he'd taken option one. Died in prison anyway.

Ari Stirling hadn't appreciated how things shook out and decided to pay her a visit, with an entire fucking army on his heels neither of them saw coming until it was too late. By the time the dust settled outside her office building? Heather Blair was bleeding out next to her, Ari and most of his men were dead, and Marti... well, Marti got lucky enough to only be mostly fucked up instead of all-the-way dead. At least Lori was spared.

The shower knob creaked as Marti cranked it. Lukewarm water shot from the showerhead as she stepped in, turning the temperature higher until steam filled the bathroom. The post-op manual had warned against hot showers: not good for healing or some shit. But she needed the burn against her skin. Needed to feel something that wasn't dull aching numbness or sharp reminders of bullets that had almost done the job right.

Water cascaded over her shoulder, revealing the smooth SynthoSkin stretched across what remained of her real flesh. She ran her fingers along the seam where artificial met natural, wincing as her shoulder twinged. Her thigh bore similar marks, the muscle held together by another scaffold. Her knee: part titanium, part cobalt-chromium, moved better than before but still protested with each step. And somewhere inside, a lab-grown kidney filtered her blood, a miracle of modern science keeping her pissing.

Water stung her eyes as she reached for the shampoo. Pain or no pain, she had work to do. Getting clean enough to fake being respectable was step one.

The money situation was fucked. Henrick Katsaros had paid her for finding his parents, but she gave the money back after Andreas got murdered. Ari Stirling had hired her to find Andreas's killer, but he died in the same hail of bullets that tore Marti apart. Four hundred crisp from Victim Services covered medical bills but didn't do shit for everything else: rent, Lori's paycheck… drugs.

It didn't help that her temporary secretary stole all her money and fled to China in the hopes of murdering her husband.

Fuck.

At least detoxing in the hospital had lowered her tolerance. Small mercies while she saved up for more Shadow. But it hadn't killed the need entirely. Pauline showing up high as hell hadn't helped either. That crazy bitch had pumped Poison Ivy into Marti's IV twice before Lori caught her red-handed and had her arrested.

"It's like the universe wants me high," Marti muttered around a mouthful of toothpaste before spitting foam into the sink. "I want me high."

Another reason to get out of here soon. Lori could ruin a perfectly good high with one well-timed frown.

She pulled on clean clothes and stepped out of Lori's sister's childhood bedroom. The floral wallpaper made her eyes itch almost as much as the thought of spending time with a bunch of kids. She paused in the hallway, taking in the massive house: three floors with rooms big enough to lose yourself in forever if you weren't careful. This place barely felt like a house at all; more like an entire hotel stretched across too much space. There was even talk of some hidden basement larger than her whole damn apartment back home.

A child's voice carried down the corridor: "Hi! Merry Christmas!"

Marti braced herself before limping into the kitchen. Three small faces turned toward her from the breakfast bar, Lori standing behind them with a spatula in hand, smiling like this wasn't some cruel joke played on hungover people everywhere.

"Merry Christmas," the little girl said, because that was what you were supposed to say in houses like this. The brats burst into laughter immediately. Fucking hyenas in toddler form.

"Merry Christmas tomorrow," Lori corrected with a grin as the kids chattered about Santa and gifts and magic bullshit Marti had never believed in even as a kid.

Marti's lips parted. "You know Santa doesn't—"

"Marti!" Lori's eyes flashed a warning before she could finish ruining their innocence. "What's your problem?"

Marti rolled a kink out of her spine. "What's my problem? I dunno… but I'm guessing it's hard to pronounce." She turned away from their breakfast bar shrine and headed back toward blessed solitude.

The bedroom window stuck before giving way with a hard shove. Cold air rushed in, carrying the scent of freezing rain: Falls City's poor substitute for snow. Marti lit a cigarette from what remained of a crushed pack, inhaling deeply as the first hit of nicotine flooded her system. Bitter cold clawed at her face while smoke curled warm into her lungs. A war between sensations she had no real investment in picking sides over.

The door creaked behind her as she lit a second cigarette.

"Sorry about that," Lori murmured, her voice closer than expected. Then warmth pressed against Marti's back as Lori leaned into her. "The kids love to talk."

Arms slid around Marti's waist. A slow movement meant to be gentle but landing somewhere between comforting and torturous.

Marti stiffened. Harder than any withdrawal she'd faced so far.

"Why are you torturing me?" She exhaled smoke without looking back.

Lori didn't budge an inch. "I've heard so many of your sex stories... Thought you might like it."

Marti swallowed. She liked telling stories. Twisting the passions just enough to keep Lori hanging on her every word. Like the time she'd been close enough to Isabella Katsaros to feel the air shift as the whip cracked against the woman's skin. She had to be sure the birthmark was there, had to confirm it was really Isabella bound and gagged in that chair, since asking wasn't an option.

Lori pulled away first, like always. They never got further than a few brushes of fingers in passing, a touch that lasted too long.

"Come eat," Lori said. "The toaster's waiting."

Marti exhaled slowly, blinking hard to clear her head. "Yeah, in a second." Maybe if she stood still long enough, the heat between her legs would go away. Probably not. Lori was making it her full-time job to drive Marti insane. Lingering too close, dropping hints, trying to convince Marti they should date.

No fucking way was Marti dating her secretary, no matter how good she looked doing shit like this.

Lori paused in the doorway. "Are you allergic to anything?"

"No."

"Eggcellent! I'm eggcited!"

Marti dragged a hand down her face. "How old are you?"

Lori's grin flashed before she disappeared into the kitchen. Marti stubbed out her cigarette and followed, cane tapping against hardwood then carpet then tile.

The scent of browning butter filled the kitchen. Marti leaned against the counter as Lori worked, butter melting into two slices of bread, each with a hole cut from the center. The bread sizzled when it hit the hot pan, and Marti's stomach tightened with hunger.

"What's your name?"

A small voice from her elbow. Marti turned slowly to find a kid staring up at her, all big eyes and boundless energy.

"Marti."

"I'm Franny! I'm five."

I don't care, Marti thought.

"Auntie Hay-Hay says you used to be a cop," another kid piped up from somewhere behind them.

Jesus Christ.

"Yeah."

"Marti was in Homicide," Lori added as she flipped one of the toast slices over. "Like Grandpa. My dad works Homicide too."

The little boy—Daniel? Douglas?—stood on his toes to see better. "In Georgetown! Twenty-eleven years on the force."

The toast hit the stove again as Lori cracked eggs into both holes.

"Slow department," she continued while sprinkling salt and pepper without looking up. "Couple murders a month, nothing crazy."

"Huh," Marti said because something seemed expected of her.

"Bacon?"

"Yep."

"BACON!" Douglas-or-whatever shouted like he'd been personally blessed by God himself.

Lori pointed toward the basement door. "Go watch Blippy and Bloopy, please."

The kids took off running, and seconds later an explosion of cartoons rattled through the floorboards.

Marti's shoulders dropped. "Your sister's kids, you said?"

"Yep. Bobbie's kids," Lori said as she laid strips of bacon onto a paper towel. "Love 'em."

Lori plated everything carefully before setting it in front of Marti, knife and fork placed neatly beside her hand like they were at some fancy brunch instead of sitting in a family kitchen at seven in the goddamn morning.

Marti ripped off a chunk of toast with her fingers and dunked it straight into the yolk.

"This is sweet," she muttered around a mouthful before taking another bite.

Lori sat beside her with her own plate, nudging paprika across an egg with the edge of her fork.

"My dad had a good solve rate," she said after a moment. "Still had one case that haunted him though."

Marti kept chewing but didn't answer right away. There was always one case for a homicide detective. Always one that ate your soul.

She picked up her fork and finished one egg before speaking again: "Christmas shot?"

"It's not Christmas," Lori deadpanned.

"Fine. But since I didn't pull my gun on that kid today," Marti said, "I think that calls for a reward."

Lori's eyes narrowed over a bite of toast. "You didn't—"

"Of course not," Marti scoffed mid-chew, gesturing with what remained of a bacon strip. "Too loud anyway. And those little fuckers are fast."

"Amazing," Lori muttered as she gathered their plates and carried them toward the sink.

"I'm serious," Marti called after her, leaning back in her chair. "A drink would be nice."

"You just joked about shooting children." The cupboard door opened with a flick of Lori's wrist as she grabbed a bottle down anyway.

"I joke about all kinds of shit," Marti replied.

"You're sick."

"Yep," Marti agreed without argument as Lori set down a glass between them and poured amber liquid into it.

"My dad likes whiskey too," Lori said after taking a sip from Marti's glass instead of handing it over. "Smokes too. God, that's disgusting."

"You trying to set me up with your father?"

"No."

"You're staring like you have something extra dumb planned this time." Marti gingerly took the shot from between Lori's fingers.

"I think you'd like him," Lori admitted after a pause, a rare hesitation creeping into words that usually flowed so freely.

"Doubt it." Marti knocked back half the whiskey but didn't protest when Lori refilled it seconds later.

"You like me though," Lori pointed out with an infuriating little smile.

Marti let herself look this time, really look: took in where soft fabric clung to warm curves; traced lines from collarbones down bare shoulders before forcing herself back up toward bright eyes waiting patiently.

"I like you," she admitted eventually. "But not most people. People are terrible."

"You think you're terrible," Lori challenged, not letting it slide.

Marti cleared her throat against the tightness building there. "...You never told me your dad was Homicide."

Lori tilted her head, warmth lingering behind quiet amusement. "He's why I became an engineer."

Chapter 2

Marti slouched into the couch, lighting another cigarette with hands that still trembled from their earlier conversation. Her lungs filled with smoke, a shield against whatever was happening between them. Talking about feelings was bad enough. Now fathers? Christ. At least it was safer territory than admitting she wanted to kiss that knowing look off Lori's face. Bad idea. Disaster waiting to happen.

"My dad drank," Lori said, her earlier warmth hardening as she stared at the TV screen like it might offer escape. "Drinking doesn't make you a bad person. But when he drank..."

Marti exhaled a cloud and waited, smoke curling between them.

Lori's fingers worked at a spot on her jeans, scrubbing invisible stains. "He got angry. Used to throw things. Vases, plates, whatever was in reach."

The image flashed vivid in Marti's mind: porcelain shattering against drywall, the sharp intake of breath before the next explosion. Different ghosts had haunted her childhood, but she recognized the familiar specters in Lori's eyes.

"He thought I should be a cop," Lori continued, voice tight. "Follow in his footsteps." A bitter sound escaped her. "Who wants a job that makes you bitter and hateful?"

"Not you," Marti offered, cigarette dangling from her lips as she grinned.

Lori's mouth twitched but didn't commit. "I used to think he was the most messed-up person ever." Her gaze slid sideways, landing on Marti with something unreadable in its depths. "At least, until I started working with you."

Marti arched an eyebrow. "Oh yeah?"

"Yeah." Lori sighed, stretching her legs until her knee bumped against Marti's. Casual, unthinking, maddening. "You're so fucked up, you make my dad look normal." Her tone danced on the edge of teasing, but something darker lurked beneath the surface.

"I set high standards for dysfunction." Marti flicked ash, watched it scatter.

Lori's hand darted across her face, quick and furtive, but not quick enough to hide what Marti glimpsed there.

"You know what always helps a shitty day get better?" Marti stubbed out her cigarette, lunging for the remote. "A movie."

"You don't watch movies." Lori's brows knitted together.

"Sure I do," Marti lied with ease. "I've heard they're cathartic or some bullshit like that."

Skepticism radiated from Lori, but she snatched the remote from Marti instead of calling her bluff. Not worth fighting over something this trivial, not when everything else between them was built on battlefields.

"My choice?" Lori's finger hovered over the buttons.

"Unless you want porn," Marti shot back, reflexive.

"My choice," Lori repeated, cutting her off before that particular suggestion could take root.

The screen flickered to life with some drama about widows and daughters and terminal illnesses. Marti checked out after the first five minutes of dialogue-heavy suffering masquerading as art. Sunlight tapped against the window, slipping through a crack to mingle with the stale popcorn smell. The room felt comfortable in ways Marti wasn't equipped to handle without eventually destroying.

An hour passed before a muffled sound pulled Marti back to awareness. She turned to find Lori crying silently beside her, tears tracking silver paths down her cheeks.

"What the hell are we watching?" Marti muttered, snatching a tissue from the box and thrusting it toward Lori without ceremony.

Lori took it wordlessly, tears continuing to fall as though some internal dam had cracked open, refusing to be patched.

When the credits finally rolled, silence filled the space between them, broken only by the static hum of the television. Marti blinked, startled to find her own face damp.

She scowled, scrubbing roughly at her cheek with her sleeve. If she refused to acknowledge it, maybe it hadn't happened at all.

Beside her, Lori's shoulders trembled beneath a weight neither of them would name.

Marti's arm moved before her brain could veto the motion, wrapping around those shaking shoulders. Lori melted against her side, warm and solid and breaking.

They sat frozen as morning light crept through the blinds, painting stripes across the floor.

Neither moved first. Neither spoke. Maybe this was catharsis after all. Or maybe catharsis was just another word for getting sucker-punched by emotions you weren't ready for.

Either way: fuck movies. Never again.

Lori grabbed another tissue. Then another. By the fourth, Marti sighed and rubbed circles against her back, some half-remembered cooing noise escaping her throat. It didn't help.

Merry fucking Christmas to me.

"Alright," Marti shifted, muscles stiff from holding still too long. "Do you want me to hold you, hear you, or help you?" She'd learned this years ago through trial and error. There were only four ways to handle someone falling apart: hold, hear, help, or get the fuck out. The last option was her specialty, but with Lori already nestled against her, that ship had sailed.

Lori's breath hitched against Marti's ribs. "I don't... I don't know where this is coming from." Fresh tears soaked through the thin fabric of Marti's shirt.

Marti tightened her grip and continued what seemed to be working: holding. Her fingers traced patterns through Lori's hair, across her cheek, down her arm in slow, steady strokes until the sobs quieted to hiccups. Lori drew in a deep breath, released it slower. The storm had passed.

Marti turned back toward the television, grateful for the distraction.

The screen flashed with an AI-generated advertisement. Colors too bright, voices pitched just wrong enough to crawl under the skin. Georgetown's latest middle-class security fantasy filled the screen: a massive black truck prowling neon-lit streets while digitally enhanced families smiled from behind reinforced glass.

"Three rows of seating! Projectile-proof glass to keep your family safe!" A metal cage enclosed the truck bed like something designed for transporting dangerous animals. "Keep your belongings safe!" The crowning feature: a gleaming bullbar built for plowing through anything, or anyone, that got in its way. "Keep yourself safe!"

Georgetown's sanitized version of Falls City might swallow that fantasy whole, but the real Falls City would strip that truck to its frame before the financing paperwork cleared. Gang-owned chop shops operated with brutal efficiency.

Thundering footsteps overhead shattered the moment. Children stampeding across floorboards, shrieking and tumbling with the coordination of baby elephants on a tightrope. Whatever had been happening between them evaporated like smoke.

Lori peeled herself away, face still blotchy but smiling as she headed upstairs to corral the chaos into something resembling order. Minutes later, Christmas music blasted through the house. Too loud, too cheerful. Lori twirled between strands of tinsel like someone who'd escaped from a holiday greeting card. Children's laughter echoed off the walls as Marti sank deeper into the couch cushions, mimicking a possum's death response in hopes the festivities might pass her by.

They didn't.

"Come on," Lori called, voice lilting as she draped another string of lights around an already drowning tree. "Join us!"

Marti's eyes drifted toward the door. Outside meant cigarettes and silence, or at least fewer decibels per square foot, but the effort of moving through cold outweighed the potential rewards. She stayed put, thumb scrolling mindlessly through her phone while her eyes rolled at the forced merriment surrounding her.

Twenty minutes later, when lunch appeared, Marti finally enacted her escape plan. Even that simple meal dissolved into more chatter, more laughter, more of everything that made her skin itch. Her fingers picked at her sandwich crust while her gaze kept returning to the whiskey bottle on the counter: amber salvation in glass.

Her throat burned with anticipation; she licked her lips as her hand reached forward...

"No."

Marti's head snapped toward the voice. Aiden, the oldest kid, watching her with disapproval etched across his face. Her lips pulled back in something caught between a grin and a snarl. "I wasn't fucking asking." The bottle clinked against the counter as she poured a double, making a point that didn't matter.

Lori shot her a look that could have stripped paint, but redirected before launching into a lecture. Apparently, it was time for games or gingerbread houses or whatever holiday ritual came next on her Christmas checklist.

"I'll think about it," Marti lied, already plotting her escape.

Minutes later she stood on the porch, whiskey warming her belly, cigarette burning between her fingers as rain misted around her. The nicotine did nothing to clear her thoughts.

Through the window, Lori laughed with the children, fitting into their storybook world like she belonged there.

Marti planted her feet on the wet boards, watching. Pretending it didn't bother her. Pretending it wasn't nice. Pretending anything at all.

None of it worked.

"Let's go to the park," Lori announced after the games ended. The children scrambled for coats and boots, a tangle of limbs and excitement.

Marti leaned back, muscles loosening at the prospect of solitude. Finally, peace and—

"No playing with yourself while we're gone." Lori's breath tickled her ear, warm and close.

Marti's lips curled. "Me? Never dream of it. But why not?"

"Because Bobbie might walk in, and I do not want that conversation."

"Is she hot?"

Lori groaned. "God, you're impossible. Just keep it clean. Please." The look she gave Marti could have melted steel before she herded the children toward the door.

Marti kept it clean. If whiskey and cigarettes counted as clean. A few shots, a few smokes, then she surrendered to unconsciousness on the couch. The sooner this holiday nightmare ended, the better.

Dinner arrived with all the subtlety of a Broadway production: gleaming table, perfect turkey, mashed potatoes swimming in butter, cranberry sauce that still held the shape of the can. Bobbie appeared. The children vibrated with excitement. Lori glowed with joy like she'd swallowed

Christmas lights. Marti shoveled food into her mouth and calculated how many hours remained until freedom.

After dinner, Lori, Bobbie, and the kids clustered around the tree, tying ribbons and wrapping last-minute gifts that would be shredded within hours. Lori's laugh floated above the chaos. Soft, contented. And something about it crawled under Marti's skin. She mumbled an excuse and slipped onto the back porch, seeking refuge in nicotine and darkness.

Cold air slapped her face: a welcome relief after the cloying warmth inside. She inhaled deeply, letting smoke scorch her lungs like an antidote to all that happiness. Her chest tightened, but she ignored the urge to reach for her inhaler. The last thing she needed was to give Lori another reason to lecture her tonight.

When she finally returned inside, Bobbie and the children had vanished. She had vague memories of nodding goodbye as they filed past her. Lori hummed a Christmas melody while elbow-deep in soapy water, looking disgustingly content with her domestic scene. With the house finally quiet, Marti collapsed onto the couch and released the breath she'd been holding all evening.

Minutes later, fabric rustled behind her. A whisper of sound followed by warmth settling across her shoulders: a blanket, draped gently by hands that lingered a heartbeat too long.

The couch dipped as Lori settled beside her, lips curved in a smile that suggested secrets. "Hey."

"Hey."

"You've been a real Grinch today."

Marti drew on her cigarette, exhaling slowly as if smoke could smother whatever unfamiliar feeling crept at the edges of her consciousness. "Christmas isn't really my thing."

"I know," Lori said, voice dropping to something intimate. "But you being here? Means a lot."

Silence stretched between them. Not uncomfortable, not awkward, just present, expanding until Marti became acutely aware of Lori's knee barely touching hers, of snow falling soundlessly beyond the window while inside, everything held perfectly still.

Marti risked a single glance just long enough to catch something warm flickering in Lori's eyes before looking away, unwilling to examine what it might mean.

She crushed out her cigarette and mumbled about being tired. The warmth of Lori's presence followed her down the hallway like a persistent ghost. She needed distance. Needed something else to focus on besides the way Lori had looked at her, besides how easy it would be to just…

Chapter 3

Marti dragged herself into the bedroom, exhaustion weighing heavy on her shoulders. She kicked off her jeans and slid between the cool sheets with a sigh. Her mind drifted to Ha-Yoon handing her those delicate, dirty panties at the hospital. On nights like this, their soft fabric against Marti's skin became a cruel surrogate for the touch she craved but couldn't have.

She traced Ha-Yoon's underwear over her nipples, which hardened beneath the fabric. In her mind, a woman (Linda, as serviceable a name as any) materialized above her. Faceless at first, then dissolving into nothing but hungry lips and a probing tongue. Marti squeezed her own breast, and in her fantasy, Linda sucked and pulled in response.

Marti's tongue darted out, tasting the phantom heat of Linda's mouth. The imaginary kisses trailed down her neck as sheets rustled beneath her restless body. She thought of that woman who used a microphone when she fucked, capturing every wet sound. Her own fingers slipped between her lips as Linda circled her nipples with that hot mouth.

A tremor ran through Marti's muscles at the memory of hands stroking inside her. Her fingertips journeyed down until they found the moist heat between her thighs. In her mind, Linda's velvet tongue licked there while Marti stroked herself. She pressed Ha-Yoon's panties to her face and inhaled, eyes fluttering closed.

She spread her legs, waiting with anticipation for Linda's expert touch, surrendering to the vivid fantasy unfolding behind her closed eyelids. Her fingers curled against secret spots until, drunk on pleasure, she begged the empty room for more.

The pressure coiled tighter in her core as she pushed deeper into her fluttering depths. Hungry for release, she rolled her hips to meet each flick of her own fingers.

That's it baby, Linda purred in her mind, as Marti rubbed circles over her clit with a slick thumb. Take it all.

Those imagined words sparked an inferno. Marti came hard enough to see stars, her back arching off the bed as aftershocks shuddered through her trembling limbs.

"God, I'm good," Marti said, rolling onto her stomach to hide the blush scorching her face. The sheets stuck to her sweat-slicked skin.

"That was...fuck..." she breathed out. "I'm doing that again."

An hour later, she peeled herself from the bed and hobbled to the bathroom, thighs still quivering.

The bathroom's orderliness mocked her disheveled state: face cloths stacked, towels hanging just so, hair products lined up like soldiers. She scrubbed her hands, then wiped herself down, wincing at the lingering sensitivity.

On her way out, she grabbed a dry towel and stuffed Ha-Yoon's panties back into the pocket of her coat hanging on the chair. She tossed the towel over the damp spot on the sheets before crawling under the covers on the other side, not done yet but wanting to avoid more wet spots.

Her shoulder throbbed in protest, her thigh joining the chorus of pain. Not from pleasure this time, but reminders of her fucking luck. She rolled onto her back, waiting for her muscles to release their grip. Grabbing a pillow, she shoved it under her left hip for cushioning. As her fingers dragged through tangled hair, exhaustion replaced arousal, settling over her like a weighted blanket.

Marti woke with restlessness clawing at her ribs. She stumbled to the window for a cigarette, then padded toward the kitchen, craving leftover turkey. Barefoot, she winced as her soles met cool wooden floors. The house stood quiet except for the refrigerator's low hum and old pipes groaning in their sleep. The stovetop light cast just enough glow to navigate the shadows.

But her night wasn't as empty as she'd hoped.

Lori was there, curled into one of the kitchen chairs, fingers wrapped around a steaming mug. The air hung thick with chamomile and honey, warm and cloying.

Marti hesitated, one foot poised to retreat. Too late.

Lori glanced up, hair mussed and sleep-dazed but still falling in those soft waves that made Marti's jaw clench.

"Thought I heard you," Lori murmured, voice rough with leftover dreams. "You stalking the halls like some insomniac ghost?"

Marti ignored the question, heading to the sink. The tap squeaked as she filled a glass with water. The first sip chilled its way down her throat, washing away the lingering taste of sleep.

"Depends," she said, leaning against the counter. "You?"

Lori shrugged, her mug meeting the table with a quiet clink. "If something needs handling."

Marti cocked an eyebrow. "Handling?"

A smirk tugged at Lori's lips. "Like now. I'm handling my inability to sleep with tea and self-reflection."

Marti took another sip, unimpressed. "Self-reflection? Christ. Must be dire."

Lori exhaled and stretched back in her chair. The worn fabric of her sleep shorts shifted up just enough to expose the curve of one thigh. Marti's gaze flicked down, then away.

"When I was saying goodbye to Bobbie and the kids earlier," Lori said, dragging her fingertip around the rim of her mug, "I saw a neighbor sneak an entire bag of trash into someone else's bin just to dodge pickup fees." Disgust curled underneath her flattened tone. "I went to pull it out and dump it back on their yard, but Bobbie stopped me. Said it wasn't our problem."

Marti rolled her glass between her palms, a smirk creeping in. "So now we're losing sleep over garbage justice?"

Lori rolled her eyes, tucking a loose strand of hair behind her ear. "It's not about the trash." She shook her head. "It made me think how much Bobbie's like you. If something's not your problem, you let it slide."

Marti set her glass down with a sharp click. "That's called picking your battles."

"Or avoiding them," Lori countered, tilting her head.

Marti snuffled. The kitchen smelled of old wood and dish soap, undercut by the lingering sweetness of Lori's tea. Outside, branches scraped against the window as the wind picked up, scratching like fingernails.

"If people want to screw themselves over, that's their business," Marti said.

Lori didn't blink. "Yeah? And what if someone makes a mistake that will cost them? What if you see it coming and don't stop them?"

Marti held her gaze, feeling the space between them tighten with quiet tension. "If it's my place, I'll try. Otherwise, they have to live or die with it. You've seen that in action."

Something flickered across Lori's face. Annoyance? Amusement? Both, probably. She lifted her mug, took a slow sip, let the moment stretch before swallowing. A slight smirk touched her lips.

"I hope you never have to find out what that feels like," she murmured.

Marti didn't answer. Didn't move. The wind slammed against the window, rattling the frame like it wanted in. The pipes groaned in protest somewhere deep in the walls.

Lori drained the rest of her tea and set the mug down with a quiet clink before standing. Her chair scraped against the floor. "Try to sleep, Marti," she said, voice softer now, no edge left to cut on.

Marti watched her go, barefoot steps soundless against the floorboards. When she was gone, Marti stayed put, staring at nothing, the taste of cold water still on her tongue and something heavier, something unnamed, settling in her chest.

Chapter 4

The morning light assaulted Marti through half-closed blinds, too bright and ordinary for the weight still sitting in her chest. Lori's words from last night echoed as she forced herself up, body protesting every movement. The window had stopped its rattling, but the memory of that howling wind lingered, matching the storm still churning in her gut.

"Marti? Breakfast."

She grunted, stretched, and groaned deep in her throat as reality dragged her back under its boot. The ceiling swam above her before she shoved herself upright. Every muscle screamed their disapproval. Fuck, her body was a graveyard. Metal shards nestled in her flesh like buried bones, aching with each step toward the bathroom.

The mirror didn't pull punches. Jagged scars mapped the wreckage of her face while waves framed sharp, predatory eyes. Feral. And yeah, she liked it that way.

Still, maybe it was time for a cut. Something half-respectable, not that she gave a shit what respectable people thought. Would Athena be working today? She smirked at the thought of a 'special' appointment.

Cold water shocked her face as she splashed it on. She ripped a brush through her hair: good enough. Then she pulled up Athena's Palace on her phone. The ringing registered over the ghosts rattling around in her head. A parade of hospital visitors flashed by: Athena looking almost ordinary next to Mure; Ha-Yoon dropping flowers and that pair of underwear; Lia's clockwork visits. Others had come too: fast fucks and fellow addicts, cops who owed her or wanted something in return. But they rarely mixed.

Athena's voicemail cut through: closed for the holidays. The screen went dark before she could decide if she was disappointed or relieved. Didn't matter now. The smell wafting up from downstairs made all other decisions for her.

She followed it down to the kitchen, rubbing sleep from her eyes as she slumped into a chair. "Merry Christmas. Smells good."

Lori's fingers brushed her shoulder on the way past, lingering just a second too long before sliding a plate in front of her. Fruit, yogurt, home fries. All arranged as if this wasn't wasted effort on someone who just wanted toast. "Merry Christmas."

Marti stabbed at something pale and took a bite. "Apple," she identified through the chew. "Thanks. Looks delicious." She glanced around the kitchen. "Your kids around?"

"They're Bobbie's," Lori corrected, the words automatic as she settled with her own plate.

"Uh-huh." Marti popped another bite into her mouth, watching Lori's face. "Where are they?"

"Home with Bobbie opening presents." Something warm flickered across Lori's face before she smothered it with coffee. "They'll be back later today." Her eyes found Marti's over the rim of her mug. "You going home? You could stick around, watch 'em open what's left."

"Home," Marti confirmed, leaning back with a sigh that pulled from somewhere deeper than her lungs. "It's been a while." She stared at the ceiling, picturing her apartment. "Food left out. Might be a moldy, putrefying nightmare."

Lori's expression hovered between fond and horrified. "That's disgusting."

"You offering to help?"

"No."

Marti smirked around another bite but set down her fork after swallowing. Three pieces of fruit and half a dozen home fries were effort enough when all she wanted was burned bread and butter grease clogging her arteries like nature intended.

Lori's mug hit the table with a sharp click. "Have you been paying attention to what's going on in Falls City for the last little while?" Her voice strained for casual and missed by miles.

Marti ran her tongue over her teeth, tasting the sweetness of fruit against the bitterness of morning breath. "Since I got shot? I hear things."

Three weeks of mayhem boiled the city into a horror show. People weren't just disappearing; they were getting taken right off the streets in broad daylight. A woman snatched from outside a grocery store, the receipt in the bag the only way to identify her. A man who stepped outside for air and never made it back in. Another lifted from his own stoop, nothing left but a cigarette.

Parents now moved through the city hollow-eyed, those who lost children, even grown ones, wretched in their grief.

Marti's fingers drummed against smooth wood as she watched Lori's face. Falls City had folded fast, dragged under by its own paranoia after a couple high-profile murders. Drug barons shot down in the street. Mayor Seibert bleeding out on the courthouse steps. Nobody felt safe anymore: crooks, politicians, moms grabbing diapers at midnight. All targets now.

The trouble was, nobody knew who was pulling the trigger.

"Been keeping up?" Marti asked, reaching for her cigarettes.

Lori scraped eggs into the trash, her movements precise. "Yeah. Ari's murder kicked off a turf war. At least, that's what it looks like." The water ran as she rinsed plates, her voice flat against the background noise. "Fifty-six deaths in three weeks. Three Federal agencies in town."

Marti lit her cigarette, the ritual steadying her hands. "That include FUCT?" Her lips twisted around the ridiculous acronym. Federal Unified Crime Taskforce. One of the few things about this mess that amused her.

"Yep." Lori's mouth tightened, an eye-roll. "And word on the street is, Falls City PD and some of your Feds are involved."

Smoke curled from Marti's nostrils as she snorted. "Yeah? My Feds? And where'd you get this 'word on the street'?"

Lori glanced over her shoulder, shoulders stiffening. "I have sources."

Marti raised an eyebrow and waited.

"Rat stopped by the office looking for you," Lori admitted with a sigh.

Laughter burst from Marti's chest. "Oh yeah, real credible witness."

"He knows things," Lori insisted, crossing her arms.

"He 'knows' that cops are dirty?" Marti took another drag, letting smoke curl from her lips like punctuation. "Big shocker there."

"You need to be careful going home," Lori said, her voice softening. "More than usual."

Careful? In Blightwood? Where half the neighborhood had been carrying since they could afford their first piece? Where dealers and addicts made up most of the population? Marti exhaled, letting the silence answer for her.

"I'll be fine," she said. "Ari was the target that night, not me." She tapped ash from her cigarette before lighting another one just because she could. "For once."

Lori stood by the sink, running a towel over her hands. Her hesitation filled the room like smoke, too careful with her words before she even spoke them.

"Before you go," she said, "can we talk? About last night?"

Ah, fuck's sake. Marti took another draw and lifted an eyebrow, granting permission.

Lori crossed the kitchen, her loose robe dipping off one shoulder as she moved. "I was touched," she said, slipping arms around Marti's waist. Her lips pressed against Marti's forehead, warm and dangerous in their gentleness. "You've been here a week. I've gotten to know you."

"Nah," Marti muttered, heat rising where it shouldn't. She dropped her cigarette into what used to be oatmeal but was now an ashtray by default. "You think you know me." Her eyes betrayed her, dipping to the exposed skin at Lori's collarbone before forcing themselves back up. "I'm not nice."

Lori pulled back just enough to meet her gaze but kept her hands where they were. A mistake neither seemed willing to correct. "You're sweet."

A scoff escaped Marti's throat as she shook her head, dislodging Lori's hands before stepping back. "I'm a self-centered addict with impulse control issues and a gun." The words formed a barrier between them, a warning sign Lori seemed determined to ignore.

But Lori just watched her. "Sweet," she repeated.

Marti sighed hard enough to disturb the remnants of breakfast.

This was going to be a problem. Not in the fun way.

Lori laughed and pulled Marti into her chest, arms tight around her as if she was trying to squeeze something real out of the moment. Marti let herself sink into the warmth, just for a second, before reality crawled back in.

"Oh, shush. I like you, Marti. I like you."

Marti exhaled smoke over Lori's shoulder, the burn in her lungs easier to focus on than the warmth in her chest. "I—"

"I think we get along well," Lori said, voice steady. "I'd like to keep this going."

"This?" Marti pulled back just enough to see Lori's face. "Living together?" The words tasted wrong in her mouth, foreign and impossible. Martina Starova didn't settle down.

"No, sorry." Lori shook her head. "I meant us. Dating. Being a thing."

Marti's fingers itched for another cigarette, something to occupy her mouth besides words she shouldn't say. "I'm not the kind of person who settles down." Settling down ruined lives: hers and other people's.

Lori snorted. "Oh, I know that. Fish will climb trees before you even think about it." Her voice softened. "But we could date? See where it goes? Just casual."

Marti clicked her tongue and stepped away from Lori's heat. "Oh no," she said, shaking her head. "I'm not monogamous. You get that, right? I've got a sex drive like a freight train."

Lori leaned against the table, amusement playing at her lips. "Yeah, I know," she said dryly. "You're sleeping in Bobbie's room, right next to mine. I hear you every night."

"You're welcome," Marti shot back before she could think better of it.

"I'm not asking for monogamy," Lori said. Her voice remained steady, but vulnerability lurked beneath it, making Marti want to look away. "Just... dating. Because you make me feel good."

Marti had been hoping for sex since she first laid eyes on Lori: since the first eye roll, the first insult thrown across the office. But this wasn't just sex anymore. Her gaze fixed on Lori's lips, parted as if waiting for something; pleasure waiting there if she just took it.

So she did.

She kissed Lori hard. Pressed in close and swallowed that gasp against her mouth, hands gripping hips as if she could pin down whatever this thing between them was supposed to be. Lori's breath quickened against her cheek, fingers curling into Marti's shirt as if they could hold her here forever if they tried hard enough.

Marti broke away first, smirking to cover the tightness in her chest, and wiped the taste of lipstick from her mouth with the back of her hand.

"What now?" Lori asked, eyes half-lidded.

Marti swallowed something jagged and forced out a grin that didn't reach her eyes. "What happens now is: I go clean my apartment." She grabbed her jacket off the chair and slung it over one shoulder, a casual gesture that took more effort than it should have. "Make it nice enough for you to come over sometime."

Lori raised an eyebrow, a challenge lurking beneath her amusement. "Well, aren't you practical?"

Practical wasn't right, but Marti let it slide. Explaining would mean saying things better left unsaid. Things like I don't ruin good things on purpose; I just can't help myself. Instead, she kissed Lori once more, quick and biting, and walked out before staying could become an option.

Outside, her fingers found cold metal in her pocket. The Shadow inhaler hissed as she brought it to her lips: one short hit to take off the edge without sinking too deep. By the time she reached her car, she was chilled to the bone.

Marti sat back, eyes half-lidded, waiting for the hit to wash over her.

Nothing.

The familiar warmth, that soft slide into oblivion. Gone. A faint buzzing, some dry mouth, but no release. No weight lifted. No edges blurred.

She stared at the inhaler, then at the roof, then at her vintage watch. The second hand made its lazy rotations on her wrist, counting out seconds that stretched like hours.

"You son of a bitch," she muttered to the drug itself. "We had a deal."

The resentment gnawed at her ribs. The one thing that had always come through for her, now just another liar in a long list of liars. She wanted to throw the damn thing out the window but didn't. That would be giving it too much dignity.

Her fingers found the cigarette pack without looking. The smoke scratched her throat, harsh and reliable. At least that still worked. At least something did.

She took the scenic route home, avoiding the new 15-lane highway where traffic was a nightmare run by lunatics who couldn't read giant red Xs over reversing lanes. Every day someone fucked up; every day someone died playing chicken with angry commuters.

No one took this road anymore. The old cracked highway lined with century homes and farmland still holding onto its last breath before sprawl swallowed everything whole. But Marti preferred it: quiet and forgotten.

She crossed Three Falls Bridge where tourists in bright plastic ponchos snapped pictures of rain-drenched waterfalls, oblivious to the fact they stood above one of Falls City's best body dumpsites.

Falls City, ugly and unrelenting, was still home.

And home had never felt more dangerous than right now.

Chapter 5

Marti stared up at the three flights of stairs, raindrops sliding down her leather collar and seeping cold against her neck. After weeks in Lori's spotless suburban sanctuary (where danger meant choosing the wrong throw pillow) this felt like being shoved face-first back into reality.

Three fucking flights.

Each one mocked her with memories of why she'd stayed away, why Lori's soft, carpeted staircases had felt like such a goddamn refuge. Two choices lay before her: climb, or abandon everything and vanish to another city, maybe another country altogether.

The thought of leaving behind her curated collection of sex toys made the decision for her. Some things were worth fighting for.

The stench hit her halfway up the second flight: a wall of rot that grew thicker with each step. By the time she reached her door, she was breathing through her mouth, gagging as she wrestled with her keys. She yanked her t-shirt over her nose as a makeshift gas mask and shouldered the door open.

One step inside and she froze. The apartment reeked with a presence almost physical. Brown-tinged misery hanging in stagnant waves, coating her tongue and crawling down her throat.

"Jesus Christ," she muttered, kicking the windows open with more force than necessary. Cold air rushed in, cutting channels through the miasma.

She grabbed a trash bag and attacked the evidence of her neglect. Moldy bread disintegrated between her fingers. Coffee cups harbored ecosystems of slime. An overflowing ashtray (its only crime being proximity to the disaster zone) went straight into the bag. The fridge surrendered its contents without a fight: milk that had evolved into cheese, leftovers now unidentifiable, something green that might once have been edible. When only a jar of pickles and an unopened bottle of vinegar remained, she hesitated, then tossed them too. No memory of buying either; no point in keeping them now.

An hour later, sweat beading on her forehead, she surveyed her work. Still a shithole, but at least she could breathe without gagging.

Ravencrook Street wasn't glamorous living. More like choosing to exist inside someone else's nightmare. But it came with perks. Cheap rent. Anonymity. A bodega three blocks down where Carlos would sell you cigarettes, whiskey, and information, all without a flicker of judgment crossing his face.

She peeled off her damp clothes and found something clean in the back of her closet. Her fingers brushed against the cubby behind her bed, and cold metal sent a jolt through her system; not from craving but from something heavier, closer to dread. Ten inhalers lay lined up, her emergency stash bought just before everything went sideways. The touch of them loosened something in her chest.

Just in case, she told herself as she slid one into her sock. Like carrying a spare knife or an extra clip. Not because you want to use it, but because some part of you knows you might need it.

The gun went into her jacket pocket, its weight familiar and reassuring.

Night had transformed Falls City into something recognizable. Not asleep but sedated under neon haze and flickering streetlamps. Junkies drifted along cracked sidewalks, some lost in chemical euphoria, others hunting with hollow-eyed desperation.

Marti drove past them without slowing, the streets growing darker and emptier as she approached Carlos's bodega. She killed the engine, noting the silence. Not peaceful, but the tense quiet of trouble crouching behind drawn blinds. A dried pool of blood stained the pavement two doors down, its edges flaking in the night breeze.

She reached for the door. Locked. Carlos looked up from inside, waved, and hit a button. The lock buzzed open.

"Carlos, what's with the mag lock?" Marti stepped inside, the familiar smell of cigarettes and cheap alcohol a strange comfort.

"Miss Innocent Bystander!" He gave her a once-over, eyes lingering on the cane. "Saw you on the news. You alive under all that damage?"

"Barely." She leaned against the counter. "Wrong place, wrong time."

"What do you need?"

"A bottle and a carton of smokes." She gestured at the door. "And an explanation. What's happening out there?"

Carlos reached under the counter, pulling out his worst whiskey (stuff that could strip paint and kill brain cells in equal measure) and set it beside a carton of cigarettes.

"It's war now," he said, voice dropping. "Your shooting kicked it off. That guy who died? Ariel something? Chain reaction." His fingers drummed on the counter. "On this block, three bodies since then. Drugs got expensive, money ran out, people got desperate." He tapped a security monitor. "Got robbed four times in two weeks before I installed these. Cameras too."

His laugh held nothing resembling humor. "Falls City's a real warm-and-fuzzy place these days."

He rang up her order and slid the receipt across the counter. "Sixty bucks," he said, then pushed the whiskey toward her. "This is on the house."

Marti blinked. "Why?"

"Because you'll be dead soon anyway." His grin stretched too wide, too sharp.

"Great," she said, handing over cash for the smokes. "Appreciate your faith in me." She pocketed them and nodded toward the door. "Anywhere I should avoid?"

Carlos stared past her, eyes unfocused as if consulting some internal map of danger zones. He muttered, "Yeah: outside." Then he buzzed her out without another word.

The city really had changed in her absence. Combat gear had become street fashion. Automatic weapons slung over shoulders like accessories, dried blood pools part of the urban landscape no one bothered to clean up anymore. The whole place felt like one long execution waiting to happen.

Marti turned onto a familiar street and exhaled when her office came into view. Martina Starova Investigations, somehow still standing while everything around it crumbled. She parked close, calculating the shortest path to the door. Close enough to safety that she let her guard slip; a mistake when rain-slick pavement sent her boot sliding. She caught herself on the cane, cursing under her breath.

Inside, she locked the door behind her and inhaled. Familiar air thick with leather, Shadow residue, stale cigarettes, and human sorrow soaked into the walls.

"This place needs a goddamn exorcism," she muttered, shrugging off her jacket.

The office looked untouched except for Lori's presence lingering at the desk: a coffee mug with lipstick on the rim, papers organized in neat stacks, a half-empty pack of gum. Marti sank into the chair, feeling the ghost of Lori's perfume rise from the leather, and woke the terminal.

Two new folders blinked on-screen: Your SignOff and Your Work.

She clicked the first one, scrolling through Lori's reports. The woman was too smart for secretarial work, but she stayed here anyway, keeping Marti's sinking operation afloat with sheer competence.

Thanks for sucking at career choices, Lori's dad.

Three cases flagged as complete. Marti scanned through them:

Eastman. Guy wanting dirt on his fiancée before dropping ten grand on matrimony. Lori had dug deep and found nothing but boring legitimacy. Marti approved the report with a digital signature. Easy money.

Roger Granger. Eighteen years old and lost in Falls City's drug vortex. Lori had tracked him down through Rat, without even having to ask nicely. Kid had been tweaking too hard to argue when Lori made him talk. Proof of life recorded and forwarded to his mother. Five grand in the bank. Done.

The Telliridge case. Another missing son. Lori found Andy slinging lattes in North Sydney, alive and determined to stay estranged. She'd given him restraining order information instead of betraying his location, then sent his parents just enough to know he was alive but wanted no contact. No happy ending, just expensive confirmation their kid hated them.

Marti's fingers lingered over Lori's detailed notes, her precise language, her thorough documentation. She wondered how much she paid her, then remembered Lori set her own salary and figured it was fair.

A pathetic meow cut through her thoughts. Bertha Tinkledorp sat in the window, fur plastered to her skinny frame, yellow eyes accusing Marti of arranging the rainstorm. Marti exhaled smoke at the glass, matching Bertha's stare for a long moment before hauling herself up to open the window.

"Shouldn't you have better places to be?" she muttered as Bertha strutted inside like she owned the place, leaving wet paw prints across case files.

A shout echoed between buildings. Sharp, urgent. Then came the gunshot, splitting through the night air. Marti leaned out just as another shot screamed past, ricocheting off the fire escape in a shower of sparks. She yanked herself back inside with the rapid reflex of someone who'd been shot once and wasn't eager for a repeat performance.

Back at her desk, she pulled out the whiskey bottle, twisted off the cap, and took a long pull straight from it. Freedom tasted like malt liquor and bad decisions, almost as intoxicating as Shadow itself. No one to stop her if she wanted to get high before breakfast, drunk before noon, or pass out on the couch until tomorrow. No one except Lori, who would just sigh and keep doing perfect paperwork anyway.

Another sip burned down her throat before she stuffed the bottle into the desk drawer. Bertha watched from atop a pile of case files, tail flicking with judgment.

The inhaler felt cool against her palm as she pulled it from her jacket pocket. Just one hit: enough to take the edge off without dissolving. The familiar hiss, then heat sparked under her skin as reality bent sideways.

Colors pulsed with impossible vibrancy. Sounds stretched and warped, each raindrop against the window a symphony of tiny explosions. The chair beneath her melted away until she floated, weightless, in a universe where gravity was just a suggestion. Her thoughts unraveled into patterns too vast for language, each neuron firing with electric significance only Shadow could translate.

Her body hummed with pleasure. Not sexual but something purer, like being kissed by light itself from the inside out. Every cell vibrated in perfect harmony with a universe made sensible, made beautiful.

Then it faded (too fast, always too fast) leaving behind that afterglow, that slick satisfaction humming beneath her skin even as normal reality reasserted itself around the edges.

She sighed, deep and slow, dragging out the moment before it slipped away, and opened her eyes to what remained of her city.

Chapter 6

Shadow's electrifying buzz still shimmered beneath her skin as Marti lit a cigarette and exhaled smoke into the windshield. Through the grime-streaked glass, the city bled into view: a nightmare of hunting grounds. Traffic crawled. Horns blared. Someone yelled something obscene three cars back.

Falls City in full bloom: neon signs shot to shit, roads slick with more than just water.

She drummed her fingers on the steering wheel, eyes flicking from one ruin to the next. The drug wars had done a number on this place, but it had been circling the drain for years. She just got to watch it swirl in real time now.

Gang tags layered on gang tags, marking turf as small as a doorway. A fresh threat every other block. Bullet holes in windows. Blood turned brown on the pavement until nature reclaimed it. The police had stopped pretending. Uniforms still blue, but now sporting insignias of whatever faction owned those particular streets.

The underbelly of Falls City wasn't under anything anymore. It was out in the open, sprawled across every surface as if it owned the place. Addicts scuttled between shadows, skeletal figures illuminated for half-seconds by headlights before disappearing again. They moved like bad wiring: jittery, unpredictable, ready to short-circuit at any second.

Death was fine. Dying, though, that could go real sideways real fast.

Coffee wasn't much better, but she wanted some anyway. Needed it, maybe, not for the caffeine so much as for the ritual of something hot and bitter cutting through all this shitshow of a cityscape.

She scanned the street for somewhere that sold something resembling coffee and spotted a convenience store squatting under flickering streetlights: a P-Mart, its sign so faded it whispered its own name instead of screaming it like it used to. Sold coffee. Tasted like gasoline runoff and regret, but fuck it; she'd had worse mornings this week.

Pulling over was its own gamble. Her car kissed the curb too hard, but she made it work. The brakes screeched and she killed the ignition and peered into cracked windows.

Marti grabbed her cane and shoved open the door, making a break for P-Mart's entrance before she could think twice about it.

The bell above the door dinged cheerily when she pushed inside.

Liar.

Inside, the fluorescent lights hummed their shitty anthem, casting shadows over half-stocked shelves. The cashier looked up from his phone, flicking through whatever kept him from dying of boredom. Marti ignored him and made a beeline for the burned coffee in the back, the bitter smell promising salvation, or at least a fix.

She grabbed a cup and filled it to the brim, steam curling into her face. Her gaze lifted to the convex mirror angled above the counter. The cashier stood behind his plexiglass shield, slouched, looking as if he'd rather be anywhere else.

The door chimed. Another loser looking for gas-coffee, snacks, or cheap smokes.

As she reached for a lid, her fingers brushed against the stack of grimy plastic. The whole mess toppled like a house of cards.

"Fuck." She muttered it more from habit than frustration. The pile had fallen half a dozen times today, each time some poor bastard picking them up only to make things worse.

Her eyes flicked back to the mirror just as she caught it: the glint of a gun.

Adrenaline snapped through her like a live wire. She set her coffee down, slow, and shifted toward the aisle's edge. Moving quiet. Unthreatening. It was funny how fast her body remembered what to do, like muscle memory trained on years of being a fucking cop.

"Give me the fucking money!" The guy's voice cracked, young, panicked, like he'd seen too many movies but never thought this part through. "Now! Move!"

The cashier froze for half a second before his hands fumbled with the register buttons. Marti closed in from behind. Steps, steady breath. Close enough now to see the jitters in his grip, the way his fingers twitched against the trigger as if he hadn't decided if he wanted to pull it yet.

First-timer. Had to be.

The piss hit her nose before she registered the stain spreading down the cashier's leg. Poor kid was terrified, shaking so hard his teeth might start rattling next. Must be a first-timer too.

Bad night for you, buddy. Worse night for him.

Marti sighed and drew her own gun in one clean motion, closing the last few steps between them before he even knew she was there. Then she struck: fingers clamping around his wrist in an iron grip, twisting downward and hard enough to send pain shooting up his arm. The gun slipped loose and clattered to the tile floor with a metallic clang.

For all of two seconds, he hesitated, then lurched forward like an idiot trying to reclaim lost ground. Marti didn't even think about it; she jammed her barrel between his eyes before he could get any bright ideas about continuing this life choice.

"Stop that shit," she said.

"You fucking bitch..."

Marti fired past his ear without blinking, letting the shot ring hot and loud against concrete walls and cheap shelving units stocked with expired candy bars. He yelped and tripped over himself scrambling backward into lighter-fluid displays and off-brand chips that crunched underfoot in protest.

She cocked her head as she adjusted her aim lower, not quite fired-up-enough-to-kill-him low, but ruin-his-month low, and let her exhale slide out slow between her teeth. "What did you just fucking call me?"

He swallowed but didn't answer fast enough for her liking, so Marti helped him along by snapping out a booted kick into his knee cap. He went down hard with a strangled noise that wasn't quite words but sure sounded like regret hitting all at once.

"You do what the fuck I tell you," she said, as if she hadn't just sent him sprawling face-first onto convenience store tile that smelled of mop water and disappointment.

She turned toward the counter without taking her eyes off him, the old cop trick of watching everything at once, and flicked two fingers at the kid behind it.

"You," Marti snapped, "call 911."

The cashier jolted as if he'd forgotten how phones worked before scrambling into motion, yanking it from his piss-stained pocket with fumbling fingers.

Marti shook her head as he dialed.

Fucking amateurs everywhere tonight.

"Name?"

"Louis," the cashier stammered.

"Louis, you got security cameras?"

"Y-Yeah. Three."

"Fuck."

"You don't want cameras?"

"I... fuck."

"I can delete it. The footage," Louis offered.

"You'd do that for me?" the thief asked.

Marti rolled her eyes. "Shut the fuck up, no one's talking to you, dipshit." She turned back to Louis. "Get some duct tape and tie this fucker up."

The thief started to get up as if he had an idea, so Marti fired another shot. She wasn't aiming for him, but he didn't need to know that. He dropped back down as Louis skittered off and returned with tape in hand.

"Tie his ankles," she said. "Now hands behind his back, yeah, around and around and around. Good enough."

The thief swallowed hard. "What are you gonna do to me?"

Marti ignored him, working through how much of a headache this shit was about to be. The last thing she needed was more attention after the triple shooting she was still trying to scrub from her record. Tomorrow's headlines would scream Bystander Turns Hero or Ex-Cop Redeemed!

Fuck that noise. She stepped in because amateurs like this punk made her nervous, not because she wanted a medal for saving dumbasses from their own stupidity.

With the guy trussed up like a fucked-up Christmas present, she holstered her gun and shook out a cigarette. Lit up, took a long drag, exhaled smoke toward the ceiling. "I don't want to be part of this shitstorm when it hits," she said. "I think I hear sirens. You got a back door?"

Louis hesitated before nodding toward a door behind the counter. "Through there, then storage room leads to the alley. Thanks." He frowned as if thanks wasn't the word he wanted but couldn't find a better one.

She smirked and took another hit of nicotine. "No worries. Delete the video, yeah?"

The sirens wailed closer now, blue lights flickering against the street outside. Time to go. She grabbed her coffee, shoved the lids into the trash, wiped down her prints without thinking about it too much, and slipped out the back just as the front door bell jingled behind her.

Cold wind slapped against her hoodie as she stepped into the alley, glancing around quick and sharp before spotting them: the green cop gang rolling in slow from the other side of the street. One car parked nowhere near hers, both cops still inside, dicking around on their terminals before stepping out into the mess waiting for them inside Louis' shitty P-Mart convenience store.

Marti tucked her chin deeper into her hoodie and limped fast but casual toward her car. No sudden movements when cops were around if you wanted an easy night. Slid inside without incident, pulled out just as another cruiser came barreling up from two streets over. All this because of a fucking coffee, she thought as she took a turn too sharp and sloshed lukewarm coffee onto her center console like an asshole.

As she cruised the streets, she let out a breath only to realize adrenaline was still thrumming beneath her skin like static electricity. Her phone rang through it all, a welcome distraction from thoughts spiraling between stupid-kid-could've-gotten-himself-killed and I-don't-need-this-kind-of-heat-right-now, so she answered without checking the name flashing across the screen.

"How are you?" Lori greeted her.

"Listen... I... Asshole!" She cut herself off mid-sentence as some pedestrian wandered into her lane at a red light despite having right of way, so of course she leaned on her horn instead of stopping like any law-abiding person would.

"Asshole!"

Lori's laughter crackled through the speaker like static on an old radio line.

"Becoming self-aware, I see," Lori teased.

"Yeah yeah," Marti muttered around another pull from her cigarette. "Why are you calling?"

"Because you're running late," Lori said. "Wanted to make sure you weren't dead in an alley somewhere."

Marti smirked despite herself. "Not dead," she acknowledged, shifting gears as traffic picked up again. "Not in an alley either." A pause while she checked mirrors and cut across two lanes without signaling. She had to stop doing that, but whatever, no sirens yet meant no consequences today.

"I'll be there in five."

"Just don't kill anyone on your way," Lori said.

"No promises."

Lori sighed, but Marti could hear the smile in it anyway.

"I'll meet you when you get here." A car horn blasted as Marti ended the call. Perfect. Because what this day needed was more fucking noise.

Chapter 7

True to her word and her driving, Marti made it in four minutes flat, though her hip screamed from that last sharp turn. Rain pelted the windshield as she squinted through the blur at Lori, who stood by the café entrance, umbrella open, wearing that familiar smug expression of someone staying perfectly dry.

Marti shoved the door open with a grimace, rainwater already seeping through her hoodie. "Why aren't we in the office?"

"Because," Lori tilted her umbrella to shield Marti as she hobbled up, "once a week, update meetings somewhere that doesn't reek of cigarettes and your questionable life choices."

"Did I agree to that?"

"Yes."

"Was I sober when I did?"

Lori's mouth quirked. "When are you ever?"

Inside, a handbill taped to the glass door caught Marti's eye. She stopped, jabbing her cane at it. "This kid."

The missing person's poster showed a seventeen-year-old Hispanic boy with dark eyes that sparkled with something Marti recognized: that particular glint hovering between mischief and trouble. A face she knew.

"César López," Lori read, shaking raindrops from her coat. "Missing since November 10."

Marti stared, time peeling away like old paint. Suddenly it was '48 or '49: Severo's case, Natalia's grief-heavy sobs when they caught the bastard who'd killed her son. Now another son missing?

She exhaled hard, anchoring herself to the present. "Worked his brother's murder when I was on the force. Thought that family had suffered enough."

"That's a lot for a mother to take," Lori murmured. "You wanna call her? See if we can help?"

Marti's cane tapped against the floor. Once, twice. "Nah. We've got enough on our plate. Maybe if he's still missing in a few months and I'm... functional again."

"You? Functional?" Lori scoffed. "That'll be the day."

Marti smirked but didn't argue, limping toward the counter where she ordered two coffees while Lori snapped a photo of the poster.

They settled into a booth near the window, steam rising from paper cups that promised more than they delivered. The scent of fresh pastries (croissants, cinnamon, warmth) drifted through the air, and with it came welcome memories.

"Billie used to bake like this," Marti muttered, staring into her cup.

Lori glanced up. "Billie River? The baker?"

"Yeah." Marti swirled what passed for coffee but tasted like burned regret. "Good with her hands in more ways than one."

Lori frowned, sorting through old memories. "Think I met her once or twice." She fidgeted with her cup. "You know it makes me nervous being in a coffee shop with you."

"Yeah?" Marti's lips curled upward. "Why's that?"

"Wild things tend to happen whenever we get caffeine." Lori took a cautious sip, then recoiled. "Jesus Christ," she groaned, setting it down as if she'd been betrayed.

"When is it not shit?" Marti took another sip anyway, then made a face of disgust. The cup hit the table with a hollow thud. Worse than the P-Mart even.

She leaned forward, voice dropping. "But you know what always makes coffee better?"

Lori raised an eyebrow.

Marti held her gaze. "Whiskey."

Lori exhaled: half laugh, half resignation. "You know what my guilty pleasure is?" she countered, mirroring Marti's posture.

"Oh, please. Enlighten me."

"A dash of cinnamon."

The silence stretched between them.

Marti blinked once, slowly, before letting out a laugh. "Cinnamon."

"It adds depth!" Lori insisted.

"Depth," Marti echoed, voice flat as pavement.

"Oh screw you," Lori laughed, nudging Marti's arm. "Not everything is about getting high and drinking."

Yet they both lifted their cups again, grimacing through another sip.

Marti pushed hers away. "I can't take this. Meet me at the office."

"Marti."

"Lori."

A sigh, fingers rubbing at her temple. "Fine. Office. Few minutes."

They parted ways outside the café, Lori heading to the office while Marti ducked under an awning three storefronts down. She flicked her lighter, inhaling deep as smoke curled around her head. The Shadow inhaler came next: half a hit, just enough to blur Falls City's hard edges.

The rain intensified, drumming against metal and concrete, washing cigarette butts into gutters clogged with fast food wrappers and used condoms. Under a flickering streetlamp, a hooker leaned into a car window, red lips stretched into a smile that never reached her eyes. A junkie slumped against brick, vomit pooling at his feet. Further down, a girl (far too young for this neighborhood) huddled on the sidewalk, knees pulled under her coat, watching the world slide past without seeing her.

Marti watched them all through Shadow-hazy eyes before limping toward the car.

Ten minutes later, the door creaked open to reveal Lori pacing, phone pressed to her ear, each step radiating the kind of principles Marti had abandoned years ago. Ignoring her, Marti headed for her office where Bertha stretched across the couch cushions, tail flicking with casual disdain.

Marti nudged the cat with her cane. "Off."

Bertha rolled onto her back instead, fluffy belly exposed in pure defiance. Another nudge. Nothing.

"Fucking cat." She collapsed into her chair, taking another hit of Shadow. The high settled behind her eyes as she ran her cane through Bertha's fur, watching light ripple over slick black strands.

Had the cat always been black? Was this even the same cat?

The cat purred, tolerating the attention until Lori entered. Then she shot through the open window as if she'd been caught mid-heist.

Yep. Same cat.

"You scared off my pussy," Marti muttered, head resting on her desk.

Lori didn't miss a beat. "I doubt anything could drive pussy away from you."

"And yet," Marti gestured toward the window, "here we are."

Lori rounded the desk and hopped onto it, ankles crossed with an elegance that made Marti's mouth go dry. Her eyes traced the line of Lori's thigh (taut muscle under smooth skin), wondering what secrets lay beneath that dress. Her gaze lingered on the hemline, cataloging the invisible hairs catching the light.

"Up here." Lori's fingers tipped Marti's chin. Her gaze landed on cleavage instead. Another tap redirected her attention upward until their eyes locked. "Look into my eyes."

"That's what vampires say," Marti mumbled, sitting up to dig another cigarette from her crumpled pack. The lighter sparked to life, flame dancing between them as she took a slow drag and exhaled through parted lips.

Lori's smirk held volumes. "You can't help yourself, can you?"

"Hey," Marti said around the filter, "I'm not the one sitting inches from a pervert while wearing a skirt that short."

"So it's working then?" Lori's fingers slid through Marti's hair, gentle but deliberate, sending heat pooling low in Marti's body: a sensation even Shadow couldn't dull.

Marti groaned, leaning back before temptation got ideas. "If by 'working' you mean making me horny? Yeah."

Lori's nails dragged against Marti's scalp before withdrawing. Too soon, too late, all at once. "What else would I mean?"

"You? I have no idea what else you might mean." Smoke curled from Marti's lips in a slow, deliberate stream. "Did you come in here just to fuck with me? As it were."

Lori uncrossed her ankles, then recrossed them, shifting against the desk. "César López. I want to talk to his mother."

Marti flicked ash into a paper coffee cup, watching embers die in yesterday's sludge. "And you're telling me because...?"

"I'm thinking we take the case." Lori waved her phone like a flag. "Unless you have concerns?"

"You think I don't have concerns?" Marti's voice hardened.

The silence stretched until Marti broke it.

"Severo López. Shot April 2048." Her words came clipped, each one a bullet point in a case file she'd never forget. "Nineteen years old. Runner for the 36th Street Robber Riders: mean motherfuckers, every last one." She stubbed out her cigarette with enough force to tear the cup. "Killed by Bernardo Villegas, sixteen-year-old B Street King who couldn't keep his mouth shut. His bragging got him picked up hours later, and kicked off a war that wiped out every King except him." A pause, heavy with unspoken violence. "They got him in jail two weeks later."

Lori rubbed at her arms as if the room had chilled. "And César?"

Marti leaned back, chair creaking. "His younger brother. Could be gang-related, could be something else. His mother would know."

"But if gangs are mixed up in this..." Lori's voice dropped. "We're walking into something dangerous."

A short, harsh laugh escaped Marti's lips. "Oh yeah. Fucking dangerous."

"Getting-shot-four-times-walking-out-of-the-office dangerous?"

"Funny how my worst injuries happen when I'm doing nothing at all." Marti's smirk didn't reach her eyes.

Lori shifted, her gaze flicking down to where her shirt covered an old scar beneath layers of fabric and time. "Remember when I got shot? That hurt like hell," she murmured.

The silence between them thickened. Marti's fingers drifted over Lori's knee without thought, until she felt the tremor in her own hand and yanked the desk drawer open instead, grabbing her whiskey bottle.

She poured a shot and knocked it back before Lori could object. "Look," she said, voice steadier now, "I don't mind when you take on the easy stuff: cheating husbands, runaway dogs. But tracking down the missing brother of a murdered gang kid? Not you."

Lori nudged Marti's shin with her foot, the movement hiking her hemline higher. "So we do it together?"

Marti shook her head, but the refusal died before reaching her lips.

"Have you even asked Ms. López?" Marti tried instead. "If she could afford me, she'd already be calling."

"Not everything is about money," Lori fired back, sliding off the desk with purpose carved into every line of her body. "This is about a mother whose son is gone." She raised the phone between them like a challenge and hit dial before Marti could find another excuse to not care today.

Marti's sigh felt ancient, too heavy for someone only thirty-six years old. Or thirty-eight, maybe.

Thousands of mothers with thousands of missing sons.

Lori met her gaze as she tapped speakerphone.

The line clicked. "Hello?" A woman's voice: cautious hope wrapped in exhaustion.

"Ms. López? My name is Lori Harring." Steel threaded through that honey-smooth tone. "I work with Martina Starova."

A pause.

Then: "Martina? Oh, Martina! Yes?" Relief flooded those syllables, making Marti's chest tighten.

Lori squared her shoulders as if bracing for impact. "We saw your son César is missing," she said firmly. "We want to help."

Chapter 8

Marti stretched out across Lori's desk like it was a goddamn chaise lounge, trying to shake off the weight of that phone call. Another missing kid. Another desperate mother. At least she knew this one, even if the circumstances were shitty.

Lori didn't look up from her screen, but that same steel-honey voice from the call now held an edge that could've flayed skin. "Get off."

"I'm comfortable."

"I can't move my mouse."

"Use the keyboard."

A beat. Then Lori shoved at Marti's hip until she grudgingly slid over an inch.

"César López disappeared November tenth of this year," Lori said, back to business. "Nat said he left for work and never came home. She doesn't know where that job was. It was a second gig, casual. His main job was at a bodega, part-time."

"What time did he leave?"

Lori clicked through windows with more force than necessary. "Didn't ask. We can follow up."

Marti rubbed her temples, headache creeping in. "And let me guess: he was a saint?"

"Responsible, hardworking, not in any gangs," Lori confirmed without looking away from the screen.

"They're always angels." Marti's mouth twisted. Families had a way of smoothing over inconvenient truths when someone went missing or worse. Like if they admitted anything real, it somehow made them responsible for the worst-case scenario. "What else?"

Lori tapped the screen with her nail. "Copy of the missing person's report. Looks normal."

Marti lit a cigarette, watching the flame flicker against her fingers before snapping the lighter shut. Smoke curled toward the ceiling as her gaze drifted briefly to Lori's neckline before flicking back up again. "Getting intel is like pulling teeth these days."

Lori swatted at the smoke invading her space. "Don't you have connections in the force? Buddies?"

"Hamilton's dead," Marti said flatly. "Gudas retired to some nowhere town in Texas. McNabb... maybe, but I'd trust a Magic 8-Ball before I'd trust him."

"What about Kendra?" Lori asked absently, still clicking through files. "That woman you helped out?"

"Keira," Marti corrected without missing a beat. "She headed out west." She stretched in emphasis. "Took stamina to fuck that woman."

Lori's chair scraped back as if physically removing herself from this conversation might help. "What about Agent Blair?"

Marti finally sat up properly; or at least sat up halfway, slouching into the guest chair instead of draping herself over Lori's workspace. "She hates me. I hate her."

"But she wanted to get coffee when you last saw her," Lori pointed out with irritating accuracy. "You can't blame her for getting yourself shot."

Marti tapped ash into her palm and ignored Lori's judgmental glare. "No," she admitted after a moment, watching specks of gray drift down onto her jeans before rubbing them away. "I blame coffee."

Lori rolled her eyes and turned back to her screen. "I set up a meeting with Nat López."

"When?"

"In an hour." A pointed pause. "Why do you think I came to get you?"

Marti grinned lazily, dragging one knee up onto the chair. "Wow. Someone's got a clock fetish."

"I worry about you sometimes," Lori admitted, not snide or teasing but quieter than usual, arms folded across her chest like bracing for whatever excuse might come.

Instead, Marti laughed, a little forced but functional, and stood abruptly. The chair legs scraped against the floor, shattering whatever moment had started brewing between them.

"Alright," she said breezily. "I'll grab a shower and change before we go."

"Clothes will be on the couch," Lori said after another beat of silence, letting it go because that's what they did: let things go until they couldn't anymore. "...And deodorant."

Marti smirked as she stubbed out her cigarette in an already overflowing ashtray. "Thoughtful as ever."

Lori was behind the wheel by the time Marti slid into the passenger seat. The car smelled like vanilla air freshener fighting a losing battle against cigarettes.

"Nat said she's bringing friends," Lori offered, eyes on the road as they pulled away from the curb.

Marti exhaled sharply. "Friends? You didn't mention friends."

Marti drummed her fingers against her thigh, watching Faircrest Heights slip past in the rearview. Their office building had already vanished into dusk. She glanced at Lori.

"You gonna tell me where we're headed?"

Lori's eyes never left the GPS. Her knuckles whitened against the steering wheel as they turned north onto Meridian Avenue. No answer.

The manicured lawns of Faircrest gave way to Baldwin Vista's tired storefronts. Half the neon signs flickered like dying heartbeats. The other half had given up entirely. Marti cracked her window and lit a cigarette, drawing the smoke deep into her lungs. The familiar burn calmed her nerves more than she wanted to admit.

"You've been quiet since we left," Marti said, flicking ash out the window. "Having second thoughts?"

Lori's jaw tightened. "Just concentrating."

Twenty minutes in, the GPS chirped directions in its cheerful mechanical voice. Eagle Rock District. Boarded windows. Chain-link fences. The streetlights came on early here. well, the ones that still worked.

A group of kids scattered from a corner as their headlights swept across broken glass. Marti watched them disappear between buildings, remembering what it felt like to run from headlights. She took a long drag, ash falling onto her dark jeans.

They passed through Eastwood District like ghosts, abandoned lots where weeds pushed through cracked concrete. A few souls moved through the gloom with the careful steps of people who knew which blocks to avoid after dark. Lori slowed at a four-way stop, hesitating longer than necessary.

"Left," Marti said before the GPS could. "And don't stop at the next one unless someone's coming."

Lori shot her a look but followed the direction. "You know this area."

"I know lots of areas." Marti's cigarette had burned down to the filter. She crushed it in the car's ashtray, noticing how Lori winced at the action. "Places I never send you."

By the time they hit Redspan District, the sun had dipped below the horizon. Buildings leaned against each other like old drunks sharing secrets, their brick faces tagged with territorial markings. Even the air felt thicker here, weighted with a familiar desperation that Marti recognized in her bones.

Shadows stretched across their path like bad omens. Marti's fingers resumed their drumming against her thigh. "Where the fuck are we meeting her?"

Lori shrugged. "She gave me an address. I'm just following the map."

"You didn't check where we're going? Didn't think to look up the neighborhood?"

Silence. Telling silence.

Marti snatched Lori's phone from the dashboard and checked the address herself. Then she laughed.

Lori flicked her a wary glance. "What's funny?"

"You'll see."

"What—"

"It's Diego's Dive." Technically true, and that was all Lori needed to know for now. First time taking her there, too. This was going to be fun.

Marti checked the time. At least one checkpoint before they got there, possibly more. Minutes wasted while some Robber Riders' guard decided what price they had to pay for passage. She could handle it without bleeding too much, but maybe she'd let Lori sweat a little first.

They turned onto 36th Street as distorted neon reflected in puddles along the curb. Holiday lights framed a familiar shape up ahead: the checkpoint, glowing like a bad memory. Marti's shoulders tensed. This place had been here before everything went to hell: before the cops fractured, before López got himself killed.

A small black car in front of them rolled to a stop. A hand snaked out, flashing an orange card. They were waved on.

"We don't live here, no orange card to bypass the checkpoint. Pull up to the white line and stop," Marti instructed. She popped open the glove box and grabbed two Shadow inhalers, tossing them onto the dashboard.

Lori eyed them warily. "What is this?"

The white line cut through cracked asphalt, thick and slapdash. Above it, a rusting arch sagged under a mess of holiday lights. Off to the side, a bus shelter squatted on the sidewalk. At first glance, nothing special; until you noticed who was watching.

Lori slowed the car as two men stepped out of the shadows.

"Window down," Marti said. "And stop."

The first guard barely glanced at her before shifting his attention to the dashboard.

The second circled the hood, then let out a low whistle. "Hey; look at this."

The first guy leaned in. Lori flinched as his rifle strap bit into her shoulder, the barrel jostling against her cheek. Marti snatched up the inhalers and dropped them into his waiting palm. He reeled back with them like a snake uncoiling.

He pulled out a strip of green paper, blank, and slapped it under the windshield wiper before rapping a knuckle against the hood and waving them forward.

Lori rolled up the window as they drove through. "Two inhalers? Those things aren't cheap."

Marti barked out a laugh, flat, humorless. "Supply chain's fucked. Going rate's a crisp apiece." She shot Lori a look that could've peeled paint. "One of many reasons you should've checked the damn meeting spot first. We could've gone anywhere. Instead, I just burned two grand for your shitty bar in Robber Riders' turf." A sharp exhale. "And Nat López probably won't be reimbursing me."

Lori winced. "Shit, Marti; I didn't know." A beat passed. "What happens if you don't stop at those checkpoints?"

Marti shook a cigarette loose from her pack and lit it with one flick. "You keep driving," she said around the filter.

Smoke curled past her face as she took a long drag. The memory surfaced unbidden: Raymond Oswald walking past that checkpoint ten years ago, cocky and oblivious. His friend Joe Hancock hesitating on the safe side while Oswald strutted forward. One block later, five rounds at close range. Oswald stumbling halfway into 36th Street, bleeding out under flickering neon, eyes wide open but seeing nothing.

She'd caught that call: body cooling on wet pavement, blood pooling in every crack and pothole like the street itself was feeding. Just another case that went cold fast, another ghost swallowed by this city.

Fiona Sanders came next in the parade of ghosts. Mother of three who left home for cookies and never returned. Garbage collectors found her a week and a half later. Two days to ID what remained. Six months to pin DNA on the bastards who'd done it.

"Sick fucks," Marti muttered.

"Huh? What did I—"

"No, not you." Marti yanked open the glove box, fingers closing around nothing. Right. Gave away her last inhaler. She slammed it shut harder than necessary. "We close?"

"Five minutes." Lori took a turn sharp enough to make the tires groan, flicking Marti a concerned glance.

Marti ignored it, watching the street roll by: low-slung cars creeping like hungry strays, buildings looming tall and ruined over busted pavement.

"That it?" Lori nodded at a squat concrete block behind thick steel bollards.

Diego's Dive. Every Latino in Falls City knew it: Officially JJ's now, but his father and grandfather had stacked those cinderblocks forty years ago. Long and narrow, cheap as hell, ugly as sin, with barred windows that'd keep people in just as well as they kept them out.

The 36th Street Robber Riders treated it like a second home: moms, girlfriends, half the damn family packed inside like an unofficial clubhouse for people who knew better than to ask questions they didn't want answered.

No rivalries, no turf wars, no blood feuds dragging through the door. If trouble followed you in, it got a bullet before taking a seat. Drugs? Personal use only, just enough without inviting heat unless you were JJ's son, Big Man. JJ ran the joint; his grandma Maria kept things tight. Cops had bigger fish to fry, and Maria hated bloodshed almost as much as she hated cops.

Lori squinted at the numbers peeling off a bollard. "So that's it?"

"Yeah." Marti scanned their surroundings: burned-out buildings slumped against each other, chain-link fencing half-collapsed across the street. "Park there." She pointed at a spot barely ten feet from the entrance.

They stepped out just as some guy shuffled past, clocked the green paper on the car, and kept moving without a word. Cold drizzle speckled their shoulders as they reached The Dive's sagging awning. A wooden door with thick iron hinges waited: scarred, solid, damn near medieval-looking.

Marti hesitated before grabbing the handle; habit. But Lori didn't waste time stepping inside first. Two steps in, every single face turned toward them at once.

Marti nodded toward one of only two tables with women: five of them crammed together over mismatched glasses and sullen faces. "There."

Lori lit up and waved on instinct, her pale skin easy to track in Diego's perpetual gloom.

The smell hit Marti next: sweat and stale tobacco baked into woodgrain, cheap tequila seeping into every crack like bloodstains no one bothered scrubbing out. It smelled like something that'd been hibernating too long and just woke up pissed off and starving.

The murmurs started before they made it halfway across the room, low at first, then rolling louder like distant thunder before someone called out from the back:

"My Shadow Queen!"

Heads snapped so fast they might've cracked vertebrae.

Chapter 9

Marti's fingers twitched toward the gun at her hip before recognition hit. The stale tobacco smell parted around the mountain of a man like water around a boulder.

"Well, fuck me." She barked a laugh that didn't quite mask her relief.

Lori groaned beside her. "Can we not?"

"Go on ahead." Marti pushed her toward their table. "I gotta say hi."

Weaving through the Dive's uneven furniture, she stopped before a human mountain built like he belonged in an underground fight ring. "Big Man Jake. How the fuck are you?"

Jake wasn't a boxer, but his six-foot-nine frame carried four hundred pounds of trouble wrapped in sweat-stained cotton. Cops didn't waste their time trying to arrest him: not since the last guy who tried ended up with a broken spine.

His massive grip engulfed her hand, shaking hard enough to make her shoulder crack. His bulk spilled over both sides of his chair in silent challenge to the furniture's structural integrity. A beard thick enough to nest birds hung down his chest, and when he spoke, his voice rumbled against the Dive's warped walls.

"Shadow Queen." The nickname vibrated through the floorboards. "Sit your ass down."

The stench coming off him, part cigarettes, part mescal sweat, wasn't the worst Marti had encountered. She'd bought from him plenty back when Shadow was all she lived for. Not that things were all that different now.

Jake slapped the table, making empty glasses jump. "Sit," he said again.

She dropped into the chair. Across from them sat a woman Marti would fuck without hesitation, except she had a table full of PTA moms waiting for her across the bar.

"Angel, meet Shadow Queen," Jake said, jabbing one thick finger between them. "One of my best customers from Kransten."

Angel stood and extended her hand before Marti could place her face. A smirk played at her lips, hinting at secrets Marti wasn't privy to.

"I know you," Angel said. "Hi, Marti."

Marti took her hand: warm skin over lean muscle. Her brain scrambled for context. That face: sharp features framed by cropped brown hair, bronze skin stretched over solid strength. A body carved rather than born. Familiar in that do-I-know-your-cousin? way, except this cousin made Marti's pulse drop south fast enough to be embarrassing.

Brown eyes sparkled with mischief as Angel sat back down, settling into a confidence Marti couldn't quite place but wanted to explore.

"This bitch right here?" Jake's thumb jabbed in Marti's direction. "Top-tier customer. Pays without a fuss, in and out, no bullshit. Used to be a cop, too."

"Oh, for fuck's sake." Angel sighed, shaking her head. "Do you not know who this is?"

Jake squinted at Marti like he was seeing her for the first time. Marti blinked back. She was the Shadow Queen. Nothing more.

Angel laughed, slow and easy, then rested a hand on Marti's knee like it belonged there.

"That makes two of us," Marti said.

Angel's grin widened. "Three years." Her eyes dragged over Marti as if searching for something beneath the surface. "You were fucked up back then. Comadrine, wasn't it?"

Marti glanced toward where Lori sat scribbling notes across from her gang of moms, their voices murmuring over glasses in the smoke-hazed air. With effort, she pulled her attention back to Angel. Hot as hell, sure, but nothing about her clicked into place.

"I haven't touched Comadrine in a long time," she said.

"You don't remember me?"

Marti lifted an eyebrow. "Should I?"

"Should she?" Jake echoed.

Angel smacked him hard on the arm. "We dated," she said, then winked. "Two weeks or so."

Dated? Still nothing beyond the vague, nagging familiarity of someone who'd maybe shared space with her once upon a binge. But Angel knew about the Comadrine, which meant something. Just not enough to make Marti care yet.

"Comadrine fucks with your memory." Angel snapped her fingers at Jake like he was some kind of waiter instead of a dealer twice her size. "Give her some Bright. Girl, you're going to love this."

Marti raised both eyebrows but didn't move when Jake dug into his pocket and pulled out a tiny vial of oil slick as motor grease under the dim light.

"Thanks," she said, "but I've got people to talk to." She nodded toward Lori.

Angel ignored the excuse. She grabbed a shot glass off the table and dumped in tequila like it was an afterthought. "Ten drops," she instructed Jake, who frowned as he started counting them out, slowly, lips moving like basic math was a foreign language.

"Sip it," Angel told Marti. "Not all at once or you'll be stuck wherever you land for hours." She tapped the rim with one nail. "Just stick that slick tongue of yours in there: light Bright."

Marti smirked despite herself. Jesus Christ.

Jake hit ten after a false start and capped the vial just as Angel turned back with another head tilt.

"You really don't remember me?"

Marti exhaled, letting silence stretch long enough that maybe Angel would take the hint. No such luck. Instead, Angel leaned back with an amused sigh and dragged one manicured hand through dark hair that hadn't been dark before. Not if what came next was true.

"That's fair," she conceded. "I didn't look like this three, four years ago."

"Oh fuck!" Jake's laughter boomed across the bar, turning heads as realization slammed into him. He slapped his knee hard enough to rattle his drink. "You were a fucking pig back then!"

Angel smacked him upside the head without missing a beat, harder than necessary but not enough to be serious, and rolled her eyes when he winced.

"Fuck you," she shot back before turning to Marti, all earlier hesitation gone. "I was fat."

Her shrug sent toned shoulders rolling under smooth skin: a far cry from whatever weight had sat heavier on her bones.

And just like that, memories crashed into Marti: red eyeshadow smeared too thick around desperate eyes; laughter hiding insecurity; soft, unsteady hands reaching for hers during nights lost under neon signs while drugs burned away their names before morning came.

Four years ago. Another lifetime.

Marti leaned back, arms crossed, studying the woman before her. It wasn't just the makeup: something lurked in the sharp curve of those cheekbones, the way she held herself like she expected a fight and might start one just for fun.

"Well, fuck me," Marti exhaled. "Angelina?"

Angel's grin spread wide and wild. "Yeah. Ha! Bro, you believe this shit?" She turned to Jake, slapping his arm. "Marti here? This woman was a fucking animal."

Jake's face drained white as RumChata. "Jesus Christ," he muttered. "I don't wanna fucking know."

Angel wasn't done. She grabbed his arm again before turning back to Marti, smugness radiating from every pore. "No, no: this is a big deal! First time I ever broke up with someone." She leaned in close, voice dropping. "Me. Back then. Breaking up with her."

A sharp bark of laughter escaped her as she straightened, throwing out her arms like a victor taking a bow.

"You gave me such a confidence boost, Marti. A hot woman like you? Fingering me in restaurants? Eating me out in back alleys?" She pressed a hand to her chest with mock sincerity. "Me? Back then?"

Jake looked like he'd rather swallow glass than sit through another second. His gaze flicked between them before settling on his sister with disbelief curdling into disgust. "I thought you were lying about all that."

Angel cackled, pointing at Marti like proof incarnate. "Nope! This is her." She shook her head. "Shit...you did give me a boost." Her voice dripped satisfaction. "After I dumped your ass."

Fifteen days: that's all it had been. An explosion of sweat-slicked nights in cars, elevators, alleyways. The kind of reckless indulgence that burns bright enough to leave scars. Marti had been riding the Comadrine high, skirting edges sharp enough to draw blood if you weren't careful...and neither of them had been careful. Angel soaking up attention like she'd been starving for it while Marti drowned in another vice.

Something raw flashed behind Angel's bravado before she covered it with another grin. "Marti was, hell, I don't know, a doorway or some shit." She rolled her wrist. "Someone who wanted me...my body...that piece-of-shit body I'd been stuck in for years."

That shadow crossed her face again. "And I dumped her." The last word landed victorious as she slapped Jake's arm before turning back to Marti with something softer than amusement but sharper than affection.

"You keep saying that." Marti shifted but held steady under Angel's stare, unwilling to let old ghosts settle on her shoulders tonight.

She tapped two fingers against her skull. "Confidence thing." Her grin stretched wider as she tipped an invisible hat toward Marti. "Breaking up with you gave me confidence." Her hands spread wide over herself in open display. "All this exercise...and just a little bit of surgery...and here we are!"

She nudged Marti with her elbow. "Fuck, it is amazing though."

"Glad I could be of service." Marti snorted.

"We should catch up, go back to a few of our old spots, see if we can't do it harder this time."

"Bitch you got a woman," Big Man said as he swatted at his sister.

She pushed her chair back. "I gotta run."

Before she could stand, Big Man Jake slid the shot glass toward her. The liquid inside had an unnatural shimmer, something thick and oily clinging to the sides.

"Angel's not wrong," he said. "This shit's potent. A new oil blend I've been working on. Thinking about selling it to Gardner's people." Kevin Gardner: Falls City's drug lord slash nightmare in human form. "Go slow with this. Ten drops in an ounce, maybe just stick your tongue in it."

Marti lifted the glass and sniffed before letting her tongue flick across the surface.

Heat exploded through her veins like she'd plugged into the city grid. The bar's lights flared, colors sharpening as if someone had stripped away the film of grime coating everything in this shithole. Even the darkest corners glittered like broken glass under neon. Her head spun, stomach twisting as reality yanked sideways.

Then it was gone. Ten seconds, maybe less, and the world settled back into its usual dull sludge of nicotine stains and regret.

"Holy fuck," she muttered, blinking hard against the afterimages still dancing across her vision.

Jake smirked. "I call it Bright."

"No shit." She shook off the aftershocks humming through her fingertips.

"Pace yourself," Jake said, nodding toward the other end of the bar. "Slam it down and you'll be out for hours."

"Yeah, I need to go deal with that." She stood, still feeling too light on her feet from whatever Bright had just done to her. "Thanks for the drink," she told Jake before flicking a glance at Angel. "Good seeing you again."

On second thought, she grabbed the glass. Then she turned and walked into whatever fresh hell awaited her at that table.

Chapter 10

Marti slid into the empty chair, grounding herself against the buzz of Bright still dancing in her system. She set her rescued vodka down with care, fingers curling around the glass like an anchor.

Across the table, Nat stared with that desperate hope Marti had come to hate. Marti dragged her gaze to Lori instead, who watched with tight-lipped patience: that look she always wore when Marti was about to do something stupid.

"Mine, don't touch," Marti whispered, tapping the rim of her glass.

She leaned back, chair creaking. "Nat, didn't expect to see you again so soon." A lie. She'd been waiting for this, dreading it. "What's going on?"

The bar's overhead light buzzed and flickered, stretching shadows across their faces. Stale beer and cigarettes hung in the air like old regrets. Perfect place for bad news.

"Everybody," Nat said, sweeping her arm toward the women at the table, "this is Marti Starova." Her voice clanged with something between gratitude and desperation.

Nat's hands twitched against the sticky tabletop. "She got Severo's car back from impound. Without her..." She trailed off, but didn't need to finish.

Without Marti, she couldn't have sold the car and survived that month. Severo had been their safety net. With him gone, Nat and César were drowning: rent past due, utilities hanging by threads. Marti had patched things up before walking away. Couple hundred for groceries, just enough to keep the lights on, but she wasn't running a fucking charity.

"Marti," Nat said again, voice dropping low, "I need your help to find César." Her hands curled into fists against the wood grain. "He's been gone three months. Three fucking months."

Marti exhaled smoke toward the ceiling. Was there an answer to this?

Nat's voice cracked. "I need to know what happened to him." A swallow scraped down her throat. "I need you to bring him home."

Marti let the silence stretch, her cigarette burning down between her fingers. She held it just long enough for Lori to shift beside her in quiet disapproval.

"Nat..."

"I know." Nat shook her head, wiping at one eye. "I'm not stupid." Her voice wobbled, fingers twisting against the table edge as if they might hold her together. "Three months without word. I know what that means."

She choked on the truth. Marti lifted two fingers in a lazy wave: the universal signal for 'Don't say it if you don't want to hear it out loud.'

"We're all in the same position."

The words cut through the smoke-heavy air, thin and sharp and inevitable.

"All of us are missing our sons," said Ynes Baez, the woman who'd spoken earlier. Her voice steadied as everything spilled into open air. "Will you help us?"

Each word landed like a weight on Marti's chest.

One person needing help? Easy enough to ignore. Six? That was something else.

Ynes straightened, saying it aloud giving their grief some shape beyond alcohol fumes and desperate prayers.

"One thousand each," Nat added, words tumbling out as if money might tilt the balance. "Six thousand total."

Six grand. Six kids.

Marti leaned back until the chair creaked, dragging smoke deep before exhaling with patience.

"Were they all together when they disappeared?"

"Oh no," someone said from down the table. Marti didn't catch which one; too many voices blending into a tangled mess. "It's been two or three years spread between all of us."

Not isolated, then. Something systematic. Something that had been happening longer than anyone wanted to admit. Or coincidence.

Marti wrapped one hand around her drink but didn't lift it. After a moment's consideration, she released it, reaching for another cigarette instead.

No amount of vodka and Bright would be enough for this shit.

She rolled smoke over her tongue before tilting forward again, facing their haunted expressions, tight with desperate faith in something as flimsy as hope.

Faith in a drug-addicted PI who'd rather be anywhere else but here, listening to their wreckage unravel across cheap wooden tables.

Marti took another drag, letting smoke drift toward Lori just because she could, then lifted a finger toward Ynes.

"Go ahead," she said, bracing for whatever fresh hell was about to drop.

Ynes hunched forward, arms wrapped tight around herself. Silver streaked through her dark hair, and the lines around her eyes ran deep: carved by years of worry rather than age. When she spoke, her voice rasped like sandpaper.

"My son," she said. "Luis."

Luis Baez. Fifteen when he vanished from his job at the bodega. August 21, 2052. His friend David had stopped by, seen him talking to some customer: older guy, maybe white, maybe tall. No security cameras caught it. Police came when Ynes called the next morning, took his computer because he played games online.

"They never gave it back." Ynes clutched a photo in both hands, knuckles white against the worn edges. "The police came, asked questions. Then nothing. No leads, no updates." Her breath stuttered. "Just silence."

Marti exhaled, scanning the bar. The bartender wiped down the counter on autopilot, throwing a quick glance their way before turning back to a glass that didn't need cleaning.

"You got photos?" Marti asked. "We'll need everyone's."

"I have them," Lori said, not looking up from her phone.

"Let me go next." Susanna Alvarez straightened, shoulders squared against invisible weight. Early forties, face marked by grief, hands calloused and trembling against the tabletop.

"Albert," she said.

Albert Alvarez. Eighteen. October, 2052. Vintage car fanatic who called himself a gearhead. Worked at Hands Car Co., washing vehicles until he could afford his own. Last seen outside the shop talking to some man about his car.

"A blue one. They told the police it was blue. But what kind of blue? Why didn't they get the make and model? It was blue, definitely blue," Susanna said, the words falling flat and useless. Christine and Gabriel had spotted him: friends passing by who didn't notice make or model or anything that mattered beyond color.

"They told the police it was blue, and the guy was older." Frustration tightened every muscle in Susanna's face. "That's all they said."

The cops had questioned everyone: family, co-workers. Security footage caught nothing outside.

Lori gripped her water glass, condensation dripping between her fingers. She caught Marti's eye, something heavy passing between them before Marti looked away.

Ana Córdova leaned forward, jaw set beneath features worn from fighting uphill battles her whole life.

"Not gonna lie to myself," she said, clasping her hands on the table. "My son sold pot." Her eyes swept the table, challenging anyone to judge. "He had to."

Jacinto Córdova. Sixteen. Missing since April 2, 2054.

"Look, I work three jobs but the math doesn't add up. Jacinto saw the numbers too. Kid was smarter than these cops give him credit for," Ana said.

She counted off on her fingers: Margaret, her mother. Sophie, her thirteen-year-old daughter. And Jacinto, who did what he thought necessary for all of them.

"We needed money," Ana said, voice steady despite the current underneath. "And Jacinto stepped up."

He slung dope on the corner of Danvers and Main: territory the Robber Riders let him claim. Nothing big-time, just enough to keep the lights on and the landlord away. Alejandro and Marcus had seen him around 8:45 the night he vanished, just standing there. When Ana called the cops, they told her to wait 72 hours.

"That's a lie, by the way," she said, voice sharp as broken glass. "Just some lazy cop who didn't want to do his fucking job."

By the time she called back, they shrugged her off. No case number, no file. As if she'd never reported it.

Other mothers shifted; their sons got case numbers, even if nobody was looking.

The Robber Riders hadn't helped either. Denied involvement but did nothing beyond that.

Adriana Hernandez leaned forward next, elbows braced against the scarred table. Early thirties, but weariness hung about her like a shroud. When she spoke, her voice carried something dangerous beneath the surface.

"My name is Adriana Hernandez," she said. "My son Mateo was sixteen, and police are assholes."

No argument there.

Mateo scrubbed hospital floors part-time and sold Shadow and Fentafill when rent got tight. "He was a good boy," Adriana said, jaw clenched around each word. "Had a daughter: Maria, just two months old." Her breath hissed through her teeth. "She's still with me and Darlee, his girl. Stole milk for Maria that day."

Security footage caught him leaving work June 6th with nothing but a plastic jug from some corner store: the last time anyone saw him.

Adriana's hands clenched into fists, then forced themselves open. "When I reported him missing? The cops were sympathetic at first." Her mouth twisted in disgust. "Then they found that camera footage. And you know what those bastards did? Issued an arrest warrant! For stealing milk!"

Her laugh cut like steel: the sound of someone with nothing left but rage.

"I told them where they could shove their fucking warrant," she said coldly. "My son would've come home no matter what. They think he'd stay missing just 'cause of some petty theft charge? Bullshit." Her voice dropped. "But they don't care about him or Maria or me." A pause heavy with unspoken grief. "Nobody cares about a fucking container of milk."

Silence settled across the table until Lori shifted beside Marti, scribbling into her notebook. Marti dragged hard off her cigarette, eyeing her vodka.

Carmen Molina spoke next: 54 years old with gray streaking through dark curls pulled back from an anxious face.

"Antonio was my magical baby," she said softly before clearing her throat, as if admitting love in front of strangers felt too raw.

Fourteen when he disappeared: the youngest wound at this table of open ones.

"I don't know," Carmen admitted, fingers twisting her silver earring. "Maybe he ran away? But Antonio's a good boy, he wouldn't just... I mean, he knows I worry. He knows I pray for him every night." The sigh that followed carried the weight of sleepless nights.

She hadn't called police, hadn't seen the point, but after hearing the others, she figured Antonio deserved someone looking for him too.

"Last I knew...he went over to Nicolas Coffer's house, but Nicolas swears he never showed up."

Her other sons had searched everywhere: Chester checking alleyways, Lucas knocking heads when needed, but found nothing.

"It's like he just..." Her voice faltered. "It's like he just walked away."

"When?"

"April, '52."

Lori hummed under her breath: a sound barely anyone noticed, but Marti did. Watched her fingers trace grooves cut into cheap wood, as if grounding herself in imperfections made any of this easier.

It didn't. It never did.

Nat was the last.

"Marti, I don't know what to do." She crushed a napkin in her fist. "You remember César? He was ten when Severo died. It wrecked him. But he always said, 'Mama, I'll stay with you my whole life.'" Her voice cracked. "Now he's gone."

Marti flicked ash onto the floor and waited.

"Last time anyone saw him, he was talking to some gringo: light hair, slick smile." Nat swallowed hard. "César wasn't a saint. He ran for the Robber Riders. Whatever you needed, he'd get it. Take the money, run, trade the drugs, run back."

"I know what a runner is." Marti crushed her cigarette under her boot.

"Right." Nat exhaled. "He was seventeen when he disappeared. Already had a record, so I didn't go to the police. I went to the Riders instead." A bitter laugh scraped from her throat. "They didn't give a shit. Called him 'some little rat chasing cheese.'" She spat onto the floor. "That's what I think of them." Her eyes blazed. "I can't call the cops; I can't ask the Riders, but you found Severo's killer, Marti. You can find César."

The neon sign buzzed against Marti's ears, bar lights cutting sharp as she reached for her glass. Outside, rain smeared the windows in jagged streaks: ugly weather for uglier business. She touched her tongue to vodka, felt the stab of light behind her eyes, warmth in her stomach, then gone. She shivered, pushed it away, and lit another cigarette.

Beyond the haze of smoke, Lori watched her as if she already regretted dragging her here.

Marti exhaled and turned back to the table. "Alright," she said. "I've got questions." Her gaze swept across them: Nat, Ana, Adriana, their silence thick as old blood. "Your kids sold drugs. Anyone else?"

Nobody answered.

"Are any of your sons addicts?" Still nothing. "Any of your sons gay for pay?"

Ynes inhaled, disgust twisting her features. "That's repulsive." Her lip curled over clenched teeth. "That is the vilest insult you could throw at my son."

Marti leaned back, stretching her legs under the table. Something ugly and familiar settled in her chest. "Oh? And here I thought his worst quality was being dead." She crushed her cigarette, grinding ash into concrete. "Lori, scratch Ynes off our list."

"What?" Ynes jolted forward. "Why?"

"Because you're a piece of shit," Marti said.

Color flooded Ynes's face, her body vibrating with fury. "Don't you fucking dare," she hissed.

"I dare," Marti drawled, watching her unravel.

"You, you're disgusting! You're filth! You think you're better than me?"

Marti laughed, sharp and breathy and full of smoke, and then grinned. "You wanna fight about it?"

"I should beat your ass," Ynes snarled.

"Please do." Marti crossed one leg over the other, elbow resting on the chair back. Just another Thursday night talking about missing kids and lowlife gangs and now yet another woman who wanted to kill her.

Ynes lunged, wild-eyed and furious, but froze when cold steel pressed against her cheekbone. Marti's gun had appeared without warning, steady as a surgeon's hand.

The bar went silent.

"What?" Ynes spat through clenched teeth. "You gonna shoot me?"

"Yes," Marti said, thumbing back the hammer. Not a threat. A promise.

"Marti!" Lori's voice sliced through, low but urgent. She didn't move closer. She never knew if tonight would be one of those nights when Marti pulled the trigger.

Ynes stood breathing hard, steel against bone.

Marti smiled, slow and mean, before easing off just enough to holster her pistol.

"Get lost," she said.

"Fuck you both," Ynes snarled, blasting past other tables to the door. Daylight sliced the room before vanishing again. The bar resumed its usual hum: drinks clinking, quiet deals passing through smoke.

Marti sprawled back into her chair. "Meeting's over. Lori will be in touch. And for the record? Ynes is out." Final. No debate.

The remaining women gathered their things without a word, eyes avoiding Marti's as they muttered thanks and shuffled out. Only when the last one disappeared did Lori turn on her, glare sharp enough to cut glass.

"What the hell is wrong with you?" She planted herself beside Marti, fists on hips. "That was out of line! You just pulled a gun on a mother looking for her missing son."

Marti exhaled, unimpressed. "And?" She nudged her shot of vodka closer. Tempting.

Lori scoffed. "And? You think this is how we handle things?"

"This is a shit job you took on, Lori." Marti's fingers curled around the glass. "I've blown through damn near the whole budget just getting us in here." A shrug. "Ynes is out."

Lori shook her head, lips tugging into a frown before she snapped her laptop shut. "You didn't have to pull a gun on her," she muttered, then reached across the table and snatched Marti's vodka as if she had every right to it. "Let's move this along. We aren't staying here any longer."

In one smooth motion, she tipped it back and swallowed.

Marti's stomach dropped through the floor, muscles coiling tight as she watched the glass tip back. The vodka, her special blend, caught the light as it disappeared between Lori's lips. Each heartbeat thundered in her ears as realization hit: Lori had just swallowed Bright.

Chapter 11

The empty glass clinked against the table as Marti lunged forward, her chair scraping across the floor.

"Oh, fuck! Ohfuckohfuckohfuck!" She stretched across the table like she could snatch the vodka and Bright back out of Lori's throat through sheer desperation. "Big Man! Fuck! Big Man! She drank my shit!"

Lori stood frozen mid-motion, fingers still curled around a phantom glass. Her pupils dilated until black swallowed brown, lips parting on a breath that never escaped. One heartbeat. Two. Her body went rigid: a mannequin with cut strings, seconds from collapse.

Big Man Jake's boots thundered across the floorboards before Marti could scream again. "What?" His massive hands went up defensively. "What the hell you yellin' about, Queen?"

"She drank my fucking stash," Marti hissed, one hand hovering near Lori's shoulder, afraid touching her might shatter something irreplaceable.

Jake whistled low, the bastard amused. "She'll be fine. Give it four, five hours. She'll enjoy the ride."

"The fuck she will." Marti snapped fingers inches from Lori's face; not even a flinch. A thin line of drool traced Lori's chin. Marti cursed and wiped it away with rough tenderness. "Lori? Hey! Hey, stay with me." Her voice rose, panic edging in. "She doesn't use! She doesn't even drink!"

Marti whirled on Jake. "Are you fucking kidding me? Angel! Get the Dark!"

Angel was moving: a blur toward the back room while Big Man barked orders, returning seconds later with an auto-injector clutched in trembling hands. No hesitation as she jammed it into Lori's thigh, thumbing the trigger until the syringe emptied with a mechanical hiss.

Three seconds of nothing. Then Lori convulsed once before collapsing as if her bones had liquefied.

Marti caught her before she hit the grimy floor, cradling her with gentleness. Lori's head lolled against her chest, deadweight and burning hot.

Angel hovered nearby, guilt etched into every line of her face, muttering apologies Marti couldn't be bothered to acknowledge.

"Don't just fucking stand there," Marti growled, stroking damp hair from Lori's forehead. Another shake; nothing beyond shallow breathing and twitching fingers.

She swore under her breath. This wasn't how things were supposed to go. This wasn't supposed to happen at all. But here they were, and for once in her goddamn life, Marti had no plan beyond the urge to punch fate square in its teeth.

Big Man moved, scooping Lori's limp form into arms the size of small trees. Relief flooded Marti's chest, but it wasn't enough. Not enough.

"Grab your cane and whatever else matters. We're moving," Big Man commanded, hiking Lori up like she weighed nothing.

The bar wasn't built for a man his size. Tables scraped aside, chairs tipped, patrons scattered: a human tide parting before him. Angel and Marti trailed in his wake, fast enough to keep up, not stupid enough to try to lead.

The back room smelled of old grease and cigarettes, a stark contrast to the bar's new grease and pot smoke. Big Man laid Lori on a sagging couch with care, like she was some passed-out princess instead of a junked-up mess.

"The fuck is this?" Marti's hand found her gun, fingers wrapping around cold metal. Nothing about this situation felt right.

Angel didn't flinch. "That's what Bright does when you overdo it: melts your brain into soup." She crouched beside Lori, pressing fingers to her neck. "Leaves you trapped inside while your synapses keep rewiring themselves."

She glanced up at Jake. "Appreciate the Dark, man."

Jake nudged Lori's foot with one massive hand. "No problem. You good?"

"Yeah. Got it."

He grunted. "Tell your fuck-friend to keep her girl away from that shit." Then he was gone, the door swinging shut behind him with surprising gentleness.

Only then did Marti see where they were: a cramped apartment carved from the bar's back rooms. Faded floral wallpaper peeled at the edges like dead skin, revealing patches of fresh paint underneath. Mossy green and crisp white battled years of neglect. Overhead lights buzzed too bright, casting harsh shadows across a space that couldn't decide if it wanted to be forgotten or remade.

Lori sprawled unconscious on a couch that had seen better days, her head propped on a garish pink pillow: the only vibrant thing in the room.

Angel gestured toward the battered kitchen table without looking up from Lori. "Sit down. She'll be fine." Her voice carried that same fuck-it confidence Marti remembered from years ago, like the world might be burning, but Angel had calculated which direction the wind was blowing. "I'll grab beers."

Marti lowered herself into a chair without taking her eyes off Lori's still form. Angel popped the caps off two bottles, shooting them into the blue crate by the fridge with precision.

"She'll be fine," Angel repeated, sliding a bottle across the table. She leaned forward, pulling up her pant leg to reveal a thick scar encircling her ankle. "Tried flying once." Her grin turned sharp as she met Marti's gaze. "Didn't work out."

Marti stared a beat longer than necessary before taking a long pull from her beer because what the fuck else was there to do?

Angel traced the rim of her bottle, contemplating something before jerking her chin toward Lori. "She won't remember shit," she said. "Three, four hours and she'll wake up clueless." A pause. "What's her name?"

"Lori." Marti reached out, brushed aside a strand of hair from Lori's face. Watched her chest rise and fall, slow and steady now. Alive.

"She'll remember everything up to the Bright hit," Angel explained, propping herself against the counter. "Then nothing. Dark blocks the neural pathways Bright lights up. Stops the process cold."

"She gonna be okay?" Marti couldn't keep the concern from leaking into her voice.

"Yeah. No lasting damage. We cut it off early, so no cravings. Just needs time for her system to reset."

Marti exhaled, fingers fishing a rumpled pack of cigarettes from her pocket. "Fuck me," she muttered, shaking one loose and placing it between her lips. The first drag burned familiar and necessary.

"Still smoking, I see," Angel observed, something like fondness creeping into her voice.

Marti's lips curved around the cigarette. "Got enough addictions for both me and Lori."

Angel tilted her head, studying her. "That your girl?"

Marti's laugh came out harsh and sudden. "Her? Hell no. She's my secretary." She dragged smoke deep into her lungs, letting it seep out between her teeth. "Fuck. We met some clients before this shitshow."

Angel nodded like that made perfect sense, like their lives hadn't just collided again after years of unaware distance. She reached across the table, fingers brushing against Marti's forehead, pushing back stubborn strands of hair that fell back into place.

"You ever cut this shit?" she asked, amused at the futility of her efforts.

Marti snorted, flicking ash into an empty bottle. "You looking to sell Bright on the streets now?"

Angel leaned back on her elbows, relaxed in a way that made Marti's chest ache with something she refused to name. "Big Man Jake runs distribution. I just know the chemistry, not where it goes after." A small smirk played at her lips. "My girl don't like drugs."

"So you're deep in Bright but dating a saint?" Marti chuckled. "That's some poetic bullshit right there."

Angel laughed, the sound warming the cold corners of the room. "Robin 's amazing," she said, flexing an arm with pride. "Met her at the gym a few months back. Real healthy type."

Marti raised an eyebrow as Angel lifted her shirt just enough to reveal carved-out abs where softness used to be: terrain Marti had once mapped with hungry fingers and greedy mouth, pressed against car doors and squeaking mattresses. The landscape had changed.

"Damn," Marti whispered, then whistled low. "That is one hell of a glow-up."

Angel's grin widened, teeth flashing as she stretched, fingers laced behind her head. The position pulled her shirt higher, revealing more skin: deliberate in a way that made heat pool in Marti's stomach.

"When we dated..."

"For two goddamn weeks," Marti interjected.

"When we dated," Angel repeated, eyes glinting mischief over her bottle, "you were something else."

Marti took another drag, smoke curling between them like a living thing. "Yeah? You liked?" The words slipped out before she could stop them.

Angel leaned forward, voice dropping to a register that vibrated along Marti's spine. "Mama's bed," she murmured, watching Marti's reaction. She was rewarded when Marti's smirk cracked into laughter at the memory of ancient springs screaming beneath their tangled bodies.

"And the car," Marti countered between gasps. "Belt buckles. My ass never recovered from those goddamn buckles."

Angel winced but didn't deny it; just let her grin spread slow and wicked. The tension between them shifted, old memories bleeding into present desire.

"And the roof," Angel added, voice honeyed with suggestion.

"That fucking tar paper roof," Marti groaned, rubbing her lower back at the phantom pain.

A heartbeat of silence.

Then laughter spilled between them, warm and dangerous as spilled whiskey: something they shouldn't touch but couldn't resist.

"And that restaurant," Marti mused, cigarette dangling forgotten between her fingers.

Angel groaned, covering her face as if that memory burned brighter than all the rest.

"Broke my wrist," she admitted through muffled laughter.

"I damn near stabbed myself with my fork trying to look normal," Marti added, grinning so wide it hurt.

Angel peeked through her fingers. "Oh, that waiter knew."

The memories flowed between them without need for explanation; their shared past deeper than words could capture. But Angel still chuckled before adding:

"And the park."

A beat of silence.

"Holy fuck," Marti wheezed, laughter sharp enough to cut.

"My poor innocent elbow," Angel lamented with flair.

"Innocent?" Marti snorted, ash falling unnoticed. "I recall an elbow begging me to hump it."

Angel gasped in mock outrage, clutching her chest. "Hump it? You were a damn menace!"

"A menace who stumbled upon the softest, most inviting elbow in existence."

Their laughter melded together, settling warm in Marti's chest, making her forget, just for a moment, the mess of everything else.

"You made use of every part of me," Angel mused, her voice softening to something intimate.

Angel tilted her head, considering. "You may have ridden me like a cowgirl, but there's one thing we never did."

"Oh?" Marti arched a brow. "Do tell."

Angel moved closer, the scent of her (cheap soap and expensive perfume) filling Marti's lungs more than smoke. "I've wanted to sit on this pretty face of yours," she murmured. "To feel you under me."

Marti frowned, confusion breaking through desire. "Really? I went down on you all the time."

Angel tsked, shaking her head. "Not like that." Her fingers traced Marti's jaw, nails scraping just enough to raise goosebumps. "I was bigger back then. Worried about crushing you." Her thumb brushed Marti's bottom lip, pressing until Marti's mouth parted. "But I wanted to."

"Yeah?" Marti's voice had gone rough.

"Yeah," Angel confirmed, voice dropping lower. "Wanted to fuck your face until I couldn't think straight."

Marti caught Angel's wrist, drawing her index finger into her mouth with slowness. She sucked hard, watching Angel's pupils dilate before biting down (not hard, but enough) then releasing with a wet sound that echoed in the quiet room.

"Jesus," Angel breathed, closing the distance between them.

Their lips met with the familiarity of old lovers and the hunger of strangers. Marti groaned as Angel swung a leg over her lap, settling her weight with ease. Lori, asleep on the couch, saw nothing.

"I've thought about this sometimes," Angel admitted against Marti's mouth, rolling her hips in a slow, deliberate tease.

Marti's fingers dug into Angel's waist, gripping hard enough to bruise as she looked up through heavy lids. Her lips curled into something wicked and wanting.

"Then stop thinking."

The words hung between them, heavy with promise and the weight of their shared history, as Lori lay forgotten on the couch behind them.

Chapter 12

The familiar scent of Angel's perfume mixed with leather as Marti yanked her in by the neck, muscle memory taking over where hesitation had lived moments before. Their mouths crashed together, and Marti's other hand found Angel's nipple, rolling it between her fingers before giving it a sharp twist: clockwise. Angel liked clockwise.

"Oh fuck, I love that," Angel mumbled against her lips. "Harder."

Marti obliged, squeezing until Angel hissed through her teeth, then let go just long enough to tear Angel's shirt over her head. Angel didn't waste time, tugging at Marti's own shirt as if it was keeping them from oxygen. Marti barely got it over her shoulders before Angel shoved her toward the bed, eyes dark with intent.

"You gonna let me eat you?" Marti teased as she landed on the mattress.

"Let you?" Angel scoffed, yanking Marti's jeans down her legs. "I'll fucking force you." Angel's phone was thrown down, clattering against Marti's, forgotten among their scattered clothes.

Marti scrambled back to the center of the bed, arms raised in invitation. Angel shed her own pants in one fluid motion and straddled Marti's waist. She glanced down at herself: black cotton torn at the seam, and smirked. "These aren't my best," she said, fingering the rip. "Didn't think anyone would see them."

Marti traced a teasing fingertip along the split fabric and into the heat beneath. Angel jerked, sucking in a breath as Marti pressed deeper, stroking through cotton and slick skin alike. Her thumb found its way to Angel's clit, rubbing slow circles through damp fabric until Angel gasped and grabbed a fistful of Marti's hair.

"Eat me," she ordered. "Just like this."

Marti didn't need to be told twice. She gripped Angel's hips and pulled her forward until wet cotton pressed flush against her mouth, soaking into her lips as she dragged teeth and tongue along the damp seam. She groaned deep in her throat and shoved aside the fabric with her tongue, mouthing at burning flesh beneath.

Angel rocked against her face, light at first, tormenting them both, before pressing down harder with each pass of Marti's tongue.

"Harder," Marti murmured against slick heat, voice lost between Angel's thighs. She dug fingers into soft flesh and pulled Angel closer, urging more weight down onto her mouth.

Angel let out something like a growl and shifted forward, grabbing the headboard for leverage before dropping her full weight onto Marti's face. Marti groaned as warmth smothered every inch of her mouth: lips, chin, nose, while she licked deeper, stroked faster. Salt slick spread across her tongue as she moved lower, teasing the edge of Angel's entrance before plunging inside with strokes.

Angel choked out a curse and lifted herself off Marti's face just long enough to tear off what little was left of her underwear before slamming back down again with force.

Marti barely had a second to breathe before wet heat crashed over her again. Bare this time. A flood against lips and tongue as she sucked deep against swollen flesh.

Above her, Angel was unraveling fast.

She ground forward with abandon now, chasing pleasure as sweat gleamed down the slope of her stomach and along trembling thighs.

"Fuck," she gasped out, hips jerking above Marti's eager mouth. "Right there! Fuck yes!"

A low groan rumbled from deep inside Marti's chest as she flicked faster over Angel's clit, drinking in every moan and tremor like they belonged to her.

Angel bore down so hard Marti could barely breathe. But that only made it better.

"I wanna come all over you," Angel panted through clenched teeth. "Wanna drown you in it."

Marti slid one hand up; found soft curls and curled two fingers inside without warning.

Angel clenched her thighs tight around Marti's head, riding hard, relentless. "Fuck me, Marti! Harder!" Her voice broke on the last word, her hips pressing down, demanding more.

Marti gasped against slick heat, fingers tightening around Angel's thighs. Her lungs screamed. No air. Her vision swam. Orgasm hovered just out of Angel's reach, but Marti was drowning. She pushed at Angel's hips once. Twice. But Angel was too lost in it to notice.

So Marti shoved back. Hard.

Angel yelped as she toppled backward onto the mattress, legs sprawling beneath her. Barely a second to process before Marti surged up for air and then dove straight back in, tongue fucking deep while her fingers rubbed circles over Angel's clit.

Angel arched off the bed with a strangled moan. "Oh fuck... fuck! I—" Her body locked up, every muscle tensing, then breaking apart all at once. She grabbed for Marti's hair as pleasure wrecked her in pulses that left her shaking.

Marti licked through each aftershock, sucking until Angel whimpered, too sensitive to take any more. She pulled back just enough to breathe and swipe a hand over her face before grinning at Angel's glazed-over expression.

"Say what you want about being thrown mid-orgasm, but that shit worked." Angel groaned and threw an arm over her eyes. "What the fuck even was that? Judo? Wrestling? Some kind of assassin move?"

Marti flopped onto her side next to her. "Survival instinct." No way she was admitting she nearly passed out between Angel's thighs. No way was she admitting she was just fucking Angel to forget about Lori. Not when that feral grin was creeping across Angel's face.

"Jesus fuck." Angel huffed out a laugh that barely had enough energy behind it to count as one. "Stay there." Her voice was wrecked and breathless against the sheets. "Lie on top of me."

Marti smirked but obeyed anyway, stretching herself over Angel's back until their bodies aligned: legs tangled together, breasts pressed flush against rippling shoulders still damp with sweat from their exertions. She nuzzled into the crook of Angel's neck and kissed whatever skin was available until they both remembered how to breathe again.

Then, because Marti could never leave well enough alone, she slid off of Angel just far enough to snatch up her phone from where she'd left it on the nightstand.

Click.

Angel cracked an eye open just enough to glare at Marti over one shoulder.

Marti grinned at the freshly captured shot: a perfect view between strong thighs leading right up to where all that pleasure had happened just moments ago.

"That," she said smugly, snapping one more for good measure, "is my new wallpaper."

Angel rolled her eyes but didn't protest, reaching past empty beer bottles to check her phone before settling back against the pillows. The screen showed no messages. Yet.

Chapter 13

Marti stared at her new phone wallpaper. It was going to come in handy later. The exhaustion had barely settled around them when Angel's phone buzzed: a soft chime that shattered everything.

"Fuck!" Angel jolted up, kicking the blanket off and slapping a hand over Marti's mouth before she could make a sound. "Shhh." Her other hand swiped across the nightstand, knocking over a half-empty lube bottle before closing around her phone. The liquid pooled across the surface, dripping onto the floor in a steady rhythm.

Marti groaned into Angel's palm and pried it off her face. She squinted at the clock. Two hours. They'd gone at it for two fucking hours, and Lori still had another hour of sleep before she'd stir. Plenty of time for round three, if…

"It's my girlfriend," Angel hissed, eyes wide with panic. "Shut up." And then, into the phone: "Hey babe... Huh? Locked?"

Angel's gaze locked with Marti's as she mouthed: Get dressed.

"Yes, yep, just gimme a second." Angel hung up and flung herself toward her scattered clothes. "Move! She's outside!"

Marti scrambled, yanking her jeans from the floor and shoving her feet in without bothering to unbutton them first. The denim scraped against her skin, still damp with sweat. Angel tore through the room as if someone had lit a fuse in her spine. Bed straightened with one violent yank, track pants on, T-shirt over her head. Marti's fingers fumbled with buttons as sweat slicked down her back, breath coming too fast, but fuck it, she wasn't dying here over a goddamn shirt.

She spotted her bra hanging from the chair just as Angel grabbed the doorknob. No time. She shoved it into her pocket instead and barely managed to skid across the room before Angel wrenched the door open.

Marti dove onto the couch and landed with a soft thud beside Lori, who stirred just enough to drape one leg over Marti's lap like she belonged there. Perfect cover. Casual as hell. The couch cushion still smelled of cigarettes and cheap beer, masking any evidence of what they'd been doing.

Angel moved to intercept Robin in the doorway with a kiss that was maybe too eager, but hey. Damage control was an art form.

"Hey babe," Angel purred, leaning into the kiss with ease.

Robin stepped inside, her boots clicking against the hardwood. She clocked Marti on her couch looking too comfortable under Lori's legs. Dark brows lifted in suspicion as she crossed her arms over her chest, her leather jacket creaking with the movement.

"Oh," Robin said, eyes flicking between them like they were items on a discounted menu. "Hello?"

Marti stretched out as if she hadn't just sprinted across the fucking room seconds ago and offered a lazy salute with two fingers wrapped around an unlit cigarette. Her heart hammered against her ribs, but her face remained a mask of indifference.

"This is Marti and Lori," Angel said, too fast for comfort.

Robin hummed in acknowledgment but didn't move past the threshold. "Hi," she said, voice cool enough to make vodka jealous. "I'm Robin." She leveled a look at both of them before settling on Marti. "Angel's girlfriend."

The words landed sharp, deliberate: a blade testing how deep it could press before drawing blood.

Marti lit her cigarette with deliberate slowness, the flame illuminating her face in orange light. She exhaled a cloud of smoke and adjusted Lori's leg so she could reach the beer bottle beside her on the table. It was empty but she could make it look like it wasn't and that this was where she had been sitting all along, not that Robin seemed convinced by any of this bullshit attempt at normalcy, anyway.

Robin turned back to Angel with narrowed eyes and just enough acid to melt through steel beams when she asked: "What's going on?"

Angel stalled for half a beat, her mouth opening and closing without sound. Marti jumped in before the silence could grow incriminating.

"My wife took too much Bright," she said, taking a slow drag off her cigarette as if this wasn't an escalating disaster zone. "Big Man Jake told us to let her sleep it off here." The lie rolled off her tongue with ease, despite the absurdity of calling Lori her wife.

Robin's posture stiffened. She wasn't buying it for a goddamn second.

"Oh?" She tilted her head like a predator sizing up prey dumb enough to wander too close to its den. "Her brother told you to hang out here? With my girl?" Her fingers twitched toward her phone before anyone could stop her. "Let's ask him."

Angel tensed beside her as Robin dialed with all the confidence of someone who knew what answer they wanted and was daring reality to say otherwise. The ringtone echoed through the quiet room, each chime cranking the tension higher.

"Hey Big Man," Robin said when he picked up on speakerphone, not even bothering with pleasantries or pretense as she angled the camera at Marti like evidence submitted for trial. "You know this bitch with Angel?"

Marti smirked and wiggled her fingers at the camera lens in greeting while exhaling another curl of smoke into the air just because she could. Inside, her stomach knotted; this whole situation balanced on a knife's edge.

"Queen?" Big Man Jake barked through shitty speaker quality, his voice coated in amusement that dripped through the call like molasses made of bad decisions and worse company choices. "Yeah, I know her." A beat of silence stretched before he added: "What's the problem? Aside from her being an asshole."

Robin gestured toward everything with her free hand. "Why are they in my home?"

Big Man Jake snorted on the other end like this was all beneath him but still entertaining nonetheless. "I gave

Queen some Bright," he admitted, like recounting what he had for breakfast rather than handing out illicit substances like party favors at Christmas dinner. "Blondie drank it all in one go." His tone dipped toward something close to impressed, or maybe just baffled by sheer recklessness alone, before he continued: "Angel gave Blondie some Dark after that and figured y'all should let her sleep it off instead of letting me deal with it." Another pause followed before he asked: "Is Queen being an asshole?"

Marti broke, snorting out a laugh before calling loud enough for both parties on either end of this conversation to hear:

"Always!"

Big Man Jake laughed right back at full volume like they were sharing beers instead of covering each other's asses over possible infidelity accusations mid-break-in scenario gone wrong at fuck-o'clock in the morning.

"Queen! Fuckin' right!" He hollered out between chuckles like this was his favorite joke all week, or maybe just because fucking with Robin was his personal pastime whenever possible. "She's good, Robin, she's good." Then after another pause that dragged out just long enough to be unsettling: "But keep her gun until she leaves."

"The fuck? Fine. Thanks, Jake," Robin muttered, hanging up. The sudden silence felt heavier than before. She didn't look convinced, but Big Man Jake's word wasn't up for debate. She set the phone on the counter with a sharp click and turned. "Your gun?"

Marti tipped her chin toward her jacket draped over the arm of the couch. Robin's mouth flattened into something resembling a paper cut as she plucked the gun up between two fingers, like it might bite her. Angel rolled her eyes, grabbed it from Robin, and winked at Marti before setting it on the table. The metal made a dull thud against the wood.

"Queen—"

"Marti," she corrected, blowing smoke toward the ceiling. "Only Big Man Jake calls me Queen."

"Marti," Robin snapped, eyes narrowing as they swept over her disheveled appearance. "Why is your shirt half-buttoned?"

Marti glanced down and realized she'd only managed to get three of the six done. Looked like she'd gotten dressed in a wind tunnel. She barely stopped herself from laughing out loud as she met Robin's suspicious glare.

"Buttons are hard." She shrugged, then gestured toward her jacket with her chin. "My inhaler."

Angel picked up the leather jacket, the material sighing as she rummaged through the pockets until there it was. The second Angel held up the Shadow inhaler (empty, but they didn't have to know), Robin's eyes went wide before pulling back into something that wanted to be an apologetic smile.

The drug explained everything: the odd behavior, half-dressed, the weird smell, the tension. The perfect cover story slotting into place.

"Shit," Robin said, rubbing the back of her neck. "I don't know what's wrong with me sometimes. When your girlfriend is as hot as Angel, you get a little jealous." She turned to Angel with a smirk. "I mean, look at this babe."

"No worries," Marti said, reaching for the inhaler and brushing Angel's fingers when she took it. A slow stroke along Angel's knuckles just to make Robin squirm a little more, not that Marti cared enough to push it further. She had no use for petty insecurity.

She did have a use for Lori, though: her 'wife', who was unconscious on the couch. And so Marti ran a hand down Lori's leg like she was petting a beloved dog. She didn't trust herself to be more affectionate than that without her fingers wandering somewhere dangerous in front of this audience.

"You want a beer?" Robin asked, reaching toward the fridge handle like she wasn't sure she wanted them in her home any longer than necessary. The refrigerator light cast a harsh glow across her face when she opened it.

"Nah." Marti shook the inhaler in the air like punctuation before bringing it close (but not touching) to her lips and sucking in breath through her teeth like she'd taken a deep hit of Shadow. A beat later, she coughed loudly for effect and let her head loll back against the couch. That should buy her twenty minutes of being left the fuck alone.

Didn't take long before Robin and Angel assumed she was out cold, their voices dropping to hushed whispers as they moved toward the kitchen.

"Why would Jake want them staying here?" Robin hissed under her breath, low and angry. The clink of bottles and rustling of takeout containers punctuated her words.

"I think he likes Marti," Angel said. "He seemed happy enough to see her."

"You know her?"

Angel hesitated just long enough to be suspicious before covering with an awkward shrug, like someone fumbling for words they didn't want coming back to haunt them later. "Yeah...a bit," she lied badly. "Jake carried Blondie in here himself. Just until she wakes up."

"How much longer?" Robin grumbled, the microwave humming to life behind her words.

"Maybe half an hour?" Angel's tone turned syrupy-sweet as she nodded toward the fridge instead of answering. "I saved some Chinese takeout for you, babe."

That did the trick; took all of two seconds for Robin's face to soften just enough that Angel looked satisfied that she'd dodged discovery for now. Meanwhile, Marti listened through their banal little coupledom routine and tried to reconcile this version of Angel (the one playing devoted girlfriend) with her version of Angel: the one who had shoved herself between Marti's lips with such desperate hunger that Marti had nearly blacked out from lack of oxygen and too much good sex.

Yeah, those two versions didn't fucking add up.

Time to go before anyone got too comfortable thinking they could keep Marti sidelined like a piece of forgotten furniture.

Chapter 14

She stirred and pushed up to stand, rolling her neck as if shaking off a daze instead of calculating how quickly she could get out of here without making things weird, or weirder than they were. Her joints popped audibly in the sudden silence.

"Gotta pee." She stretched with a yawn before glancing at Robin.

Robin sighed but pointed toward a door down the hall, her chopsticks pausing midway to her mouth.

Marti didn't rush exactly. Just moved quickly enough not to give anyone time to question shit while she scooped up socks from where they'd been kicked off earlier and disappeared into the bathroom. The door clicked shut behind her, and she leaned against it for a moment, exhaling slowly.

Bra back on first. Priorities. The hooks caught on her skin as she fumbled in the dim light.

Then socks, pulled on.

Then piss, the sound echoing in the small bathroom.

Face scrubbed raw under ice-cold water because there wasn't enough soap in this place to wash away every trace of Angel from her skin. The water dripped down her neck, cold rivulets that made her shiver.

By the time she emerged again into dim light and stale cigarette smoke curling through stagnant air, Lori was stirring. The couch creaked as she shifted, a soft groan escaping her lips.

Careful now.

Marti moved toward where Lori lay curled on the couch; she crouched at eye level and reached out, brushing stray strands away from Lori's face with deliberate softness. The blonde hair felt like silk between her fingers.

Lori blinked awake by degrees, lashes fluttering before settling on Marti with hazy recognition. Her pupils were dilated, struggling to focus.

"...You?" Lori murmured.

"Yeah," Marti confirmed quietly, her voice softer than usual.

Lori's brow furrowed as she caught sight of unfamiliar figures lurking in periphery over Marti's shoulder; tension stiffened every muscle in her body like someone snapping back into reality after free-floating in dreamspace too long. Her fingers clutched at the couch cushion, knuckles whitening.

She straightened and swung both feet onto the floor as if grounding herself physically would help piece together whatever puzzle was forming in fragments inside her head. The sudden movement made her sway, and Marti steadied her with a hand on her shoulder.

"I..." Lori exhaled before rubbing lingering sleep from her face with both hands like trying to erase confusion by sheer force alone. "Was I asleep?"

"You overdosed on Bright," Angel supplied from across the room.

"Huh?"

Lori blinked at that news before stretching stiff shoulders with deliberate concentration like giving herself time to process, or argue. Her joints cracked audibly in the quiet room.

She didn't remember. "So, when we came in..." Marti began, keeping her voice low and steady.

Marti spoke quietly while Lori worked through every word tumbling together inside her brain and then watched as realization cracked across Lori's face in increments: first disbelief...then suspicion...then cold anger settling into something solid behind narrowed eyes. Color rose in her cheeks, a flush that wasn't just from the drug.

By the time Marti finished recounting what had happened (including waking up here but not including fucking Angel just feet from where she laid), Lori wasn't just mad.

She was fucking furious. Then she tried to stand. Lori's eyes fluttered, unfocused. Her body was dead weight, her limbs sluggish. Marti grabbed her hand, pulled her to her feet, and barely hid a wince as she gestured toward the cane leaning against the table. Robin handed it over without a word, the wood smooth and worn at the handle. Angel hovered nearby, looking fucking guilty.

"Get me the fuck out of here," Lori said as she zombied across the floor. Angel slung an arm around Lori's waist and led her through the back of the bar. The heavy metal door groaned open, letting in a slap of cold air and the light drizzle of pre-dawn sun. The scent of filthy asphalt rose from the pavement.

Lori shivered hard enough that Angel tightened her grip, half-dragging her toward Marti's car. "Jesus," Lori muttered as she collapsed into the passenger seat, voice thick and hoarse, "how long was I out?"

Marti started the engine and shot a lazy salute toward Robin and Angel before peeling out onto the empty street. The tires splashed through puddles that never dried up, sending water cascading onto the sidewalk. "Three hours."

Lori stared at her, something sharp flickering in her eyes despite how fucking drained she looked. Her fingers tapped an uneven rhythm against her thigh. "What... I... What were you doing with that kind of drink?"

Marti didn't blink. "It was a gift." She kept her eyes on the road, tires humming low against the uneven asphalt, the sound filling the silence between them.

"A gift?"

"I was going to toss it." Marti flicked the turn signal, the clicking filling the silence between them.

"You toss a drink?" Lori's voice rose in disbelief.

"Yes," Marti said slowly, as if that should've ended the conversation. "I told you not to touch it, I thought you heard me." The streetlights cast alternating shadows across her face as they drove.

Lori's hands curled into fists against her thighs. "Oh no," she hissed through clenched teeth. "You didn't think at all."

"That's not—"

"You never fucking think." The words hit like gunfire, direct and brutal, with no room for evasion. "Not about other people. Never about other people."

Marti gritted her teeth, forced herself to keep both hands on the wheel because she had zero patience left for this shit tonight. The leather creaked under her grip. "That's not fair."

"The fuck it isn't!" Lori whipped toward her so fast Marti could feel the heat of her glare on the side of her face. "You put poison near me—"

"It wasn't poison." Marti swerved to avoid a pothole, the car dipping and rising beneath them.

"If it has an antidote," Lori spat, "it's fucking poison." Her breath fogged the window beside her.

"It was in front of me! You went drinking through my shit!" Marti's knuckles whitened on the steering wheel.

"You put it near me without thinking about me! Without thinking about anyone! Anyone could've taken that drink by mistake!" Lori's voice bounced off the closed windows, filling the small space.

Marti tossed one hand up in frustration before slapping it back down on the wheel. "Jesus fucking Christ, what do you want me to say? I told you not to touch it."

Lori laughed bitterly, humorless and edged with something dangerous. The sound hung between them like broken glass.

"You want me to say I'm sorry you did what I told you not to do?" Marti snapped before Lori could speak. "Fine. I'm sorry you didn't fucking listen to me. Or do you want me to say I'm sorry I wasn't babysitting your grown ass every second we were in that shithole bar? Sorry. I'm so fucking sorry for assuming you'd follow basic instructions like a functioning adult."

Lori's breath hitched. Her hands trembled from more than just exhaustion now; rage vibrated through every inch of her body like she was barely holding herself together by sheer force of will alone. The air inside was dry and still, except for the soft whisper of ventilation brushing across her skin.

"I could have died." Her voice dropped to barely above a whisper.

"You didn't." Marti hit the brakes too hard at a red light, sending them both lurching forward before settling back.

"You're an asshole," she choked out, voice raw and wrecked beneath all that fury.

"Sticks and stones," Marti shot back too fast, too defensive, and watched something crack behind Lori's eyes just as doubt gnawed its way into her own gut. The engine vibrated through her seat, a low, constant growl that settled somewhere beneath her ribs.

"Not sticks," Lori murmured, shaking now, not from cold but from something far deeper, something Marti didn't have the stomach to name right now.

Her voice broke wide open as she continued: "Bullets. Knives. Punches. Cars and fucking poison." Her breath shuddered between words now, but she didn't stop, couldn't stop, because there were years of hurt spilling out unchecked in the small space between them. She ran a trembling hand through her hair, damp strands sticking to her forehead.

"I've been terrorized and brutalized working for you," she whispered. "I've heard men scream as they died. And I've held you while you almost bled out too many times to count."

A muscle jumped in Marti's jaw. It was all true.

"I've taken you to the hospital over and over again," Lori pushed on, voice rising with every syllable until it filled every inch of the car like static electricity before a storm hits. "And you never fucking stop."

The streetlights blurred past them as Marti stared at a road that seemed endless. Her hands tightened on the wheel, leather warm under her grip, the faint scent of oil and old coffee lingering in the cabin.

"You got shot four times," Lori whispered brokenly now, tears slipping down flushed cheeks like silent accusations carved into flesh, "and I never left your side." Her fingers pressed against a scar visible at Marti's collar, a physical reminder of what she'd survived.

Marti's chest burned, but she couldn't look at Lori now. She swallowed hard, the sound audible in the quiet.

"And now you're talking to me like I'm some child who needs chastising?" The disbelief in her voice cut deeper than any blade ever had.

Silence stretched long between them until Lori exhaled through gritted teeth. A car horn blared, but neither of them gave a shit.

"There's no honesty in your words," she finished quietly, deadly finality settling into every syllable like cement hardening around bone.

"They're just another excuse."

The words sat heavily between them.

And for once, just once, Marti didn't have anything clever left to say.

"You're fucked up, Marti."

Lori's voice wasn't loud. It didn't need to be. The words landed hard, flat, filling the car like smoke. "You're so screwed up, you're dangerous."

Marti pressed harder on the gas. Not enough to be reckless, just enough to feel it. The road humming beneath them, the engine swallowing the silence between words as if it could chew them up, spit them out somewhere else. Somewhere they didn't exist.

"I was going to say 'dangerous to the people you care about,' but that would mean you care." Lori turned in her seat, eyes burning through Marti's profile. "You don't."

Marti exhaled slowly. Kept her hands on the wheel. Kept moving forward. Her reflection in the rearview mirror showed nothing, her expression blank.

"You don't care about anything but yourself. You're sick, and your illness is contagious."

Something cracked, not in her voice, not yet, but in the way her breath hitched at the end of it. A rough edge where there used to be patience. A tear slid down her cheek, catching the passing streetlight.

Marti's grip faltered for half a second, just enough for the car to swerve before she corrected it. A mistake small enough to ignore if Lori hadn't been watching her like a goddamn hawk.

"Look, just, take it easy..." She caught herself too late, the words hanging in the air like a challenge.

Lori exploded. "Take it easy? Take it easy?" She twisted in her seat, heat rolling off her in waves now. "How dare you?" Her fist slammed against the dashboard, the sound sharp and sudden.

Marti sighed, tipped her head back against the headrest for a second before bringing her gaze back to the road. "For fuck's sake."

"No! No, for my sake! Me! I exist! I am here! You treat me like a child when it suits you and like an object when it doesn't, like some disposable thing you can play with until you get bored!" Her hand curled into a fist against her thigh, knuckles white with tension. "I ask you out and you laugh in my face. I try playing by your rules; try being sexy, try pretending none of this matters. And you lead me on then shove me away like it's my fault for trying! And when I try showing you what real looks like, what normal could be, you threaten to shoot my fucking family!"

Marti said nothing. Just turned onto an empty road and kept driving, waiting for Lori to run out of steam or breath or both. She never should have suggested shooting those kids; it was a joke that would always haunt her. Every lane change clicked loud in her ears, the turn signal ticking like a nervous pulse in the quiet car.

But Lori wasn't done.

"You see that? See that?" Her voice cracked now, but she didn't stop; if anything, she leaned into it harder. "Aside from shrugging and agreeing. 'yep, I'm an asshole,' you have nothing to say. Nothing real anyway. No defense because there isn't one! It's all bullshit with you! Everything is some joke or some cop-out or some excuse for why none of this is your problem!" Her breath came fast now, sharp between words cutting deeper than they should've been able to in such a small space. "You are incapable of being decent because deep down you don't want to be! And worst part? You make everyone around you worse just by existing near them!"

Silence stretched between them, long enough for Marti to turn onto Lori's street and pull up outside her apartment building without looking over once. The engine idled, a low rumble beneath the sound of rusted metal.

"Get out."

Lori stared at her like she'd been slapped across the face with an open palm instead of two words. "Are you fucking kidding me?" The disbelief in her voice was palpable.

"This is your place." Marti reached across her lap and unlocked the door with one press of a button before leaning back against the seat like she was alone again. "Get out."

Her fingers tapped once against the steering wheel as she waited for movement beside her, for footsteps on pavement and for a door slamming shut, but Lori didn't move right away. Didn't leave without one last swipe at something raw inside Marti's ribs first:

"You know what?" Her voice had cooled again, not soft this time but hollow: the kind of exhaustion that sank into bone when you accepted someone was never going to meet you halfway no matter how far you stretched yourself trying first.

"You'll never have more than this," she said before opening the door and stepping out into the night without another word, slamming the door behind her. The night embraced her as she walked away, not looking back even once.

Marti sat alone in the car, watching Lori's silhouette disappear into the building, the only sound her own breathing in the empty space Lori had left behind.

Chapter 15

Marti lit a cigarette and stared at the office door like it might explode, her fingers still stiff from gripping the steering wheel too tight last night. The light was on. Lori was in there. That was either a good sign or the beginning of a spectacular fucking disaster.

She blew out smoke and leaned against the wall, shoulders aching with remembered tension. Last night's words still echoed: You'll never have more than this. Maybe Lori was right. Maybe this was all she deserved: standing outside her own office like a coward, waiting to face the aftermath of another mess she'd created.

The night had been loud. Lori hissing, collapsing, waking up confused, then screaming some more. A proper meltdown. Marti had bet on fury today, maybe shredded case files or wiped databases as revenge. But no, just light spilling from under the door, deceptively normal.

Marti tapped ash onto the floor and checked the time. Eleven a.m. She crushed what little hope she had left and walked in.

Lori sat at her desk, looking like an impersonation of herself. Plain gray sweater, white shirt, no makeup, no fire in her eyes. No smile. Nothing.

"Hey," Marti said as she dropped into the client chair across from her.

"Hi, Marti." Soft voice, even warm. Dangerous.

Lori's fingers drummed once against a neat stack of file folders. "Blue folder's the updated employee manual. Green has summaries of open cases with data locations on the server." She tapped the third. "Purple is research logins, sorted by specialty and alphabetized." She looked up, something unreadable flickering in her eyes before she shut it down again. "I know you like print."

Marti opened her mouth, no idea what she was about to say, but Lori held up a hand.

"No," Lori said. "You don't get to talk."

Cold spread through Marti's chest as Lori picked up another folder with unsteady fingers, trembling like it required effort just to hold on. "I've paid myself until noon," she continued, voice clipped but wavering at the edges.

"Did my own severance and prorated my bonus." A shaky inhale. "Change your banking passwords today: there's an IronPass shortcut on your desktop with priority accounts listed."

Marti flicked ash from her cigarette onto Lori's pristine desk just to see if it would make her snap, but nothing. Just more calm efficiency as she pressed on: "Medimote orders are inbound; invoices need settling when they land."

Marti rolled the cigarette between her fingers, watching embers glow red before dimming into blackened ash. "That's it?"

"Yes, Marti," Lori said, gathering a few things without looking at her again. "That's it."

Something heavy lodged itself in Marti's throat, pressing down like an unseen hand. She shrugged instead and swallowed past it all: her pride, regret, whatever else was clawing at her insides. She exhaled smoke into the space between them like that could fill the void Lori was leaving behind.

"No sense sitting around for another hour," Marti muttered. "You can go."

Lori hesitated just long enough for Marti to wonder if she'd change her mind, if she'd stay despite everything, but then she moved toward the door without another word.

Marti turned away first because losing felt worse when you saw it happen in real time. "Lock up when you go," she said over her shoulder as she stalked into her office.

The door opened. Closed. The lock clicked.

Then the mail slot flipping open. A dull clank as metal hit tile.

Marti's lungs emptied in one silent rush. She stared at Lori's key on the floor, a tiny piece of metal that somehow ripped through her ribcage like shrapnel, lodging deep where nothing could pull it free.

She stood frozen, watching the key like it might start bleeding if she stared hard enough, until one thought drowned out all others: Fuck feeling anything at all.

She reached for the Shadow inhaler tucked in her desk drawer. The familiar burn of chemicals flooded her system, reality blurring at the edges. One hit became three became five, and time stretched and folded like origami: days dissolving into disconnected moments marked only by cigarette burns and hallucinations that turned computer screens into static paintings and street signs into cryptic messages meant only for her.

And Bertha. Fucking Bertha.

The cat, or ghost, or whatever fractured piece of Marti's own brain, appeared and disappeared between moments of clarity, watching her with those knowing yellow eyes.

The phone's shrill ring cut through her fog, reality sinking its teeth back in. Marti let it ring twice, three times, four. What was left to answer anyway?

She slapped herself. Not hard enough to bruise, just enough to knock her brain back online. Her legs carried her to the bathroom on autopilot. The shower, small and claustrophobic, had been her best business decision. Turn too fast and you'd elbow the wall, but hot water on demand was worth every obscene credit deduction.

The landlord had made a hobby of lurking in the hallway for weeks after she'd installed it, pretending to check light fixtures while watching her door like he thought he'd catch her living there.

"Just checking in," he'd say, eyes darting past her shoulder, hunting for evidence of squatters.

She cranked the knob until steam curled off the tiles and stepped under the spray. Water pummeled her skull like tiny needles drilling through to her brainstem. Good. The pressure washed away chemical residue from her thoughts, leaving behind clarity she wasn't sure she wanted.

When her mind stopped feeling like it was soaking in gutter runoff, she shut off the water and grabbed a towel. Fresh clothes weren't a miracle cure, but at least now she could go five minutes without fantasizing about strangling someone.

Her desk had vanished beneath mountains of paper, all tagged Mothers of the Missing Men. Two hundred seventy-three unread emails pressed against her skull worse than last week's hangover. Her cell phone blinked with voicemails she wouldn't check, landline light flashing.

"Fuck, I need a secretary." The empty office absorbed her words without response.

Bertha appeared from nowhere, like some smug little void given form, and leapt onto the desk with ease. Marti tapped her between the ears. "Where the fuck have you been? You wanna be my secretary?"

Bertha meowed once, pure disdain, then strutted across an important-looking report before flopping onto the couch for a nap.

"Useless fuck."

Lori would've handled this mess: filtered spam, flagged anything that mattered. But Lori wasn't here because Marti was lazy, stubborn, and maybe just a little afraid of what happened when people stuck around too long.

Fine. She grabbed her cell before she could talk herself out of it.

Chapter 16

"Agent Blair." The voice on the other end was clipped, professional. "How can I help you?"

"Heather, it's Marti Starova." She kept her tone light, casual. "How are you?"

A pause, just long enough to register suspicion, before Heather replied, "Good, Marti... how are you?"

"Fine." No point selling the lie. "Listen, I need a favor."

Heather made an unimpressed noise in the back of her throat: the sound of polite rejection forming.

"From me?" Dry as dust. "If this is about that drug charge..."

Marti rolled her eyes. "That'll get dismissed; I'm not worried about that." She hesitated just long enough to give Heather an opening to cut in. When she didn't take it, Marti continued: "I'm looking into missing persons cases."

Heather's voice sharpened: "Missing? Persons? All at once?"

"No," Marti said, running a hand through damp hair as she scanned the files again. "One at a time over a couple years. All Hispanic teenagers. Young men."

Heather sighed, the sound stirring up memories Marti had no energy to face.

"I'm sorry to hear that," Heather said, federal-issue sympathy coating her words. "You want me to put in a word with Missing Persons?"

"I was hoping for something more."

Another sigh, heavier this time, irritation creeping in around the edges.

"You know I can't help you with a case."

Marti clenched her jaw so hard her molars threatened mutiny. "Okay," she said instead of arguing outright.

That got what she wanted: a pause filled with uncertainty, hesitation slipping through cracks in all that official protocol.

"Marti." Heather stretched her name out, every syllable threaded with warning. "I don't want to sound mean here... but I can't."

The inevitable rejection, wrapped up neat and tidy. She sighed back at Heather, long and theatrical, and hung up without another word, knowing it would irritate her just enough to keep thinking about it after they disconnected.

Marti lit a cigarette and took one slow drag while sorting through what came next. Each inhale illuminated thoughts better than meditation or therapy ever could. By the time she'd crushed out the second butt in an overflowing ashtray, a plan had formed beneath the nicotine haze.

She organized photos into something resembling order: faces staring back from grainy printouts, pictures of pictures of pictures.

Outside, rain hammered against thin windowpanes; wind howled past cracks no maintenance crew bothered sealing; shadows stretched long over grimy office floors as city lights flickered behind warped glass.

A shiver ran down her spine, not from cold but from something deeper, clawing at instincts dulled by exhaustion and withdrawal.

Marti tucked the photo lineup into her jacket pocket and stepped into the downpour. Rain sliced through her coat like it had a vendetta. Cold, wet, and pissed off seemed about right. The asphalt stank of rain and oil, sharp against the stale cigarettes lingering on her clothes. She didn't bother hobble-running to her car; what was the point? She was soaked before she even reached the door.

She yanked it open, tossed the cane in, slid behind the wheel, and slammed it shut. The drumming rain and her ragged breath filled the sudden silence. Her fingers clenched the steering wheel. Fuck. Lori wasn't supposed to walk out for real. Slamming doors were part of their routine. Lori leaving her wasn't.

Used Shadow inhalers glinted on the floor, telling her why. They spelled out in chemical residue that she'd fucked up one too many times, pushed too hard, pulled too far, and expected Lori to just keep orbiting around her disaster like it was normal. Turns out, not everyone found self-destruction endearing.

She exhaled hard and started the engine. The wipers scraped away sheets of water in sharp, jerky swipes that matched the static in her skull. She focused on the road, on motion, on anything except how much she wanted to turn back and fix what she couldn't fix.

The police station emerged through the downpour. Good. A case meant focus, progress, forward motion: anything but this tailspin of regret clawing at her ribs. She pulled into the lot and cut the engine before she could think too hard.

Inside, she dripped all over the constable's newspaper without apology. "Martina Starova," she said before leaning in with a smirk, "ante homicidium."

His blink told her everything: he had no fucking clue what that meant, but it sounded official enough to make him nervous.

"Don't repeat that," she added. "It's need-to-know." Then: "I need to see Agent Blair."

The guy nodded too quickly and scrambled to pass along the message. If nothing else today went right, at least intimidation and Latin still worked.

She followed him down the hall until she reached Blair's office doorway. Heather sat with her back straight as ever, eyes locked on her screen. She hadn't turned yet, but tension radiated off her like bad perfume: the rigid set of her shoulders giving away her awareness of Marti's presence.

The officer cleared his throat. "Agent Blair? Martina Starova, anti-homicidum." Formal as hell, which might've been funny if Marti had feelings left for amusement tonight.

"Anti...?" Heather took a beat before looking up. She didn't turn right away, just stared at something on her shelf like it held all the answers.

Marti leaned against the doorframe, arms crossed over her damp coat. "Ante-homicidium. I know you're busy," she said. "Got time to talk?"

Heather exhaled like contemplating murder was preferable to conversation but turned anyway, slowly, and flicked a glance at the officer with enough force to send him scurrying out.

The moment stretched between them; Heather studied Marti with those unreadable eyes (were they green?) before breaking the silence. "What the hell is it?"

"It's complicated enough that I need to sit down." She waggled her cane in the air. "So, if you don't mind..."

Heather gestured at the chair across from her desk. "By all means."

Marti dropped into it, taking lessons from Bertha and stretching out like she owned the place. Heather swiveled toward her, arms crossed.

"How's the wound?" Heather asked.

"Healing." Marti flicked two fingers toward her. "Yours?"

"Fine. A twinge here and there."

"A reminder."

"As if I needed one," Heather said.

Marti smirked. "Scars are cooler than twinges."

Heather arched a brow. "You're scarred."

"I'm cool."

"You come all this way just to compare battle damage?"

"Nah. You'd win." Marti watched as Heather's arms twitched upward, like she was about to pull her jacket tighter, then she stilled, forcing them back down. Interesting. "I need a favor."

Heather exhaled, unimpressed. "You've already asked."

Marti pulled a folded sheet from her pocket, flicked it open, and flattened it on the desk. Five women stared up from the paper. Next page, five young men with names lined beside them in neat print.

Alvarez. Córdova. Hernandez. López. Molina.

Heather's eyes scanned the two lists, her brow tightening just enough to show interest before smoothing again. "Five men's names, five women's? What is this?"

"Five missing young men," Marti said, tapping the first list with her knuckle. "And five mothers with broken hearts." She leaned forward, elbows on her knees. "C'mon, tell me you're not heartless."

Heather snorted. "Really? Emotional manipulation? That's lazy, even for you."

"It was worth a shot," Marti shrugged. "Not that it matters; I brought the wrong paper anyway."

Heather's skepticism was palpable as she leaned back against her desk. "I don't buy that for a second. Your secretary wouldn't send you here without what you needed."

Marti looked down at the page like she could will it into changing, then sighed and rubbed at the bridge of her nose. "Lori quit two days. Weeks? ago."

That got Heather's attention: a slight tilt of her head and a sharp look over the edge of the desk lamp's light pool. "Since when does Lori quit anything?"

"Since she got tangled up in something messy," Marti said. "Needed someone else to blame."

Heather hummed, a noncommittal sound that somehow still reeked of doubt, but didn't press further, just drummed one finger against the desk twice. "What do you want from me?"

Marti relaxed into the chair like they were discussing the weather. "A federal database search on my missing boys."

"And why would I bend over backwards for that?"

"Professional curiosity."

Heather cocked her head but didn't bite right away, just narrowed those sharp green eyes at Marti across the desk.

"Curiosity?"

"Mm-hmm."

"About missing people?"

"About why these mothers, none of whom can afford my rates, pooled their money together for a PI instead of calling the cops."

That got Heather to look at the photos again: the mothers first, then their missing sons. Not long enough to be sentimental but long enough to mean something before sliding her gaze back to Marti.

"You'll owe me a drink," she said.

"Dinner," Marti corrected as she reached for her phone.

Heather smirked like she'd expected that answer all along. "Send me everything."

Marti tapped out a message before looking up through dark lashes. "I did, ma'am."

Heather tilted an eyebrow skyward but didn't respond, just glanced at her phone as it buzzed on the desk beside her elbow then let out an exaggerated sigh.

"Ma'am now, is it?"

"It's ma'am whenever you want it to be," Marti muttered under her breath.

Heather's smirk widened before she turned back to scroll through the files that had just landed in her inbox.

Marti watched her work for half a beat before standing with a ragged stretch and heading for the door. She'd be back soon enough anyway. Through the office window, dark clouds were rolling in, promising the kind of weather that made her joints ache in advance.

Chapter 17

Cold slithered down Marti's spine as she limped toward the coffee shop, each step sending needles through her knee. The cigarette between her lips offered brief warmth before wind snatched the smoke away.

Heat slapped her face as she shouldered through the door. Her phone buzzed. Heather, probably. Important shit. Coffee first.

"There's no smoking in here."

The voice grated like a kazoo with delusions of authority. Marti exhaled smoke toward the source: mid-thirties, average build, thinning hair he thought no one noticed. He looked up at her with hall monitor satisfaction.

"You said what?"

He squared his shoulders. "No smoking inside." His face scrunched with exaggerated disgust.

"That's not what you said." She took another slow drag.

"There's no smoking inside."

Marti blew out twin smoke rings. "And?"

His eyes darted toward the counter. No backup coming. "What is your problem?"

"You. Apparently." She shifted her cane, reaching under her coat in a casual movement that made Kazoo freeze like prey scenting predator.

"Look," his voice thinned, "if you don't put that out, I'm calling the police."

A laugh burst from her throat: sharp, genuine relief. This was nothing. Just another self-important asshole who thought rules kept people safe.

She flicked the cigarette into his coffee without breaking eye contact.

"What the heck?" His chair scraped as he squeezed out from between tables.

Marti lifted her cane, poking him in the chest with each word: "You. Stay. Right. The fuck. Down."

He gaped. "What the fudge is your problem?"

"'Fudge'? Do people actually say that?"

"That's it! I'm calling the police!" He yanked out his phone like a holy relic.

Marti claimed his chair. "Okay." She flagged the barista. "Black coffee." A twenty hit the table. "Keep the change."

She lit another cigarette while Kazoo Man stood frozen, hands clenched.

The barista arrived just as the whiny Kazoo grabbed Marti's cup and poured it onto the floor with all the petty rage of someone who'd never won an argument.

Steam rose in accusation.

"What did you just do?" The barista's voice sliced through silence.

"She made me!"

Marti gasped dramatically before dropping to deadpan: "Jesus Christ, how old are you?"

"Out," the barista decided.

"This isn't fair!" His voice cracked upward.

"Yeah, I ruined your shitty coffee. Tragic." Marti stood, sliding another twenty across the table. The barista didn't take it.

"Don't let her get away with it!" The man grabbed her arm.

Her fist met his nose with satisfying precision. Wet crunch, yelp, blood between fingers.

"Both of you, out."

Outside, adrenaline hummed under her skin. She needed to break or fuck or feel something other than cold seeping into bones.

Falls City stretched before her, soaked in neon and decay. To her left: bodega, fast-food joint, and Adult Love Sex. The shop that somehow survived morality crusaders. To her right: twisted metal that once symbolized civic pride, now dented with bullets and stained with old blood.

Fifteen minutes later she emerged from the sex shop with a paper bag, heading home to the apartment building where she could finally park out front. Landlord folded after weeks of pestering; persistence paid when charm wore thin.

Inside, she caught her reflection. Scars cut across familiar skin, one tracing her collarbone like a signature. Her fingers followed it, considering an eyepatch, something roguish to make damage look intentional.

Her phone vibrated. She ignored it, dropping onto the couch to light up while messages piled like unpaid parking tickets.

She dumped the bag's contents onto her lap.

"What the fuck?"

A glass dildo shaped like a cat? Had she blacked out during purchase? She tossed it aside. Another bad decision in a long line.

Ambient music filled the air as she stripped off dirty jeans, drawing Shadow's inhaler to her lips.

The room melted. Colors dripped; sheets became flesh; breath turned tangible. This was going to be a good trip.

She skimmed bare skin as warmth pooled low, pleasure curling through muscles still tight from confrontation. Behind closed lids, Angel flickered: sharp hipbones and washboard abs.

Then Lori's face superimposed itself. Lori drinking the Bright, collapsing.

Marti's eyes snapped open. The room was too warm, but she pulled the comforter to her chin anyway. Music hummed in darkness, noise to fill silence.

Diego's Dive wouldn't stay buried.

Lori, angry about the gun Marti hadn't fired. Should've stopped her from drinking. Maybe couldn't have. Maybe didn't try. There was no stopping Lori sometimes. Or maybe (the thought slid in like a knife) maybe she'd wanted to see that perfect composure crack. Make her human.

Three hours in the back apartment: Lori flushed, pupils wide as moons while Marti fucked Angel because why not?

Later: Lori comatose. Then shaking. Then furious.

"Poison," Lori had called it. But the poison wasn't in the glass, it was leather jackets and dirty jeans, cigarette smoke and Shadow. It was in her heart.

"It wasn't meant for you," Marti whispered.

Tears came hot and fast. She pressed a hand over her mouth, trapping sound.

She'd lost people before: clients, friends, pieces of herself in unnoticed increments. But this carved out something vital, left hollow space no whiskey or Shadow could fill.

It wasn't Lori's efficiency or bail bond numbers. It was the knowing smirk when Marti lied badly, fingers brushing her shoulder during late nights, that perfect red lipstick leaving marks she never wiped away.

Something had cracked open, grief bleeding slow and steady. She hadn't cried since handing in badge and gun.

Tomorrow she'd armor up again, sharp words locked and loaded.

But tonight was pain and memories and regret heavy enough to drown in.

She reached for another cigarette.

Chapter 18

Three hours later, Marti slammed her office door behind her. Ghost sensations hummed across her skin, worse than the bullet wound in her side. Sweat plastered her clothes to her body: she couldn't get away from what had happened tonight.

Her coat hit the floor with a slap.

A yowl split the silence.

"Jesus fuck, Snirpa."

Bertha perched on the windowsill, yellow eyes narrowed with royal disdain. Marti shoved the window open just wide enough for the cat to squeeze through. Bertha hit the floor, performed a full-body shake that sent fur flying, then had the audacity to rub against Marti's legs, purring.

"This isn't exactly what I had in mind for a soft fluffy pussy."

Marti sat on the couch and stared at the empty chair in the other room. Lori's chair. Still smelled like her, probably.

First Billie, then Lia. Now Lori. All stuck around for longer than anyone should have.

They each had different reasons, different words, but the cause was always the same. The powder, the pills, the vials, the inhalers. The choices Marti made when no one was looking. Or worse, when they were.

She lit another cigarette, watching the smoke coil in the dead air. Relationships, partnerships, friends, lovers. Burned out like the ash at her fingertips. Each one started with patience. Each one ended at the same intersection: her and the drugs, and everyone else walking away.

"You always think you're different," she whispered, voice raw. "Think you're the one who'll handle it better, stick it out longer." The smoke stung her eyes. "You're not."

Lori had just been a secretary, technically. But Marti knew better. She'd been one more person willing to put up with Marti's shit until she couldn't anymore. One more person who'd looked at her with something like hope before that hope curdled into disgust.

The quiet stretched on. Soon she'd have to start placing ads again. Secretary wanted. Must have strong stomach and low expectations.

Marti stalked to her desk. The whiskey bottle came out of the bottom drawer. Heat chased away the chill worming under her skin as she took a long pull.

Her computer coughed to life: 428 emails, mostly spam. Probably. She lit a cigarette and clicked through them. Insurance fraud. Missing spouse. Dumbass who owed her five grand.

Reality smacked her upside the head. Again: She needed a goddamn secretary again.

Her old job posting still sat in drafts:

Secretary for Private Investigator. Seeking an organized masochist capable of dealing with my shit while managing schedules, answering calls, researching leads, and pretending not to judge my life choices. Must have working knowledge of office software and the ability to keep secrets without blackmailing me later. Experience preferred but not required; ability to tolerate assholes mandatory. Salary negotiable (starting at 120k because I'm desperate).

She clicked close. Some truths were best left in draft.

The Missing Men stared up from grainy photos on her desk. Marti stuffed them into her coat pocket alongside cash for bribes or quick getaways. Families were waiting.

Tonight, something had to give.

Falls City cracked under streetlights, broken pavement and busted neon, too many places for people to disappear. Marti worked the streets methodically, showing photos to anyone whose gaze lingered.

"Do you know any of these kids?"

"Kids" got more attention than "missing persons." People could ignore grown men vanishing, but boys not old enough to buy their own liquor hit different.

Hours of refusals followed. Some polite lies, some drenched in threats she ignored until they got specific about her body. Those assholes found themselves staring down her gun barrel until they backed off with mean little laughs.

A woman with skin stretched tight over bones shuffled up. "Got a spare?"

Marti lit one for her. "Seen any of these guys?"

"Not my problem." Another ghost in a city full of them.

Near a wall layered with tags, young guys loitered. One glanced too quick at the pictures before locking down. "Nah." Eyes darting elsewhere, eager to escape before the conversation cost him.

Fifteen hours and nothing. Marti pulled into a bodega lot, thankful she didn't have to park in the street. The coffee machine inside wheezed out something bitter enough to burn but not strong enough to wake her.

Back on the street, she spotted a man with jumpy hands.

"Looking for any of these guys. Seen them?"

He squinted under the streetlight. "Maybe. Think I saw this one? Month ago? Near Boys Town. By the G&D tracks."

"This one?" She tapped Jacinto Córdova's face.

"Yeah? Think so? But he was a white guy. 'Bout thirty?"

Hope flared and died. Still, she pressed a twenty into his palm.

Near the park, gravel crunched underfoot as she approached five men on a bench. They turned wary, ready to run.

"Any of you seen these guys?"

One of them, scarecrow-thin, eyes sharp despite sluggish movements, grunted. "Nope."

"C'mon. I bought Shadow off you last week. You recognize me. I'm not a cop. Anymore."

He grinned wide. "Oh yeah, I remember now. Still no."

"One more time." She flicked the paper.

This time he looked, nudged another guy. Silent exchange: nod, shrug. He tapped a photo with one grimy finger. "This one."

Marti's pulse jumped. César López's face. "Where?"

"East side couple weeks back. Buying off some new guy. Real strung-out type."

"New guy meaning?"

"No clue."

Someone hissed, "Shit! Cops!"

The bench scattered. Two uniforms closed in from either side. Marti ran, cane thumping, ribs screaming where one of the bullets had caught her. Behind her, a heavyset cop wheezed after her with all the grace of wet cement rolling downhill.

She wasn't even going full speed and he couldn't keep up.

She veered toward shadow, doubling back to her car. The cop gave up with a groan.

Marti slid inside, catching her breath and leaned across the seat, out of sight. Small victories counted too. She allowed herself half a smile before turning the key.

That lead on López wouldn't wait forever, and neither would the cop she'd just ditched.

Chapter 19

Pain shot through her injured leg as she slammed the accelerator. The engine snarled awake, tires shrieking against dry asphalt. Her brief satisfaction evaporated. That lead on López was worth every risk. Neon smeared across the windshield, the city a blur of light and shadow. None of it mattered. Just César López dangling out of reach.

The impact jolted through her bones before the sound registered. Metal shrieking like a knife dragged across bone.

"Fuck." She wrenched the wheel, fishtailed to a stop.

The pain knifed against her skin as she surveyed the damage. The SUV crouched there, its driver side caved in. Her own car: fender crushed, headlight obliterated.

She kicked the SUV's door three times. Didn't fix shit, but it felt good. "That'll teach you to park on the street," she muttered before climbing back in.

No witnesses visible in her rearview, but someone could've called it in. Plates flagged. Another arrest waiting. The thought made her press harder on the accelerator, her injured leg screaming.

Falls City twisted around her like an open jaw. She aimed for Parma Road's junkyards and scavenger shops that knew how to ask all the right wrong questions.

Mike's Auto Repair squatted ahead, its generic name screaming illegal side business. She honked once, sharp and impatient.

Mike emerged from the oil-stained depths, wiping greasy hands on a rag that had surrendered to filth decades ago. His eyes narrowed at the damage.

"Mike, right? Two hundred cash."

He circled her car, fingers trailing the crumpled pretend metal. "$5,200."

She exhaled but nodded.

"Office," he grunted, heading toward a scarred tool chest.

The office reeked of gasoline and shade, walls yellowed from nicotine. She dropped into a groaning chair, eyes drifting over debris until she spotted something to entertain herself with: a buck knife lying forgotten.

She flipped it between her fingers. The balanced weight steadied her racing thoughts. Jacinto Córdova, César López, Heather's betrayal... and Lori.

Mike shouldered back in, tossing two small black devices onto the desk. "Found these checking the damage. I don't know who you pissed off, but you brought two trackers to my shop."

"My fucking luck."

He held up one between grease-slick fingers. "This one's Federal." The label read: If Found, Please Contact Federal Unified Crime Taskforce – Reward Offered!

FUCT. Heather. Should've known better than to trust a Fed.

Mike rolled the second device between his fingers. "Generic tracker tag. Gun shops sell 'em. Better range than the Fed model though, about fifty miles."

Both accurate within fifteen feet. Neither should have been there.

She pocketed them and followed him to the garage floor. Her car sat gutted under harsh fluorescents.

"Can you save her?" She lit a cigarette despite the flammable surroundings.

"Easy. But two trackers? Someone's got a real hard-on for you." He crossed his arms. "Ever think about buying a scanner? One crisp."

"A thousand dollars? You got jokes."

"Nothing for the trackers this time. But next time you're paying for each one." He squatted by her front tire. "Get a TrakSafe 750C. Finds everything: bugs, GPS, recorders. I'll sell you one at cost. Nine hundred. Plus $5,200 for repairs."

Three hours later, she was threading through traffic like smoke, both trackers riding shotgun. Better to use them, make whoever was watching think they still had eyes on her.

Downtown rose in neon smears. The city hummed; so did she, wired and restless. Her knuckles whitened on the wheel. It wasn't the cops or trackers getting under her skin. It was Lori walking away, shoulders straight, never looking back. As if Marti meant nothing.

She swallowed something sharp that tasted like regret and shoved it down before it could take root.

At her apartment, she showered fast. Scalding water over tired muscles because maybe she'd get laid tonight. Dressed in black everything. The trackers waited on her passenger seat. She'd handle Heather's amateur surveillance games soon enough.

At a red light downtown, she scanned her contacts and tapped Heather's name. A horn blared behind her. The light had turned green. She waited, counted five Mississippis as it went yellow, then rolled forward, stranding the asshole at red.

"Agent Blair."

"Heather, it's Marti. We still on?"

A pause. "Hi, Marti. Yes, of course. See you in an hour."

This was a setup. Had to be. But she had things to do first.

She circled the restaurant block twice, searching for surveillance. Nothing obvious except the junkie slouched under an awning, fingers twitching. Too convincing to be a Fed.

The Belmont Heights neighborhood was going down hill since her last visit.

She parked and took a small hit of Shadow from her inhaler, just enough to quiet the paranoia. Crossing to the junkie, she crouched beside him.

"Yours?" She held up the inhaler.

His bloodshot eyes met hers. "Yeah. Must've dropped it."

She pressed it into his palm while slipping the federal tracker into his coat pocket. Let Heather's team chase him around the city all night.

"Stay clean," she murmured, walking away.

Her stomach rumbled as she headed for the restaurant. When was the last time she ate?

Chapter 20

Marti stood at Hasper's entrance weighing her options. The warm glow inside promised whiskey and leather seats and Heather looking like sin across a table. That last part made the decision for her.

The upscale joint had glass windows framed in dark wood, leather booths along one side, white-linen tables through the middle. The whole place hummed with wealth Marti didn't belong to but could buy her way into.

"Two for Rothberg," she told the host, scanning for an empty booth. Had she told Heather? Shit. She fired off a quick message.

The host led her past an open kitchen where chefs stitched together overpriced perfection. Garlic, butter, seared meat. Layers of scent that weren't why she'd come.

He stopped at a table near the kitchen door. "Here you are."

"Booth."

"The booths are reserved."

Marti held up her wrist. Everyone had a price.

"One hundred."

Asshole tax. She paid and followed him to plush leather hugging deep wood, privacy built into its design. She slid in, warm leather making her wish she was naked.

"What can I start you with?"

"Whiskey." She leaned back. "Can I smoke?"

"Of course." He pointed at a button. "Activate the filter first."

First drag slow, smoke vanishing into the wall like some ghost of bad habits past.

Then Heather walked in, and fuck if that wasn't unfair.

Every light seemed set just for her; pendants catching highlights in that red hair, green eyes locked onto Marti with intent that pooled heat low in her gut. Her dress shimmered with each step.

Marti stood, letting herself look. "You're making it hard to focus." Her voice came out rough. "You look so fucking hot."

Heather smirked, leaning close to press a kiss against Marti's cheek. "You said that kind of loud," she murmured, warm breath against warm skin.

Marti's hand found Heather's hip, fingers drifting to her waist before nudging her toward the seat. If Heather kept standing there looking at her like that, public decency was off the table.

They settled into the booth, Heather adjusting her dress while Marti collapsed with less grace.

"Hi."

"Hello. You look great when you aren't wearing your office."

"You don't look so bad yourself." Something in Heather's tone made Marti's spine tighten.

Drinks ordered—Chardonnay for Heather, another whiskey for Marti—before Heather slid a white envelope across the table. "It's not much, but it's all I could find."

Marti snagged it. "Thought we weren't talking about work."

Heather scanned the room. "Are you gonna stop staring at my breasts long enough for conversation?"

"I'm capable-ish of conversation." Marti lifted her eyes, biting her lip as the server arrived.

She snapped her menu shut. "What's the chef excited about?"

"The dry-aged rib steak. Aged on site for twenty-eight days. He won't cook it past rare."

"Good man. I'll take one rare, baked potato on the side."

Heather ordered salmon and asparagus with less enthusiasm.

Once alone, Heather sighed. "Marti? Up here. You know they're fake."

"No offense," Marti dragged out the words, "but you're making me wet."

"I'm just sitting here breathing."

"Turns out that's enough." Marti took a slow drag, exhaling toward the ceiling.

Heather groaned into her wine. "Okay, forget it. Let's talk about the weather."

"Dry outside, wet inside." If handlers were listening tonight, they were getting a show.

"Fine. Work then. These men you're looking for..."

"Moms hired me. They disappeared over the last few years." Whiskey burned smooth. "Took time to raise the crisp. They're paying me to care because cops don't. No offense."

Heather's fingertips brushed Marti's hand before pulling away. "That's kind of nice of you."

"I'm nice." Marti leaned forward. "Unless you'd rather I be naughty."

Heather blushed, pulling back. "I am so confused about you right now...I'm not used to this kind of dinner conversation."

The food arrived before Marti could tease further. Her steak sat marbled on the plate, red juices pooling where she'd cut into it.

"Fuck," she murmured around meat that melted on impact.

"It's still bleeding," Heather muttered.

"That's not blood. It's myoglobin. Protein and water." Marti swirled her whiskey. "Dead bodies don't bleed."

Heather stared. "I'm gonna check up on that later."

Marti ripped into her steak and smacked her lips as she ate.

"So..." Heather glanced around. Lots of paintings of birds. "Birds. You like birds?"

"I love birds," Marti lied.

"I like bird songs."

"You know birds only sing for two reasons: fucking and murder. 'Fuck me, please, somebody fuck me,' or 'Stay the hell off my branch.'"

Heather snorted into her drink as nearby diners turned. A waiter materialized.

"Is everything alright?"

"Delicious," Marti said. "My friend just realized what birds are saying."

"She has Tourette's," Heather gasped between giggles.

After the waiter retreated, Heather asked, "Why do you do that?"

"Make you laugh? Because you did."

"You're just so—"

"Unfiltered?" Marti asked with an arched eyebrow.

"A wild thing."

Marti gestured with her knife. "If I argued, I'd be lying."

"You can't help yourself. That's why you get caught up in bad stuff."

"I'm impatient, self-centered, and addicted to sex, drugs, booze, and bad math."

"You joke like it doesn't matter. Maybe because you're hurting." Heather took a delicate piece of salmon between her lips, Marti practically drooling as she watched.

"Are you telling me you don't hurt? I know bullshit when I see it." Marti leaned forward. "Make this about you. Family? Love life? Seeing anyone?"

"No."

"Fuck. I know that. Sorry. I'm an asshole."

"You are," Heather said, but softer now.

"So what then? Am I getting you into bed tonight?"

Heather blinked. "Is that why you invited me?"

"Of course that's why." Marti flagged another round. "If you're seeing someone, just say so. I'll stop flirting. Can I watch though?"

"Feral."

"Then why are we at dinner if you don't want to fuck?"

"Your language is something else."

"Fine. Why are we here if you don't want to engage in intimate relations?"

Pink flushed across Heather's cheeks. Marti pressed in. "When a federal agent sits down with a woman she arrested, it makes me wonder what she's after. I've got nothing but great hands and a tongue that could make your knees buckle."

Heather stabbed her asparagus. "Get your head out of your crotch."

"I've tried. Not flexible enough."

"Not everything is about sex, Marti," Heather protested as she crunched her way through another spear.

Marti lit another cigarette. "Only thing besides sex is death. You wanna talk about death?"

"Is that all there is? Nothing more?"

"Death isn't bad. Fear keeps people from living." She tapped ash onto her plate. "Everything that happens was gonna happen anyway. Food tastes better, smokes hit harder, sex—" her voice dropped, "—that much more intense."

Marti looked deeply into those beautiful eyes across the table, and smiled.

"Can you love someone while dreading their doom? Fear chokes off the best parts. If you're not afraid of losing them, you can love fully. For a lifetime or just tonight."

"So this is what you meant? Thinking about sex and death?"

"I live sex and death. And it's a good time."

"I've never thought about it like that," Heather said as she took a sip of wine.

"I'm not just a pretty face and a decent fuck."

Heather's fingers curled around hers. "Not just a pretty face. And a great fuck, if you do say so yourself."

With dinner ended, bills paid and coats collected, the pair hesitated under the awning. The night had shifted into something Marti hadn't let herself feel since Lia.

She brushed her thumb along Heather's cheekbone. Heather turned into the touch, and that was all Marti needed, fingers skimming down her jaw as their mouths met. Slow but sure, a goddamn mistake waiting to happen.

They broke apart, people moving around them rather than through them. Heather's fingers lingered like a dare.

"Goodnight, Marti."

"Goodnight, Heather."

One last glance, both knowing they weren't done, and Marti walked back into the dark city streets.

Chapter 21

Marti shook out her leather jacket before hanging it up, last night's 'almost' still clinging like a bad memory. The image of Heather's face flashed through her mind: wide-eyed and breathless when Marti had leaned in close, breasts nearly touching. Perfectly unsettling. Just the way she liked to leave cops who thought they could get under her skin.

Dirty boot prints tracked her path across the office floor to Lori's empty desk. The hollow quiet pressed against her ribs. Too much space where Lori should be sitting, typing, bitching about the cat. She tore her gaze away before the familiar acid burn of resentment could dig in deeper.

Blood smeared across the top sheet as she yanked papers from the white envelope. Antonio Molina's file now marked with her DNA, like punctuation on bad luck. She sucked the paper cut and started reading.

The names blurred together at first. Petty crimes, minor infractions. Albert Alvarez: solicitation, June 2052. Missing by October. Jacinto Córdova: speeding ticket that somehow warranted detention. Gone by April 2054. Carlos Hernandez with his yearly trouble until a shoplifting arrest in February. Vanished by June.

Smoke curled from her cigarette as the pattern emerged through bureaucratic ink stains. Each man arrested for bullshit charges. Each disappearing within months.

"Four months," she whispered, the revelation cutting through the hammering in her chest.

Four fucking months between their last arrest and vanishing completely.

The desk drawer scraped open. Amber liquid caught dim light as she poured two fingers of whiskey, burning a path down her throat while questions stacked up. Police corruption? Death squads? Some bureaucratic black prison eating people alive?

Tapping pelted the window, punctuated by scratching. Bertha glared through the glass, demanding entrance. The cat hopped in when Marti flicked the latch, shook off the disdain, and claimed the couch like royalty avoiding the help.

"Nobody gets shot for shoplifting," Marti muttered.

Outside, Falls City groaned under threats of rain. Distant thunder or gunfire, screams slicing through alleyways, and the ever-present whisper of Shadow calling.

The inhaler felt cool against her palm. One hit to take the edge off. She pressed it to her lips and surrendered to Shadow's embrace: a lover with bad intentions pulling her under.

Reality bent. Walls pulsed with impossible colors while neon dripped through ceiling cracks in slow-motion streaks. Her computer screen scrambled, letters sliding down in lazy drips before reassembling:

a blazer

travel avocado jr

tonic channeled

"What the fuck," she muttered, leaning close enough for the static glow to bite at her retinas.

Then understanding clicked: anagrams. The missing men's names, scrambled by whatever circus act her brain was staging. Nothing mystical. Just synapses misfiring while Shadow laughed behind her eyes.

She reached for another hit. Solve crime sober? Fuck that noise. At least for a while.

Reality crept back slowly until nothing remained but weak sunlight and a headache settling behind her eyes with all the grace of a wrecking ball. Bertha fixed her with a look holding zero sympathy.

"Don't fucking judge me," Marti muttered, shoving Shadow back in the drawer. Time to go.

Her phone vibrated. Nat Lopez.

She slid into her car and answered with the last dregs of energy. "Marti Starova."

"Hey Marti, it's Nat. Haven't heard from you."

"Following a lead. Didn't go anywhere."

"Right," Nat drew out the word. "I stopped by your office. You weren't around."

Marti flicked the radio on low, letting static fill the uncomfortable space. "I can be hard to find sometimes."

"Not this hard. You good?"

The warmth in Nat's voice crept under Marti's skin. She shifted, jaw clenching. The empty passenger seat caught her eye. Secretary gone, office too quiet.

"I'm fine. Appreciate you checking in."

Nat hesitated, breath catching. "Alright. Talk soon?"

"Yeah." Click.

Marti patted herself down for cigarettes. Jacket pocket, breast pocket. Nothing. "Fuck," she muttered, flipping open the glovebox one-handed.

Something tumbled onto the seat with a plastic clatter. One of the GPS trackers Mike had found earlier.

Off-the-shelf model, just another piece of bullshit someone had slapped on her car. Some overeager drug squad rookie trying to justify his paycheck was about to get very fucking lost.

A horn blared behind her. The light had turned green. Marti didn't move, an idea forming: quick, mean, perfect. The horn sounded again, longer and aggressive.

Her lips curled into a sharp smile as she threw the car into park and stepped out. The truck behind her loomed: oversized tires, chrome bumper reflecting her smug image. Inside sat what she expected: red-faced bravado in plaid, knuckles white on the wheel.

His window rolled down as she approached.

"Sorry," she cooed, voice dripping false sweetness. Her fingers pressed the tracker against his side mirror, tucking it away like a secret.

Red Face opened his mouth, but whatever he planned died in his throat as Marti turned and walked away.

She peeled toward the city center, cigarette smoke trailing from parted lips. January cold built from a whisper to steady scream: perfect weather for someone feeling sorry for themselves.

The empty passenger seat seemed wider now. Lori would've hated this weather, would've curled up on the office couch with a blanket too big for one person, pretending to work while finding excuses to stay longer than professional boundaries suggested.

Marti exhaled through clenched teeth, flicking ashes that dissolved before the wind could blow them back.

Lori was gone. Just like that.

Get the fuck over it, Starova.

Chapter 22

The silence pressed in like an unwelcome hand at the small of her back as familiar streets slid past, each one wrong without Lori bitching about her driving or playing shitty pop songs just to annoy her.

Marti needed to conjure up a break, just one little fucking break.

A different image pushed through the gloom: Ha-Yoon sprawled across cold concrete in the stairwell, one leg draped over the handrail, grinning like she knew where Marti's mind was heading.

A laugh escaped her throat as she stabbed out her cigarette in the overflowing ashtray. Maybe she'd get lucky again and Ha-Yoon would want to fuck in the rain.

The thought eased her foot off the gas before she ended up decorating the back of a semi truck like a messy Jackson Pollock. She pulled into the coroner's lot and parked around back, where no one would notice how long she stayed or why. Rain hammered against the windshield as she sat for a moment, massaging her aching knee before grabbing her cane and stepping out into the downpour.

By the time she made it inside, water dripped from her hair onto the shoulders of her leather jacket: the one Ha-Yoon gave her after dickhead got stabbed wearing her last one. His final romantic gesture; steal a jacket to impress your wife, get a free hole in your heart with it. She shrugged it off, tossed it onto the nearest chair, then dropped into another one. Her bad leg stretched out with a grimace as Ha-Yoon glanced up from her computer screen.

"You look like shit," Ha-Yoon said, eyes gleaming with amusement.

"I feel like shit."

"Maybe I can fix that." Ha-Yoon clicked 'send' on whatever email had been holding her attention and swiveled toward Marti. Her eyes darted around the room, confirming they were alone before settling back with intent. "Tell me you came here to fuck me."

Heat curled low in Marti's stomach at the anticipation in Ha-Yoon's voice, but she shook her head anyway, her knee throbbing in time with the rain outside. "Not today, the pain gets bad in the rain," she said, voice rough with regret. "I need details on unidentified white and Hispanic young men showing up in your morgue."

Ha-Yoon's eyes rolled back so far Marti could almost hear the effort. She turned away, typing something into her computer with force. "You're choosing dead men over a living woman? That's tragic." A few more aggressive keystrokes, then a sidelong glance with a smirk creeping back onto her lips. "Want me to make this official? I can register your visit."

"No problem."

"Wait. Not yet. I'm not giving up." Ha-Yoon tapped her lips, eyes locked onto Marti's. Then her smile widened. She slid her hands under her skirt and, with a gentle motion, slipped out of her underwear. She held them up between pinched fingers, letting them dangle in the fluorescent light, swinging back and forth like a hypnotist's watch.

Marti's stomach clenched. Ha-Yoon's scent hit her: warm, heady, unmistakable. She inhaled deep, let it out slowly. "What's your plan?"

"You lie down. I sit on your face. I'll be gentle." Ha-Yoon's eyes glittered. "Maybe."

A laugh escaped Marti's throat. "Yeah, okay. I can manage lying down. Just let me breath." Her eyes scanned the closed doors nearby, wondering which one would hide their indiscretion. Before she could ask, Ha-Yoon stood and walked away with purpose. Marti grabbed her jacket and followed, pain forgotten.

"My pussy has missed you," Ha-Yoon tossed over her shoulder, voice musical with promise.

"I missed your pussy," Marti replied, voice dropping an octave.

Ha-Yoon stopped and turned, her finger tracing the seam of Marti's lips before sliding along her cheekbone. Her gaze lingered on Marti's mouth for a weighted moment. Then her lips quirked and she continued down the hall. She cracked open a door, peeked inside. "This one."

Fluorescent light flickered to life with a soft buzz as they entered. "Lie here," Ha-Yoon said, pointing to an empty patch of floor. "Use your jacket for a pillow."

Marti folded the leather into a cushion while Ha-Yoon grabbed two thick reams of paper from a nearby shelf, setting them beside the makeshift pillow.

"What're those for?" Marti asked, lowering herself to the floor.

"My knees," Ha-Yoon replied. "I'm too old to last ten minutes on concrete." She laughed, straddling Marti's waist. Her hands smoothed over Marti's shirt with slowness before tugging at the buttons. "Have I ever seen your breasts?"

Marti's fingers traced the outside of Ha-Yoon's thighs, slipping beneath her skirt with intent. "I don't think so," she murmured, kneading firm muscle beneath warm skin.

"They're cute," Ha-Yoon mused, cupping them both in gentle hands. Her thumbs brushed over stiffening nipples before giving them an experimental squeeze. She bent down, kissed one tentatively, then again, lingering as if tasting something unexpected but sweet.

Marti groaned, hands sliding lower to grip Ha-Yoon's ass under her skirt.

Ha-Yoon shifted forward with small adjustments until heat hovered just above Marti's mouth, then lowered herself down, throwing her skirt over Marti's head in one fluid motion.

Darkness enveloped Marti except for fractured slivers of light filtering through the fabric: a shifting veil that turned everything fever-warm and intimate.

She exhaled against slick flesh, feeling Ha-Yoon shiver above her before diving in with eager lips and tongue. Starting slow, she kissed along the soft skin of Ha-Yoon's inner thighs, dragging teeth to hear that first sharp intake of breath.

Then she licked deep into wetness.

Ha-Yoon's breathy hum, half sigh, half moan, filled the small space.

Encouraged, Marti explored with strokes, teasing slick folds apart with her tongue before pressing deeper, alternating between broad passes and precise flicks where they were needed most.

Ha-Yoon trembled above her, thighs pressing against Marti's cheeks. The intoxicating heat against her lips made it impossible to focus on anything else as she worked slower now, more deliberate in how she sucked soft flesh between parted lips, grazing sensitive skin with the lightest touch of teeth.

Ha-Yoon's hips rolled against Marti's mouth; each movement sharper than the last, her breathing growing ragged above the fabric barrier.

The light rustle of skirt against Marti's cheek added to the sensations building between them: heat and pressure and need all tangled together in the dark cocoon they'd created.

Slick heat coated her lips as she pressed a firm kiss against Ha-Yoon's clit, tongue swirling once before flattening against the sensitive bud in expert strokes.

"Oh," Ha-Yoon's sharp gasp transformed into an unrestrained moan as she rocked forward with each stroke.

Marti sealed her lips around swollen flesh and sucked deep, making Ha-Yoon jolt forward on instinct. She groaned at the way pleasure tightened every muscle above her, hips jerking faster with each precise flick of her tongue.

"Fuck," Ha-Yoon gasped somewhere beyond the fabric veil.

Marti hummed against soaking flesh, feeling thighs clench tighter against her head, knowing without seeing that Ha-Yoon was coming undone above her.

"God," Ha-Yoon panted, desperation bleeding into every shaky breath as if coherent speech required too much focus when pleasure was so close.

Ha-Yoon arched, grinding against Marti's mouth. A broken sound escaped her throat as the paper reams scraped against the floor. With each hard suck, Ha-Yoon swayed, trembling. Every shift against Marti's tongue sent jolts through her body, pulse hammering in both their ears.

"Right there," Ha-Yoon gasped, pushing harder. Her pubic hair tickled Marti's nose, but Marti didn't stop; just tightened her lips and sucked.

Ha-Yoon's thighs quivered. "Fuck. Marti. There." Her words fractured as the tension built to breaking point. Every nerve pulled tight, her whole body rigid. Then everything unraveled at once, pleasure crashing through her in waves that left her gasping.

Marti pressed a final kiss against Ha-Yoon's clit before pulling back, tasting slickness on her lips as Ha-Yoon sagged above her. For a moment, neither moved. Then Ha-Yoon groaned and rolled back onto Marti's hips.

She stood without a word, adjusting her skirt as if they hadn't just been tangled together on the floor, and reached for the disheveled stack of papers. Marti watched her smooth out wrinkles with precision.

When Marti stood, Ha-Yoon turned to her with a satisfied smirk and wiped the corner of Marti's mouth with her thumb, tugging at her lower lip.

"You know why I like you?"

"No," Marti said. "Why?"

"You're always willing to eat me." A pause. "Any place, any time."

Marti grinned. "You're delicious." She leaned in for a kiss. Ha-Yoon turned away, avoiding the contact as she always did.

"Hold on," Ha-Yoon said, smoothing down her skirt again. "Any stains?"

Marti tugged the fabric. "None that'll show up under office lighting."

"Good."

Marti exhaled, shoving one hand into her pocket. The endorphin high was fading, leaving her knee aching again. "Listen," she said after a beat. "Ever think about working for me? Full-time secretary gig?"

Ha-Yoon blinked. Then burst into laughter so hard she had to lean against the shelving unit.

"I'm serious," Marti said, watching her. "Two hundred crisp a year because you've got skills."

That only made Ha-Yoon laugh harder.

"You're cute," she managed when she caught her breath. "But we'd never get work done."

"Oh no," Marti deadpanned. "We'd have to work."

Ha-Yoon raised an eyebrow, still grinning as she crossed her arms. "Mmm-hmm."

"I mean it," Marti insisted. "Weird hours sometimes, long ones too. Not a nine-to-five deal."

"As tempting as it is to get fucked all day long," Ha-Yoon said, "I'm not losing my pension." She jabbed a finger toward Marti's chest for emphasis before fastening the buttons Marti had forgotten were still open. "I've been in this job almost forty years. Three more and I get my full payout bonus for service time and another one for retiring at sixty-five." Her finger traced calculations in the air between them. "$4K extra a month; that's extra, mind you. And then my husband and I are taking off to Arizona so I never have to see another fucking drop of rain again in my life."

Marti nodded, weighing the logic against her need. She shrugged one shoulder and lit a cigarette instead of pushing further. "Makes sense," she admitted, exhaling smoke toward the ceiling fan.

"Yeah." Ha-Yoon's smile softened as she slipped her hand into Marti's, giving it a squeeze before tugging her toward the hallway door. "Come on," she murmured as they walked out together.

As they stepped into the dim corridor, Ha-Yoon flicked off the light behind them, a quiet chuckle lingering in her throat.

"So what happened to that blonde you had?" she asked. "Lorna? Lori?"

Before she could answer:

"Ha-Yoon! Where have you been? What is going on?"

They turned as Dr. Strickland stepped into view, clutching something at arm's length like it might be contaminated.

It took Marti half a second to recognize what he was holding.

And another half-second to bite back laughter as Dr. Strickland glared daggers at Ha-Yoon while dangling her panties off the tip of his pen like they might bite him if he got too close.

This was about to get interesting.

Chapter 23

Ha-Yoon strode down the fluorescent-lit hall toward reception, Marti limping behind her, boots echoing against tile. The antiseptic smell could mask what they'd just done. Probably.

Marti swiped at her face. Mostly dry. Good enough after Ha-Yoon's tsunami.

"Dr. Strickland," Ha-Yoon said, professional as if her lips hadn't been pressed against Marti's five minutes ago. "How can I help you?"

Strickland's face had gone crimson. He lifted the pen again, underwear dangling like an indictment. "Where were you? What are these?"

Ha-Yoon's tactical silence stretched.

"I don't understand the question."

"You're supposed to be at your desk." His grip tightened, the underwear trembling. "And...and these panties?"

"That's on me." Marti eased up beside them while Ha-Yoon retreated behind her desk. "I wanted to talk to the coroner about my friend and got lost. Scary in a way I wasn't prepared for, so I yelled for help. This woman came to my rescue."

Strickland shrank back, eyes darting between them. He lifted the pen again. "And these?"

Marti stared too long before blinking. "I peed myself so I took them off." She plucked them from the pen and shoved them into her pocket.

Strickland recoiled like she'd handed him a live grenade.

"What did you want me to do, apologize? You pull organs from chest cavities; don't act squeamish now."

Ha-Yoon watched, lips parted in stunned silence.

"You're disgusting," Strickland hissed.

"Oh, doc," Marti grinned, eyes bright with chaos, "you ain't seen nothing yet." She reached for her zipper, fingers hovering.

"Please stop," Ha-Yoon murmured through a smirk that betrayed how much she didn't mean it.

The shift came suddenly. Game over.

Marti released her zipper before glancing up sharply. "So, about my missing friend: are you the coroner? Did you rip out his heart? Eat it, maybe?"

"She is unstable, doctor," Ha-Yoon said, studying her fingernails.

Strickland blanched at the professional insult. "No! Christ, no. It was Dr. Levy. No! I don't mean he ate anything. Talk to Dr. Levy."

Marti rolled forward another step. "Right. Ha-Yoon told me where to find him, but that's where I got lost. Can you take me?"

"No," he said quickly. "Ha-Yoon will take you there! She'll help!" Then he was gone.

"That went well," Marti exhaled.

Ha-Yoon grinned. "Eat the heart? You crazy she-devil."

"For your panties, anything. Now, Dr. Levy?"

Ha-Yoon led her down one level to the morgue, stopping at the doorway like a sailor refusing to board a sinking ship. "Dr. Levy's in Room 2," she pointed down the dim hallway.

"You're not coming?"

"Fuck no. There are bodies in the hallway." She shuddered, then grabbed Marti's face and kissed her with the familiarity of lovers. "Thanks for saving my job. My pension thanks you too."

"All about serving the public," Marti deadpanned as Ha-Yoon walked away, hips swaying.

The sterile hallway stretched before her. Blue stairwell doors at each end, fluorescents humming overhead. Thirteen gurneys lined the wall. White bags for fresh ones, black for the messy ones. Falls City's dead were having a busy week.

"Can I help you?"

A guy in scrubs materialized, glaring.

"Is Dr. Levy expecting you?"

"No. I'm here about my missing son."

"How'd you get past reception?"

"Dr. Strickland told the receptionist to bring me here. Then she bailed. Got spooked."

He gave a slow nod before disappearing into Room 2, reappearing moments later. "Take a seat. Dr. Levy will see you in twenty."

She dropped into a crappy chair and wondered, only for a moment, how she always managed to mix sex and death whenever she came here. Sex and death. Always sex and death. She pulled out her phone, scrolling through the Falls City Police feed.

>Chief Franklin leads Falls City with an iron fist, necessary to keep crime under control. #IronStrong

>Three months waiting for police to follow up on my break-in, but they had time to write twenty parking tickets on my block yesterday.

The city's schizophrenic relationship with its police department played out in 280-character fragments.

>They found another body in the river with 'suicide' wounds to the back of the head: classic Falls City police.

>Officer Martinez from Falls City PD spent three hours helping us search for my daughter's therapy dog; they don't all deserve the hate they get.

Marti snorted. Rumors swirled, but nothing stuck as long as Falls City kept pretending corruption was just another flavor of law enforcement.

>Eddie Marquet, 15, last seen June 10th near 4100 South Stone Ave... #FindMarquet

Forty-three posts with that hashtag. Meanwhile, her boys had no hashtags, no digital armies demanding answers.

She locked her phone with an irritated click and tossed it onto the metal tray. The smell of death pressed against her like an unwelcome hand.

She'd stopped flinching at morgues years ago. After a decade in homicide, death became furniture, something bumped into but never really seen. She ran on sex, drugs and nicotine binges now.

A door creaked. "I'm Dr. Levy," came a voice that spent too much time around dead things.

She turned: middle-aged, white coat, tired eyes. "Marti Starova. I'm here about some missing men."

"Are you family?"

"Nope. Families hired me. Better one stranger than six grieving mothers falling apart in your morgue."

Levy hesitated. "I'm sorry, I can't discuss—"

"Cool," Marti said, thumbing her phone. "You want me to call them?"

His sigh rattled deep. "Let's not upset any grieving mothers."

She pulled out photos, creased from too many foldings. "You recognize any of these guys?"

Levy flipped through them while she watched. "Which Falls City officer are you working with?"

"Agent Heather Blair. Federal something-or-other. So... you recognize any of them?" Marti tapped on the images.

"I'm not authorized to share—"

"Falls City Homicide," she tapped her chest. "Former. Martina Starova. Check your records."

"When?"

"Left six years ago."

Levy turned to his terminal. His eyebrows lifted at the forty-plus homicide cases under her name. "Holy hell. You really were with Falls City PD."

She pulled out her ID. Levy studied it, reconciling the cop in the records with the woman before him.

"Yeah, that one." He tapped Antonio Molina's photo. "Overdose. Found under a train trestle. John Doe 56-218."

Her stomach tightened. "You want his mother to ID? Dental?"

"DNA. He's got no teeth left. And no mother should see that face."

"Got it. I'll tell his mom."

"You do this for a living? Find dead people?"

"I like them alive when I track them down. Usually." She shrugged. "Used to come here with Dr. Winterson when I was on the force."

Recognition flashed across Levy's face. "Good man. Consults now, I think."

"Hired gun. Like me."

Outside, she lit a cigarette and stared at her phone, thumb hovering over Carmen's number. The weight of what she had to say pressed against her chest.

"Hello?" cracked the voice.

"Carmen, it's Marti Starova. I spoke to the coroner. He thinks they may have found your son."

"May have? Is he… alive?"

Marti's eyes closed. "No, Carmen. I'm so sorry."

A choked sound. Somewhere behind her, a child called out. "Oh God… I knew something terrible had happened… Is it him?"

"I can't say for sure without DNA confirmation, but I gave the coroner photos of all the boys. Yours is the one he recognized."

"Do you think it's him?" Voice uneven. Pained.

"The medical examiner thinks so. John Doe 56-218. You need to call the city morgue."

"Thank you… For everything…"

Something knotted in Marti's chest. "Yeah. I'll let everyone else know."

Carmen whispered one last broken thank you and ended the call.

Marti lowered the phone, staring until the screen went dark. One mother had closure. The others still waited. And Marti? She'd keep lying to herself because it felt better than nothing at all.

Chapter 24

Falls City was a goddamn buffet of sins: exactly what Marti needed after that phone call. Her phone sat silent on the passenger seat, but Carmen's broken 'thank you' still echoed in her head like a bullet ricocheting inside a metal box. Red neon flickered nearby, advertising the night's menu: sex, drugs, booze, salvation. Three out of four wasn't bad.

Her tires splashed through potholes deep enough to swallow a man whole. Plastic bags clung to lamp posts like desperate ghosts while plywood shacks huddled against brick walls, their tarps flapping in the drizzle. The alleys ran with piss and blood.

She parked at the office and let herself in with a swift kick to shut the door behind her. Bertha perched at the window, tail twitching, waiting for her loyal fucking servant to do her job.

"Guess what the fuck just happened, Dippa?" Marti cracked Bertha's private entrance open before dropping into her chair. "Aliens landed and took off with my last good brain cell."

Bertha hopped onto the couch and started licking herself, unconcerned that she'd spent half an hour rolling in God-knows-what.

The phone rang mid-sip of whiskey. Bertha shot her a glare before tucking in again, ears twitching at every ring like a personal insult.

"Starova." She pinched the bridge of her nose as Susanna Alvarez's voice filled her ear.

"Marti, it's Susanna. Albert's mother. Carmen said you found her son? Have you found Albert?"

Hope bled into her tone like an infection. Marti yanked open a pack of smokes and lit one up. "No. It's not like that. I asked around. Coroner says one of his unidentified bodies might look like Antonio Molina."

"But no one recognized my son?"

"Nope." Smoke curled from Marti's lips. "Carmen has to submit DNA for comparison."

"But that means... Albert could still be out there? Do you think he's still alive?" Hope clung to every syllable like tar under fingernails.

Marti flicked her cigarette into cold coffee. "Susanna, I haven't found anything yet. Not a damn clue what happened to your son. Until I get something concrete, a body, I won't have answers for you. You won't hear about who I talk to or where I go unless it matters. And most of it won't."

It took another ten minutes before Susanna ran out of ways to make herself believe Marti wasn't holding something back.

The phone hit the desk harder than necessary. The screen lit mockingly: two missed calls.

Then they came in waves. Carmen must've told them all at once.

Did you find my son? No.

Have you made progress? No evidence yet.

Are you still looking? Yes.

By the time Marti hung up on the last desperate mother, her skull felt like someone had taken a crowbar to it. She knew how this night ended: pills, whiskey, a staring contest with the ceiling. But tonight, that wasn't enough.

Get off your fucking ass, Starova.

She lit a cigarette as she limped into some dive crammed between a pawn shop and a condemned building. Inside, sweat and stale beer hung in the air. A table of men laughed too loud in the corner, all sharp edges and ugly intentions.

Marti dropped paper photos in front of them. "You seen these guys?"

A muscle-bound fuck with ink from wrist to shoulder shoved them back without looking. "Fuck off, lady."

She exhaled smoke into his face, slow and deliberate. "Try again."

The table shifted, bodies tensing. A wiry bastard leaned in. "We don't know shit. Walk away, bitch."

Fine. She swiped the photos back and turned for the door. If they had anything worth knowing, they weren't giving it up.

Outside, cold made the photos in her pocket crinkle. Marti pulled her collar up and moved deeper into the city's broken heart, where streetlights flickered like dying fireflies.

Falls City swallowed people whole: cops shaking down tourists, rich kids playing at being gutter trash, junkies stumbling toward their next fix like broken wind-up toys.

She spotted a cop at the corner. "Fentafill," she said. He nodded at the darkness.

A kid darted from the shadows, snatched her cash, and dropped a bag in her palm before vanishing. The cop never touched the drugs, kept his hands clean.

Night turned to mist as she showed photos to anyone conscious enough to focus. A topless woman with pockmarked cheeks grinned wide enough to show missing teeth. "Haven't seen 'em. You want your dick sucked? Twenty bucks."

"Nah."

Further up, motion caught her eye: a kid in an FCU varsity jacket dragging an unconscious woman by the ankles. Blonde hair smeared dark with gutter water, limbs limp as rags.

Something stabbed beneath her ribs. Her brain made connections it shouldn't have: Lori on the ground instead of some nameless girl. Lori being hauled off where no one would find her come morning.

No. Not ever.

Marti dropped her cane and moved fast, ignoring how each step jolted pain up her bad leg. "Hey!" She raised the gun one-handed.

The kid's hands shot up. "No, it's fine. She's my girlfriend."

Marti cocked the gun.

He dropped the girl's ankles. "Really? I wasn't gonna hurt her."

She squeezed off a shot into the wall. Brick sprayed across the alley as he scrambled away.

She hauled the girl's dead weight to the dirty cop and held up bills. His frown disappeared.

"One hour," he said.

By the time she limped back, some asshole was twirling her cane like a parade baton. Not worth it. She'd steal another later.

Three blocks later, she dropped onto the curb next to Rat, who sat frozen, eyes glossy with whatever had knocked him sideways. First time she'd seen his sorry ass in a while. Kind of surprised he was still alive.

"Poison Ivy," a woman across from them explained.

Marti showed her the photos. "Seen any of these guys?"

The woman pointed to Albert. "Albie. Did a four-piece, just got out. We talked about getting a place together when we got clean."

"And when you got out?"

"Gone. Thought maybe he went home." She paused. "He used to crash in Boystown."

Marti left two Fentafill pills for Rat and continued her search. The alley smelled like alleys smell. A couple sprawled across the lane, fucking with all the passion of a grocery list. She stepped over them.

Ten minutes of sleep against a wall before a junkie's retching woke her. She checked her phone. Nothing from Heather. Nothing from Lori. Nothing from anyone. No one at all.

The woman from the couple had moved to smoke. When Marti showed her the photos, she said: "Kids are vanishing, and the cops are in on it."

Marti had heard it before, back when she was looking for Serra Stanfield. That case had ended with three bodies and a new tooth. Since Damien Kane had protected Rufus Montgomery, someone else might be covering for another perp now.

She left feeling worse than when she'd walked in for the nap. Rain misted against her skin as neon signs threw smeared reflections across puddles.

She settled beneath a pawn shop awning and pressed the Shadow inhaler to her lips.

Falls City cracked wide open like a neon wound. Light bled into every corner, twisting streets into tunnels of color that flickered wrong at the edges. Car horns screamed beside her instead of blocks away. Voices twisted together in whispers through rain-slick alleys.

She pressed her palm against concrete to remind herself which way gravity worked, then squeezed her eyes shut till black spots popped behind them.

Reality hadn't fixed itself yet.

Fuck it. She could stand here until everything stopped breathing around her.

Chapter 25

A thirty-minute trip, and the Shadow was wearing off. Reality reasserted itself as the buildings finally stopped breathing around her.

Marti's fingers still tingled as she followed the helpful spray-painted arrow: SEX ~>. Through half a mile of industrial wasteland toward Boystown: rusted beams reaching skyward like arthritic fingers, cracked pavement splitting beneath her boots. Overhead, the train tracks groaned with passing weight, showering rust flakes like diseased confetti onto boys too young to look this tired.

They clustered under flickering streetlamps. Stray dogs waiting for scraps. Their faces hungered for nothing but the quiet promise of eventual death. This wasn't a place that traded in love or lust; just survival. Sex as currency, no refunds or returns.

A few noticed her approach, gazes sliding over her until they landed on her chest. She pulled the photos from her pocket. "Know any of these guys? Their moms hired me."

Laughter rippled through the group: dry and sharp like crushed glass.

"Bullshit," said a bleach-blond kid with track marks peeking from beneath his sleeves. "Nobody's mom is looking for them."

Another blond didn't look up from his cigarette. "Everyone's mom is looking for them. Just looking in the wrong places."

A bald guy squinted at her, calculating. "Someone paying you for this?"

Marti caught where his thoughts were heading. "Shit money. Less than you make in twenty minutes."

Baldie grinned. "Why take shit pay? You're cute enough to work tricks yourself." He reconsidered. "Well... maybe not here."

"My secretary set it up." The lie tasted half-true now. "I heard Albert Alvarez used to work here four years back."

A kid who couldn't have been older than twenty-one laughed. "Four years ago? Hell, I was in grade school four years ago. Try the older guys down by the water."

Gravel crunched as a car rolled down the street. Before the driver could speak, she cut him off: "Fuck off." He hesitated, then reversed toward the group behind her.

The Henner Falls overflow spilled into deep currents ahead: quiet water with a fast pull that could take anything you wanted gone forever. Between concrete pillars, makeshift homes patched from stolen sheet metal and scavenged wood had developed their own ecosystem. Unlike crude tags elsewhere, these columns wore real graffiti: birds caught mid-flight, tangled wildflowers bursting like fireworks against rot.

A man with a dog blocked her path. "No cops."

"Not a cop." Marti kept her hands visible.

"No women."

She exhaled smoke at his feet. "Looking for someone who knew Albert Alvarez. Four years gone."

Movement from deeper inside caught her eye. Another man materialized from the shadows. Hole-ridden boxers hanging from sharp hipbones, torn undershirt, yellow foam slippers marking him as state-shelter stock. His lips parted around a name: "Albie."

Before she could press further, he retreated into shadowed firelight. The dog growled, barbed wire sharp.

"Can I show you pictures?"

"No."

"Can they see?"

Another shake.

Fuck it. Marti held up the photo. "One photo. Albie."

The man's eyes flicked down, then up. Half a smirk. "Blue 5."

Color-coded street signs stamped concrete pillars: Orange 3, Yellow 7, Blue 5. The "homes" sprawled chest-high at most. Coffins with rusted edges. Yellow foam slippers sat outside Blue 5's corrugated door, stained with oil and blood.

She rapped against the metal. A sleepy voice drifted through: "Yes?"

"I'm looking for Albie Alvarez."

"C-come in."

Marti dropped to her knees and shoved her head into darkness.

"I meant all the way in," the voice rasped. "If you leave your ass hanging out, someone will fuck it."

Charming. She crawled forward until face to face with something awful.

The man sat cross-legged on a thin mat, rail-thin with scabs crusting his arms. Sores oozed around his ankles. His skin carried that telltale tinge: Grease blue. A year, maybe, before his lungs forgot how to breathe.

"Albie Alvarez. You know something."

He blinked in slow motion. "Say again?"

"Albie. I'm looking for him."

"Four years too late. Never came back."

Heat pressed thick with unwashed bodies and dying soul. "He's probably dead, then."

"Looks like it," the Greaser said.

"I want his body."

Something flickered behind his eyes. "You don't know where it is." Pleased about it.

She waited. Sweat, or tears, glided down his hollow cheeks until he rasped: "Love. He loved me."

"What happened?"

His eyelids fluttered. "He went out one night and never came back."

"He loved you," she said, throwing out bait.

His lips twitched. "Why do you care?"

"His mother loved him."

That landed deep. His breath hitched. "I'm almost dead."

"Yeah. Looks like it."

"His mother loved him."

"Forever. Like Albie loves you forever."

A sound clawed up from his throat. Half grief, half withdrawal. He dug through crumpled clothes against the wall, producing an old phone and a glass vial filled with thick black Grease.

"This is all I have left." He pressed the phone into her palm, fingers damp and shaking.

She pocketed it without ceremony, then watched him uncork the vial and tip it back. No hesitation. Just that spiral toward nothing.

Marti rolled herself out before rigor mortis set in for real.

Cool air slapped her heat-damp skin. The man with the dog was approaching. She raised a hand—I see you—then turned toward the more traveled streets.

This block wasn't as bad. The sex workers were dressed, pimps lingering nearby. The junkies weren't convulsing yet. In daylight, office drones would pretend they didn't see any of it.

Rain came down harder, turning the street into shards of broken light. She ducked under a busted awning to shake water from her coat. The air reeked of wet asphalt and rotting garbage, that sharp ozone tang storms left behind.

Phil's Diner appeared ahead, warm yellow cutting through downpour. A kid stumbled from the dark, clothes soaked, eyes blown with panic.

"You the one looking for missing guys?" Voice scraped raw. "The cops are snatching people. Ripping organs outta them."

Marti snorted but kept neutral. "Why?"

"You heard of Black Harvest? They take addicts, cut 'em up while they're still alive. Sell the parts cheap so they can get new buyers hooked on drugs plus money for replacement kidneys."

She shoved bills into his trembling hand. If he was giving her this bullshit, he was bad off. Junkie parts are useless. Time to go home and leave this conspiracy quagmire to rot.

Her fingers closed around the car door handle when a voice stopped her:

"Hey gorgeous."

Marti froze, recognition sliding down her spine before she even turned around.

Chapter 26

Marti shifted her weight to her good leg, letting the car take her burden. The same streetlight that had illuminated the junkie's paranoid face now caught Naomi emerging from the alley's dark mouth. Another night crawler, but this one she could trust, at least as far as she could throw her. Which wasn't anywhere at all. "Well, well. Look who wandered into my gutter."

The hooker with a heart of gold. Well, a unicorn that helped Marti locate a killer, so...close.

Naomi laughed, low and throaty. "I live here, baby. You're the tourist." She sidled up to the driver's side window, bracing a hand against the frame. Close enough that Marti caught floral perfume beneath something sharper:

whiskey, sweat. Streetlight shimmered along her cheekbone. "What brings you slumming?"

Marti pulled photos from her jacket. "Recognize any of them?"

Naomi flipped through the prints before shaking her head. "Nah. Should I?"

"They're missing."

"Who isn't?" Good old Naomi, who Marti had met once. Maybe twice. Had pretend sex in front of cops. What a kink.

Marti tucked the photos away and dropped her cigarette, grinding it under her boot. "You know how to hack a phone?"

Naomi arched a brow. "Are you asking 'cause you think I'm Chinese?"

"What? No." Marti glanced down the empty street. Her voice dropped. "I didn't know there were any Chinese people left in the country."

Something unreadable flashed behind Naomi's steady smile. "Then why'd you ask about hacking a phone?"

Marti rolled her eyes and motioned toward the passenger side. "Get in."

Naomi slid inside, stretching out like she owned Bertha. The interior filled with that same perfume, light and cloying. Marti cleared her throat and turned the key.

"What are you doing in this part of town? Thought you were high end."

Naomi's fingers tapped the door panel once, twice. "Was. Had to defend myself when a john got rough." Her half-smile didn't reach her eyes. "My boss decided I needed reminding who runs shit."

"So he sent you here to learn humility?"

"Something like that."

The streets blurred past, empty and slick with recent rain.

"You ever think about getting out of the game? Leaving completely?"

Naomi's laugh came sharper, tired around the edges. She turned toward Marti, resting an elbow on the center console. "My husband went back."

"He help keep you off those deportation lists?"

"My dumbass husband ran up two hundred crisp in gambling debts. Then they shipped his sorry ass back to China." Her voice was flat, practiced. "That was ten years ago. Guess who got stuck paying it off? And pimp interest ain't friendly."

Marti exhaled through her teeth. "What's the cut?"

"Twenty percent. I've been paying on my back for a decade and still owe one-sixty." She flexed her hands once, let them go loose. "That's why they didn't deport me when they took him. He wasn't worth a damn to them. But me? His debt was bought by some fucking company. GenoHealth or some shit. A casino. And they came for me. 'Pay up or your kids die.' Turn right."

Marti's knuckles whitened on the wheel. "GenoHealth? That's fucked."

"Tell me about it. Two kids gotta eat." Naomi nodded toward a run-down motel sagging under pink neon. "Pull in."

The No Vacancy sign flickered, casting tired bruises onto cracked pavement. Marti killed the engine and stepped out into air thick with heat and gasoline ghosts.

"I know a guy who might fix your phone. Cost ya," Naomi said, striding toward the sidewalk. Seven-inch heels clicked concrete without a stumble. Marti followed, feeling like a swamp creature in comparison. "What happened to it?"

"Hoping it belonged to one of my missing guys. Only other lead I got is that I found one of 'em dead."

Naomi's laugh was low as she scanned the street. "Now that's what you call a clue." She slipped through a blacked-out storefront door. Marti hurried after, pulse kicking up as darkness swallowed them.

Inside: shadows and stale air. No shelves, no stock, no people.

Marti tensed.

"They understand English," Naomi murmured, "so don't say anything stupid."

"Not my strong suit."

"No shit."

Light hit harsh through the next doorway: fluorescents washing over glass cases stacked with scavenged tech pressed into neat rows like stolen jewelry.

Behind the counter stood a middle-aged Chinese man engineered for forgettability. Average everything including how unremarkable he was. His glasses looked fake: a thin layer between him and anyone who might care to remember.

"Hi Chen," Naomi said.

Chen spared a glance.

"Show him your phone."

Marti pulled out the wreck. Screen shattered into spiderwebs, casing dented, corners chipped to raw edges. Chen weighed it like produce at market, then frowned.

"Why'd you bring a white girl here?"

"She's paying."

Chen reached for a plastic something. "How much?"

Naomi turned to Marti. "How much are you putting down?"

Marti leaned against the workbench, scanning the chaos of wires and blueprints. "Not a cent unless I get the data." She lit a cigarette, blew smoke in Chen's direction.

Chen squinted through the haze. "She's an asshole."

"More than you know," Naomi agreed.

"Two grand for whatever I pull off this thing. No promises. And if she blows smoke in my face again, I'm making it three."

"Two thousand," Naomi said. She didn't know Marti well enough to know if she spoke the language. Didn't want to take the chance.

Marti shrugged and handed over the phone. No point haggling when there was only one game in town.

Chen sniffed at the device. "Water damage." He sat, spun in his duct-taped chair, plastic bottles strapped around the wheels as makeshift stabilizers on uneven floorboards.

His desk was a battlefield where junk and brilliance fought for space. Loose wires snaked through scrap metal; microchips gleamed under fluorescent light; a can of Drive-Up Juice sweated between smudged schematics.

"Smoke for me," Chen murmured, lifting what was left of his hand: reconstructed joints fused into something more claw than fingers.

Marti slid a cigarette between the malformed digits without hesitation. He cracked open the phone with surgical efficiency, movements fluid despite his unnatural grip. A nail file replaced precision tools; a bent paperclip pried loose corroded circuits.

"Too cleanly broken to be accidental. Whoever tried killing this was an amateur. Smashed it before tossing it in water."

"So?"

"Probably salvageable. Power was off before the water hit."

Chen froze, then grinned sharp and hungry as he pried loose a tiny chip. He scanned his graveyard of tech before settling on an orange ER190, peeling back the rubber to slide the chip home.

Press. Beep. The screen gasped awake.

"Fuck yeah," Marti breathed.

"Shut up," Naomi hissed.

"Two thousand," Chen said flatly, clearly, in English. Now Naomi was really glad she hadn't bumped the price.

Marti tapped her credit device against his reader. Two grand gone in a blink. She tucked the phone against her ribs like a second heartbeat. "We done?"

"Get her the fuck away from me."

Outside, Naomi cracked the door and slipped her phone through first, camera feeding back empty street. "Clear."

They headed toward the motel lot, boots scuffing against radiating heat.

"You owe me two hour's worth."

"I just paid that asshole two crisp for fifteen minutes."

"Then make mine two crisp for two hours," Naomi grinned.

"Somewhere to drink?" Marti asked, hopeful for, well, sex of course.

"Motel bar's shit but cheap."

"My favorite."

The bar greeted them with green lights flickering above cracked vinyl, air thick with stale beer. They settled at the counter, Naomi signaling for whiskeys.

"Think I can use Chen again?" Marti asked as she lit up.

"Doubt it. Chen doesn't like new people. And he fucking hates you."

"Why?"

"You stressed him out so bad he won't shit for a week," Naomi said with certainty.

Marti narrowed her eyes. "You two were talking shit about me."

"Not as much as you deserved." Naomi knocked back her shot, slammed the glass, signaled for another. The second hit different. She coughed hard, eyes watering.

"So much for showing off."

Naomi groaned, rubbing her throat. "Fuck me." She slumped against the bar.

"How's your sleuthing ability?"

Naomi blinked slow, alcohol settling in. "I can't even spell that."

"Think you can look up some people for me?"

"You got fingers. Do it yourself."

Marti dragged a circle on the sticky surface. "Too busy with dead phones."

"Why should I?"

Marti exhaled. "Look, I know what kind of transferable skills you have. You get me good intel, real info, and I'll settle your husband's debt. You'd work for me after. For a year. As a secretary."

Naomi straightened like someone yanked a string in her spine. The alcohol haze vanished. "Come again?"

"I pay the debt. You be my secretary."

"You buy me."

"Not how I want to word it," Marti said, choking just a little.

"But that's what you're doing."

Silence stretched until Naomi barked out a laugh, knocking Marti's shoulder. "You know what that's called? That's called 'Fuck Yeah Freedom.' If he takes the cash? I'm fucking gone."

"Fuck yeah," Marti echoed.

Naomi waved down the bartender. "Yo! My guy! Bring us the bottle."

She crushed Marti into a hug that smelled like cheap whiskey and relief. "You're serious? Don't fuck with me about this."

"It's real. Most of it would've gone to some desk jockey anyway."

Naomi went still, then dropped her eyes. "You're okay with a Chinese woman? I tell people I'm Japanese."

The three-day war. The vitriol. Marti had lost a secretary to the Expulsion Act.

"Yep."

That was all Naomi needed. She grabbed the bottle and Marti's wrist. "Can you buy me now?"

"If we find your guy."

"Oh, I'll find him. But I won't rub his nose in it until it's done." She pressed the bottle into Marti's hands. "You get us a room. I'll be less than an hour. When I text you, send the money to whichever account I give you."

Something prickled at Marti's skull. Freedom had been her idea, but anonymous accounts and getting drunk? That was the oldest con in the book. And Marti had written most of them.

"Tell your pimp I want to meet. Face to face. Now."

Chapter 27

The alley reeked of sin and cold rain, drizzle now. Marti flicked her cigarette into a puddle where it died with a hiss. Naomi walked beside her, shoulders hunched, darting glances into shadows like she expected ghosts.

"You sure about this?" Naomi murmured. "Meeting JayJay might blow it."

Marti's fingers brushed her holstered gun. "If seeing my face ruins the deal, he was never gonna honor it anyway."

"Not convinced that's comforting."

"Relax. I haven't shot anyone in..." Marti glanced at her bare wrist. "What, an hour?"

Naomi groaned and nodded ahead. "Down here."

The narrow alley felt like walking into a throat. Garbage bags slumped against walls, leaking things best left unexamined. At the far end, JayJay materialized from shadow, eyes sharp despite his sluggish sway.

His gaze flicked from Naomi to Marti, darkening. "The fuck is this?"

"JayJay," Naomi started.

"Names don't matter," Marti cut in.

"You know mine."

"I know what she calls you." Her voice slid smooth as oil. "You want one for me? Call me KayKay."

"What kind of shit—"

"Let's talk business." She cocked her head toward Naomi. "I want her."

JayJay's lip curled. "Two-fifty."

"Not for an hour. I'm buying her."

He rocked back like she'd suggested eating glass. "Not for sale."

"Everything is for sale. Fifty grand."

A short laugh erupted from him. "She's worth ten times that."

Marti snorted. "Maybe she used to be good. But now? Now she's trouble. People talk."

JayJay struck like a snake, backhanding Naomi against the wall. She staggered with a choked noise between shock and pain.

Marti's gun appeared as if materialized from air itself, barrel steady between his eyes.

"Well," she said dryly, "so much for playing nice."

His hands shot up, sneer twisting uncertain. "What the fuck is this? A shakedown?"

"I could just shoot you," she mused, casual as discussing coffee.

"You won't," he snapped too fast.

"You know Dan Devall?"

A beat. "Yeah."

"Then call one of his people. Right fucking now." Her eyebrow lifted. "Ask them what happens when someone pisses off Starova."

Three heartbeats passed. JayJay exhaled. "No need for that. Fine... three hundred crisp."

Marti cocked the gun with a lazy flick. "Two hundred."

Before he could argue, she fired into the brick behind him. He lurched backward, dust sifting over his collar.

His tongue darted across dry lips, fingers inching toward his jacket. "Two seventy-five. That's my bottom line."

Another shot. Closer.

"FUCK! Stop that!"

"Now it's one-fifty."

"She owes me one hundred and sixty thousand fucking dollars," he croaked.

"You bought her husband's debt?"

JayJay nodded. "Not me, I just keep the girls honest."

"Then no. She doesn't owe you shit. Her husband did." Marti stepped forward, gun nudging his sternum. "What was the interest rate? Twenty percent? Thirty? More?"

His hand jerked toward his waistband but Marti was faster. The gun's handle cracked against his wrist. JayJay howled as his weapon clattered into a puddle.

"That was dumb." She caught him by the throat, pinning him against stone. "Last chance to be smart about this. Or I kill you. Mkay?"

He folded inward, cradling his wrist. "You don't know who you're fucking with."

Marti pulled out her phone one-handed, scrolled, pressed call.

"Devall." Static-laced growl from the speaker. "Starova? That you?"

JayJay's face drained of color.

"I got someone standing here. Think he's been cutting into your territory."

"WHERE?"

JayJay lurched forward. "She's lying! I never—"

Marti ended the call. "Oops. Misdial. Good thing I didn't mention your name. This time."

He deflated like a gutted fish. "One-fifty gets her out clean. No record. No debt."

She leaned close enough that her breath raised goosebumps on his neck. "If you or your fucking corporation bother her or her or her family… I'll make a call. And let Devall handle it."

The transfer chimed.

JayJay turned away. "Good luck with that crazy asshole."

"Come back here."

He kept walking until her gun clicked.

"I'm looking for kids working the streets. Drugs or sex."

JayJay shifted. "I only handle girls," he offered before looking at his sore hand.

"Get the fuck out of my sight," Marti snapped as she waved her hand. JayJay skittered away.

Naomi watched him disappear, shoulders dropping like she'd shed a straitjacket. "Holy shit. I'm free. Because of you." Her eyes darkened with hunger. "I gotta fuck you."

Before Marti could respond, Naomi's eyes darkened with hunger. "I gotta fuck you."

"What?"

Naomi grabbed her hand, tugging her toward the street. "Come on; we've got that hotel room." Her voice dropped, charged with something more than gratitude.

"You saved my ass, and I need to show you how much that means."

Something twisted in Marti's gut. Reward sex. That's what this was: buying Naomi's freedom and getting fucked as a thank-you note. It should've felt wrong. It should have felt degrading, transactional, whatever word she'd read in some ethics pamphlet once. But when Naomi leaned close, breath warm against her ear, whispering, "Please," Marti's objections gave like wet cardboard.

The whiskey bottle from the bar burned its way down her throat as they stumbled through the hotel lobby. Their laughter echoed off marble floors despite the receptionist's disapproving glare. The elevator ride was a blur of hands and lips and whispered promises.

Marti shoved their door open, half-dragging Naomi with her. They crashed onto the bed, limbs tangling as their mouths collided in rough, breathless kisses. Clothes disappeared in frantic motions: coats yanked overhead, shoes kicked across the room, fabric twisting under desperate fingers. Heat sparked between them, electric and urgent.

Marti hovered above Naomi, their breath mingling. A question burned in her mind: how would Naomi taste? Sweet or sharp? What sounds would she make when she came?

Naomi answered with a whiskey-laced kiss that smoldered against Marti's lips. She traced a path down Marti's neck, teeth grazing collarbones, mouth moving lower across sweat-slick skin. A groan escaped Marti's throat as Naomi's tongue circled her nipple before teeth applied just enough pressure to send sparks down her spine.

Fingers tangled in Naomi's hair, pulling her into another kiss: wet and deep, all hunger and no hesitation. Marti's jeans hit the floor in one fluid motion, underwear following an instant later.

Naomi's dress rode up as Marti's hand slid beneath it. The damp heat she found made her pulse quicken. She pressed harder, teasing through thin fabric before pushing it aside. "You want my mouth on you?" Her voice had turned to gravel.

Naomi's exhale said everything. "Fuck yes."

The dress lifted higher as panties slid lower, kicked away. Marti settled between Naomi's thighs and dragged her tongue through slick folds before focusing on the sensitive bud with precision. Naomi's taste, warm and heady, filled her senses as she worked, sucking and licking until Naomi trembled beneath her hands.

Naomi's groan vibrated through both their bodies as she pressed herself against Marti's mouth without restraint. Her hips rolled with each stroke of tongue, each teasing flick over swollen flesh. Marti slipped two fingers inside her, finding velvet heat that clenched around her.

A gasp escaped Naomi as Marti curled her fingers just right, hitting the spot that made her back arch off the bed. Marti worked deeper, twisting while maintaining steady pressure with her mouth: the rhythm building until Naomi writhed, thighs tensing with approaching release.

Then Marti shifted lower, raising Naomi's legs. A gasped curse broke from Naomi's lips as Marti's tongue pressed against the tight ring of muscle below. Marti licked slowly, firmly, before pushing deeper.

"Fuck..." Naomi arched against the mattress, pleasure surging through her like wildfire.

Marti reached around to stroke Naomi's clit while working with her tongue, alternating pressure until Naomi dissolved into shuddering gasps and broken sounds. She clenched around the intrusion as waves built higher inside her, faster and more intense.

The tension coiled tight before snapping loose: a guttural cry tore from Naomi's throat as she came hard, pulses wracking through her body while wetness flooded against Marti's chin and fingers.

Marti rode out the tremors with teasing touches until Naomi collapsed against the sheets, boneless and spent.

Breathless, Marti shifted to lie beside her, their limbs still entangled in aftershocks of pleasure and heat.

The room smelled of sweat and sex and something charged hanging between them: the kind of electricity that lingered long after the storm.

Marti wiped her mouth, lips curving into a crooked, satisfied smirk. "Yeah. That was worth shooting a wall."

Naomi laughed: a real, belly-deep laugh that seemed to ripple through the mattress. Her fingers traced aimless shapes across Marti's stomach, and for a moment, everything was still.

But stillness never lasted long.

The quiet let thoughts creep in: a missing kid, a name without a face, an open case file that hadn't stopped breathing.

Marti exhaled, eyes on the ceiling. The warmth was real, but so was the work.

Tomorrow, the chase would start again.

Chapter 28

Marti woke to the sharp scent of old smoke, which had replaced last night's electric charge with something staler, more real. The hotel room that had seemed transformed by darkness now revealed its true nature. Peeling wallpaper, a busted nightstand, sheets that had gone from silken promise to cheap cotton restraints around her legs.

Her head throbbed with fragments of the night before: JayJay's shouts echoing down the alley, Naomi's sounds, that door giving way under her boot.

Beside her, Naomi stretched with the same fluid grace she'd shown hours before, her bare shoulder brushing against Marti's. "Morning," she murmured, voice carrying echoes of last night's heat beneath the morning's amusement.

A stray curl tumbled into Marti's face, and Naomi smoothed it back, her fingers lingering against Marti's cheek. Her eyes held that knowing look: the one that said she'd seen Marti come undone and wouldn't forget it.

Marti reached for her cigarettes on the nightstand, the pack crumpled from where they'd been tossed aside. She lit one, inhaling deep enough to steady herself. Smoke curled between them as she exhaled. "Guess we should eat."

"Again?" Naomi leered, tracing a finger down Marti's arm.

"Food," Marti laughed despite herself. "I need actual food. And coffee. Lots of coffee."

They dressed in comfortable silence. Marti dragged on yesterday's leather jacket, worn soft with use, and her scuffed Docs; Naomi somehow made yesterday's clothes look fresh.

The hallway's fluorescent lights buzzed overhead as they made their way downstairs. Outside, morning light cut weak angles across the street, turning everything the color of old newspaper.

The café across the street welcomed them with the scent of burned coffee and grease. A bell jangled as they entered, drawing glances from patrons hunched over their cups like mourners at a funeral.

"Coffee. Black," Marti told the waitress, sliding into a booth with vinyl seats patched with duct tape.

Naomi ordered yogurt and fruit, smiling at the waitress like they shared a secret. When their food arrived, they ate without speaking: porcelain cups clinking against the table, tension still hovering between them, neither willing to name what had happened.

Naomi licked a smear of honey from her lip, catching Marti watching her. "Gotta go soon," she said, glancing at the clock on the wall. "Picking up my kids from my friend's before school." She hesitated. "I'll be in touch. Boss."

That last word hung between them: a reminder of boundaries reestablished, roles they were stepping back into. Marti nodded, watching Naomi gather her things. The fluid economy of her movements, graceful even when she wasn't trying.

Marti reached into her pocket and tossed her a crumpled business card that was, or maybe wasn't, current. "If you skip on me…"

Naomi stood, slung her bag over one shoulder. Leaned down and pressed her lips against Marti's cheek, a kiss that lingered just long enough to mean something before she pulled away.

"You'll hunt me down, or send Devall after me."

The bell jangled again as she left, and Marti sat alone with her cooling coffee and the ghost of warmth on her cheek.

She pulled on her cigarette, letting the smoke burn in her lungs. Last night, everything had seemed worth the risk. In daylight, she realized she was a fucking idiot. Buying a woman she'd only once before. Too desperate to replace Lori. A PI sleeping with her assistant. Threatening to shoot her pimp. A boss fucking her employee. However you sliced it, the situation was messy.

She ground out the cigarette harder than necessary, leaving a black smear on the ashtray. No point dwelling now. She had cases to handle, people to chase down. Draining the last of her coffee she walked out into the morning chill.

Her car sat where she'd left it, dew beading on the windshield. The door creaked as she slid behind the wheel, leather seats stiff with cold. She dug out her phone and dialed Dan Devall's number, pulling into traffic with one hand on the wheel.

He picked up after two rings. "Jesus fuck; it's early," Dan growled, his voice thick with sleep or last night's liquor.

Marti ran a hand through her tangled hair. "Yeah, yeah," she muttered, swerving around a delivery truck. "Listen.

My call..." She hesitated just a beat, but Dan caught it anyway.

"You mean your rambling?" he cut in. "What about it?"

Heat crept up her neck, but she pushed through it. "Sorry about that. I need to ask you something," she said, forcing her voice steady. "You know if anyone's snatching up young guys? Maybe a couple of pimps getting mean with their boys?"

"Let me guess. A case." His words hit like steel against stone, flat and final, and for a second, Marti thought she had an answer.

"You know I can't tell you that of course it is."

"No." Dan snapped like she'd questioned his humanity instead of his business connections. "Nothing large scale, like boys plural. You need to find these dudes to find someone's kids, right? I get it. You've got my blessing. Hunt them down like dogs."

Something loosened in Marti's chest: satisfaction curling through her gut.

"Good," she said, watching traffic lights blur past. "And if there's any blowback?" The question hung between them, unfinished but clear.

Dan snorted through the phone. "No one fucks with my people and gets away with it."

Marti almost laughed at that. Dan thinking she was one of his people. But she swallowed it down and ended the call instead.

Her phone clattered onto the passenger seat as she gripped the wheel with both hands, knuckles whitening. This lead had better go somewhere. Failure wasn't an option anymore.

The office building materialized ahead: a monolith of stained concrete and bad decisions. Its shadow fell across her windshield as she pulled into her spot, staring up at cracked windows that had witnessed too many long nights.

The stairwell smelled of piss and disinfectant, a combination that never quite masked either. By the time she reached her floor, the conversation with Dan had settled into something useful. He'd given her permission to hunt, which meant he wasn't involved. Or he was good at lying. Either way, she had room to move.

She unlocked the office door, shouldering it open when it stuck on the warped frame. The air inside met her thick with old cigarettes and lingering whiskey: the kind of scent that became part of the walls no matter how many times you tried to air it out.

Shrugging off her jacket, she tossed it onto the couch without looking, then collapsed into her chair like gravity had caught up.

Yeah. It was gonna be a long fucking day.

The orange phone sat on her desk: screen splintered, case battered, edges worn down like an old coin. Marti didn't give a damn about its condition. It was Albert's SIM card inside that mattered.

She rummaged through her desk drawer, pushing aside empty pill bottles and tangled charging cables until she found a compatible cord. Plugging it in, she watched the screen flicker to life, lines of static cutting across it before settling into a dim glow.

A few taps, a breath held too long, then there it was. Albert Alvarez's messages, dozens of them unread.

Her thumb hovered over the screen as a name appeared again and again: 'Mama.'

Mijo, please answer me. Please just let me know you're okay.

Albert, if you see this, call me. Come home. We love you so much.

The words punched through her chest like a fist. Marti's shoulders hunched forward as if to protect against the blow. Her jaw clenched tight enough to ache. These weren't her messages to read, this pain wasn't hers to feel, but it seeped in anyway, raw and familiar. The kind of worry that ate you from inside out until there was nothing left but hollow spaces where hope used to live.

Her fingers curled into fists, nails biting into her palms. She forced them open again, reaching for the small metal inhaler tucked in her desk drawer. One hit of Shadow: the chemical burn racing through her sinuses, down her throat, and the weight began to lift. Just enough to breathe again.

The world around her shifted. Colors bled together, the dull walls of her office pulsing with violets and electric blues. The floor rolled beneath her boots in gentle waves, as if she walked on water. Air thickened to honey around her, warm and sweet against her skin. Her body melted into the chair as tension drained away, replaced by a slow smile that pulled at her lips.

Better. So much better.

The messages blurred from memory, no longer hers to carry.

Chapter 29

A sharp knock yanked Marti back too fast, back to grays and peeling paint and the stale scent of cigarette smoke. Another knock, this one impatient.

Marti pushed herself up, the chair rolling back as she crossed to the door. She opened it to find Naomi's bright grin, too sharp for morning, too cheerful for this place.

"Good morning, Ms. Starova!" Naomi breezed past her, floral dress swishing against her thighs as she surveyed the office with enthusiasm. No trace of last night's intimacy in her manner: just the assistant, ready for work. "I can't tell you how excited I am to be working with you. I've followed your work for years. I think we'll make a great team."

Marti rubbed at her temple where the last traces of Shadow still hummed under her skin. "Don't make me fire you before lunch," she muttered, voice rough with the aftereffects of the drug.

Naomi didn't flinch, just cocked an eyebrow as if she'd been waiting for the gruffness. "You can't. You own this ass for a year," she said, slapping her own backside before following Marti across the room toward a door tucked into the corner. Unremarkable except for the keypad mounted beside its handle.

Marti punched in four digits without thinking and pulled the door open. Hinges protested with a long creak.

"Medical supplies," she explained as Naomi peered inside at rows of bandages, Fentafill, Medimotes, and Stim Gum standing in neat little rows alongside glass vials with labels Naomi didn't ask about.

"The code?" Naomi drawled, arms crossing over her chest as she turned back toward Marti with disbelief. "It's 1234? Bold choice."

"Shut up." Marti grabbed a thick binder from one of the middle shelves and shoved it at Naomi before she could continue.

Naomi accepted it but didn't step back; just stood there with the binder tucked against her hip, watching Marti through dark eyes that maybe held last night's memories.

Marti waved at the binder. "This has all the crap you need to know," she said, stepping back to create distance between them. "Employee handbook, contact lists, that sort of thing. Read it, memorize it, live it."

Naomi raised the binder, hugging it to her chest with mock solemnity. "Thank you so much for this opportunity, Ms. Starova," she said, voice dripping with earnestness. "I won't let you down."

Marti waved a hand. "What the fuck is with this Little Miss Sunshine routine?"

Naomi stuck out her tongue, a flash of the real person beneath the act, and dropped into the chair across from Marti's desk. She flipped open the employee binder, somehow making even that look like a performance.

Marti returned to her own desk where Albert's phone sat next to an empty whiskey glass. Both stared up at her like accusations. She picked up the phone again, forcing herself past the mother's messages, muttering under her breath. "Mom, mom... more mom."

Then something else caught her eye.

A message from a private number, dated the day Albert vanished.

$250. The Iron Vault. Tonight. 10 p.m.

Her jaw tightened. But it was the photo beneath the text that made her stomach flip. A close-up of a man's dick filled the screen: pale, freckled, familiar in a way that made her skin crawl. Her gaze snagged on a port-wine stain birthmark along his thigh. Unique. Identifiable.

A holy grail of evidence.

"Naomi," she called out, sharp enough to slice through the quiet. "Get in here."

Naomi appeared in seconds. "Is that how it's going to be? You just yell for me?" Her eyes narrowed at Marti's tone.

Marti turned the phone toward her, grimacing at what was on display. "I think I found one of the last men to see Albert alive." She flicked two fingers toward the screen. "Whoever owns this dick."

Naomi leaned in, nose wrinkling before her expression shifted, registering what Marti had seen. Then the birthmark. Her dick disgust transformed into calculation. "Yeah," she said slowly. "That's not something you see every day."

"Redhead or blond," Marti noted, setting the phone down but still staring at it. "And The Iron Vault? It's a men-only dive in the Warehouse District. Right near Boystown. Seedy as hell. Been around forever."

Naomi straightened, crossing her arms. "You think Albert met him there?"

"Either that or he was supposed to," Marti murmured, running a thumb over her chin. "This message: it's time-stamped just hours before he went missing."

Naomi exhaled and handed back the phone with a dry look. "And this is from the same phone Chen resurrected for you? Fun times."

"Welcome to the world of private investigation," Marti said, tossing the phone onto her desk with a dull clatter. "Nothing says 'vital clue' quite like an unsolicited dick pic."

Naomi laughed as she headed back to her desk. "I'll get up to speed on the Albert phone thing," she called over her shoulder.

"So you know what to do? As a secretary?" Marti asked,

"Sure , same skill set. Fast fingers, good stamina, and the ability to handle multiple jobs at once," Naomi said as she flicked her fingers in the air.

"Okay. File is called Moms and Missing Boys, or some shit. I don't know. Lori..." Marti's voice caught on the name. She swallowed hard and turned to her computer. "Lori named the file."

Marti glanced over at Naomi, now hunched over her own desk, reading through case notes with the same intensity she'd shown in other, more intimate moments.

The memory of last night flickered through Marti's mind: Naomi's hands, her mouth, the way she'd...

Marti shook her head. "Hey, let's send this picture to Johnny Tangle," she called out, grabbing her own phone. "I'll copy you."

Naomi didn't look up this time. "Johnny Tangle?" she echoed. "You know someone named Johnny Tangle?"

Marti tapped out a quick message: Can I send you a dick pic?

The response came: Is there something you need to tell me? Let me see! Send it!

She chuckled and snapped a photo of Albert's birthmark friend, then attached it with a follow-up text: Have you seen this penis?

Her phone buzzed seconds later: LOL, then: Can't say I have. Yours?

Fuck off. I want to know who owns it, she typed back.

I'll send it around. Ur weird.

Marti grinned and leaned back in her chair, letting out a slow breath as Naomi looked up from across the office, eyebrow raised. "You playing detective with dicks?"

Marti tossed her phone onto the desk and stretched. "Johnny's on it," she said. "If anyone can ID that dick, it's him."

Naomi didn't look up from her screen, but one brow arched higher. "Not sure if I should be impressed or unsettled."

Marti smirked. "Please. You know more pervs than he and I do combined. Which is a fuck ton." She cracked her knuckles, wincing at the sound. "And it's not like we have better leads. If we can find the last person who saw Albert alive, we're one step closer."

The hours crawled by, turning into days. Naomi caught on fast, using her mom skills more than she ever anticipated. She settled into a rhythm of research and questions that kept them both moving forward.

By the time Johnny called, Marti was unwashed, slumped at her desk, an empty whiskey bottle standing sentry beside her overflowing ashtray. Bertha curled against her ankle, purring. The cat flicked her tail in disdain when Marti nudged her with a boot.

The phone rang, sharp and insistent. Marti snatched it up, knocking over the bottle.

"Marti Starova, private instigator," she slurred into the receiver.

Johnny snorted. "I've got something for you about that photo you sent me."

Marti sat up straight, alert. "Better be good."

"Well," Johnny said, amusement coloring his voice, "nobody seems to know his name. Asking around too much gets you banned from the Iron Vault. But word is he's there every Friday at ten on the dot. Been a regular for a long time."

Marti groaned and rubbed her temples, where a headache threatened. "So that means this Friday? As in two days from now? Goddamn it."

Johnny chuckled low in his throat. "Look, I don't need to know why you're chasing this guy down, but if you're thinking about strolling into the Iron Vault? Not happening. No women allowed."

Marti let out a slow breath. "Yeah, yeah. Appreciate it, Johnny." She hung up and stared at the ceiling, piecing together what came next. Staking out a club full of men every Friday night until she caught sight of a specific dick wasn't appealing, but if this lead got her even an inch closer to what happened to those kids...

Bertha jumped onto the desk with grace for her size and yowled in Marti's face. Marti scratched behind her ears, earning a rumbling purr in response.

"Guess we're going undercover," she murmured, fingers moving through Bertha's thick fur as possibilities formed in her mind. She glanced at her reflection in the computer screen: sharp jawline, hollow cheeks, her hair a mess of curls. "You think I could pass with a mustache?"

Chapter 30

Two days after Johnny's warning, Marti scowled at her reflection, tugging at the fake beard itching against her jaw. Bertha watched from her perch on the filing cabinet, tail twitching. It was never fucking still. The whole getup felt wrong: hot, stiff, unnatural, but it had to be dark-bar perfect.

Johnny's follow-up text still ran through her mind: "Falls City's men-only bars don't just discourage women; they'll throw you out on your ass if they catch you. And that's if you're lucky."

Naomi lounged in Marti's chair, scrolling through her phone. "You'll need a chest piece," she mused. "And a dick. Beard down your neck to hide the lack of an Adam's apple." She looked Marti up and down. "You want broad shoulders or a beer gut?"

Marti groaned. "Beer gut's more common."

"Yeah, but your arms and legs would give you away. You'd look like a dude who timed his Twink phase badly." Naomi added a silicone muscle suit to the cart. "Congrats, big guy. You're getting jacked."

Marti's fingers fumbled for her cigarettes. The nicotine would calm the twist in her gut that came with knowing she'd be shedding her skin soon. "Brown contact lenses too."

Naomi nodded. "Done. Big dick or small?"

Marti exhaled smoke through her nostrils. "Small. If someone cops a feel, I don't need them getting ideas."

Naomi grinned. "Shame. You give off serious big-dick energy."

"Right, because walking into a room with a monster in my pants is subtle." Marti stubbed out the cigarette, grinding it into the ashtray hard enough to bend the filter. "How much is this going to cost me?"

Naomi checked the total and whistled low. "Five thousand. Ready in an hour."

"Where?"

"Eve's Red Apple over on Placer." She smirked. "I've been there before; it's solid."

Marti snorted. "Picked up a new dildo there last week."

Naomi laughed, stretching like a cat. "I'll hitch a ride with you: need to pick up something fun for myself."

"Sure," Marti muttered, peeling off her beard and collapsing onto her office couch. "Wake me in forty-five."

The neon sign outside Eve's Red Apple flickered pink-red across the rain-slicked sidewalk as Marti pulled up to the curb. The cheerful jingle of the door bell mocked her sour mood. Inside, harsh fluorescents bounced off tile floors and glass display cases, leaving everything too bright, too sterile for the sin that lined these aisles.

Soft jazz curled around racks of leather harnesses and lace corsets. The air carried notes of plastic and perfume: synthetic desire clinging to every surface. Vibrators in impossible shapes gleamed under artificial light like candy at an adult mad confectioner's window. Lingerie fluttered from hooks in shades of blood-red and midnight black, all satin and bondage straps.

The clerk, sharp-featured with a spiky pixie cut and enough piercings to set off TSA alarms, looked up as they approached the counter.

"I'm here for an online order," Marti said, sliding cash across the counter. "Starova. Number 56834."

The clerk tapped at the keyboard and nodded once before disappearing behind a curtain marked "staff only."

Marti turned to find Naomi running her fingers over expensive lace.

"This place is nice," Naomi mused, holding up a sheer teddy against herself before tossing it back onto its hook. "Way classier than some of the dumps I used to haunt." She grinned. "You know... like yesterday."

Marti ran a finger along the curve of a glass dildo, watching light refract through its smooth surface. "Only the best for my employees. And, of course, for my personal collection."

Naomi leaned against the display case, one brow arched. "Oh yeah? Just how extensive are we talking?"

Marti smirked. "A woman never reveals all her secrets." She gave a slow blink, deliberate. A tease. The thought of breaking in something new later sent heat curling low in her stomach.

Naomi wandered toward the back shelves and stopped short. "Well, well." She reached out and plucked a monster of a dildo from its stand: over a foot long and thick as her wrist. She turned it in her hands like an art critic sizing up a masterpiece. "Check this out: veins and everything."

Marti let out a low whistle. "Damn, girl. Subtle."

"One of my regulars would lose his damn mind over this." Naomi ran two fingers along the thick shaft like she was testing the grip on a dagger, mischief glinting in her eye. "He's begging me to find him something bigger to stuff in him."

Marti paused, fingers hovering over a leather harness. "You still going to see clients?" She kept her tone casual, but something tightened in her chest.

Naomi shrugged, tucking the behemoth toy under her arm. "Just a couple. The nice ones; the ones who treat me right." She grinned. "Anyway, it's not like you are going to pay me. I have kids to feed. Think I'll get him a little something special."

A sleek chrome box caught Marti's eye as they moved down the aisle. She turned it over in her hands. "'PowerSucker 5000,'" she read aloud, a slow smile spreading across her face. "This looks promising."

Naomi peered over her shoulder. "You like those gimmicky things?"

"Oh yeah," Marti said without hesitation. "Nothing gets me off like a good clit-sucking vibe."

Naomi wrinkled her nose. "Never did much for me."

"That's 'cause you weren't using it right," Marti said, eyes glinting with challenge.

Naomi folded her arms. "Alright then," she drawled. "Educate me, a prostitute, go ahead, I dare you."

Marti leaned in, dropping her voice. "First time I tried one, I got it out of the box before slapping it on my clit at level one. Nothing happened: just this weird little hum." She shook her head. "Got frustrated and cranked it to six."

Naomi raised an eyebrow but didn't interrupt.

"Then I realized I should use lube." Marti's hands made an exaggerated slicking motion. "Got it all set up, but this time, I aimed right." She positioned her fingers with surgical precision, "I hit the sweet spot."

Marti snapped her fingers. "BAM! My eye started twitching so hard I thought I'd seize. My leg shot out stiff as a goddamn switchblade." She demonstrated, knocking against a display of flavored lubes that wobbled before settling.

"Came so hard my whole body locked up: washer-on-spin-cycle levels of shaking," Marti declared.

Naomi pressed a hand to her mouth, shoulders shaking with suppressed laughter. "And that wasn't enough humiliation?"

"Oh no," Marti replied. "See, I'm trying to turn it off, but I'm shaking too much; hit the wrong button instead."

Naomi inhaled.

"Cranked it higher," Marti confirmed. "Must've blacked out by the third orgasm. Next thing I know, I'm lying there, panting and drooling, while that demonic little toy skitters across the hardwood, still buzzing. Like it just committed a crime and was making a run for it."

Naomi doubled over with laughter, clutching the veiny monstrosity to her chest. "Holy fuck," she wheezed. "I'm sold. Gonna get me one too. I could use an out-of-body experience."

They staggered to the register, Marti tossing the infamous stimulator onto the pile while Naomi added her own haul. The clerk rang them up without so much as a raised brow.

Outside, rain transformed the sidewalk into a canvas of reflected neon. Marti glanced at Naomi: lips still curved with laughter, eyes crinkled at the corners.

Too rare, Marti thought. Moments like this didn't come easy for people like them.

She bumped her hip against Naomi's, playful, solid. Another burst of laughter, softer this time, warmer.

Yeah. She could get used to this.

Friday night found Marti emerging from a cloud of steam, towel skimming across healing gunshot wounds. Pain sparked along her nerve endings, sharp and sudden. She hissed through clenched teeth and tossed the towel aside.

The sex shop bag on the office couch spilled its contents like evidence from a crime scene: harnesses and silicone limbs nestled between chest hair and what Naomi had taken to calling "the sex vacuum."

Marti's fingers trembled as she grabbed the sleek black harness briefs. The presence of the faux phallus settled against her thigh: too real and not real enough all at once. She stared at her reflection, at the strange bulge between her legs. Her throat tightened.

Next came the torso. She ran her fingers over sculpted abs and pecs dusted with disturbingly realistic chest hair. The craftsmanship was impressive. The reality of what she was about to do settled in her stomach like a stone.

She gripped the silicone and pulled it overhead. Halfway through, resistance clamped around her shoulders. Panic flared cold in her chest as she struggled, trapped between identities: neither herself nor this fabricated man she needed to become.

For one breathless second, she fought against synthetic flesh as if she were a drowning woman in a sea of silicone.

Then, with a wrench and an audible pop, her head broke free. Wet hair stuck to the inside lining as she stumbled forward, gasping.

"Naomi!" The name tore from her throat.

Footsteps approached, then Naomi appeared in the doorway, arms crossed. She took in Marti's predicament.

A beat of silence.

Then Naomi cackled, bracing herself against the doorframe.

"Oh, fuck off," Marti growled, strands of damp hair hanging in her eyes. "Help me."

Still laughing, Naomi wiped at her eyes and sauntered forward. "My sincerest apologies, boss," she drawled, tugging at stubborn edges of latex.

Together they worked it down over Marti's body until it settled against her damp skin. Too tight. Too foreign. Something essential seemed to vanish beneath the artificial flesh: a hollowing out that left Marti breathless.

Naomi stepped back, head tilted. "Not bad. You make a damn convincing pretty little man."

Marti adjusted herself under the harness, scowling. "Let's hope convincing is enough." She exhaled, steadying herself. "What's next?"

"Beard," Naomi said, grabbing the fake facial hair and spirit gum. She worked with efficiency, as though this were just another Tuesday instead of Marti's first foray into drag-or-die.

Marti sank into the armchair. Naomi dipped a brush into the adhesive and painted it onto Marti's chin. Cold and clammy against her skin, tacky too fast. Naomi pressed the first strands of synthetic hair into place, her fingers warm and sure.

The room quieted except for the faint rustle of fake hair and distant traffic. Naomi arranged each strand methodically, mimicking natural growth patterns. Her hands moved with precision: the same hands that had once sold touch for money now crafting a new identity with unexpected tenderness.

"There." Naomi stepped back, tilting Marti's chin up with two fingers. "You could pass on any street corner."

Marti turned to the mirror. A stranger stared back through familiar eyes. Her stomach knotted while something electric buzzed under her skin. Fear? Adrenaline? She buried it all beneath determination.

"Let's just hope I can pull this off," she murmured.

Naomi smirked as she tidied up discarded brushes. "In this game? Adapt or get left behind."

She handed over the brown contacts next. Marti slid them in, blinking against the sting. The world shifted to sepia tones, another layer of distance between herself and reality.

"How do I look?" Marti asked, fidgeting with a button on her shirt.

Naomi looked her over before flashing a wicked grin. "Like a handsome thirty-something businessman." She reached out and gave Marti's fake cock a playful tweak through her jeans.

Heat rushed up Marti's neck as she swatted Naomi's hand away. "Cut it out! This is serious."

"My apologies," Naomi said without an ounce of sincerity. She grabbed the cane from against the wall and held it out.

Marti shook her head. "Too distinctive."

Naomi arched a brow but shrugged, twirling the cane once before setting it aside. "Your call." Her gaze swept over Marti one last time. "Just don't oversell it. You'll pass in a dark bar, but not a high noon showdown."

Marti rolled her shoulders back and tested her gait: uneven but not theatrical. Natural enough to avoid unwanted attention. She paused at the threshold, glancing back. "Think anyone'll notice I've got a rubber cock shoved in my pants?"

"Oh no," Naomi deadpanned, arms crossed as she leaned against the desk. "Completely unnoticeable." A beat passed. "Now get going before you make me piss myself laughing."

The weight of her new identity settled over Marti as she reached for the door handle. Tonight, she would become someone else. The thought sent equal parts thrill and dread through her veins as she stepped toward the threshold of her most dangerous masquerade yet.

Chapter 31

Marti adjusted the prosthetic dick against her thigh as she descended the office stairs, Naomi's laughter fading behind her. The swagger in her step lasted right up until she reached the curb and saw her tire.

Slashed. Fuck. Did FUCT suddenly switch tactics from tracking her to inconveniencing her?

She pulled her jacket closer, the night air slicing through the fabric like a whisper with teeth. 9:45 p.m. Just enough time to make it to the Iron Vault before her target walked in, if someone hadn't decided to leave her a message carved into her Goodyear.

Fun and fucking games.

She exhaled, straightened, and flagged down a taxi.

Rain lashed against the windows as the cab rolled through downtown. Neon signs bled into the downpour, smearing the glass like war paint. The city blurred past in streaks of gold and blue. Marti's fingers drummed against her knee. Her mind was at the club, pushing through sweat-slick bodies under stuttering strobe lights, hunting for a ghost dick she wasn't even sure existed anymore.

The cab jerked to a stop. She tossed bills over the seat and stepped into the alley. The 'Iron Vault' sign flickered overhead, a sickly pulse that illuminated the dozen figures huddled near the entrance. Shadows draped in wet leather and cigarette smoke, rain pooling at their feet.

Johnny Tangle's words came back to her: Fridays at ten. The man who sent that last message to Albert had been here before, four years ago, but rumors said he still showed up like clockwork.

Marti slipped past the waiting crowd, keeping her head low, hands buried in her pockets. Eyes followed her: some with interest, some with something lustier curling behind them. She pulled out a cigarette and let the familiar burn ground her as she took a slow drag. Smoke curled around her lips before dissolving into rain-heavy air.

The bouncers stood like concrete walls, thick arms crossed over thicker chests, scanning each patron for weakness. They checked IDs and ran heavy hands over bodies, searching for weapons. A couple guys got turned away; their frustration flickered brief and ugly before they disappeared back into the night.

Beneath her feet, the music vibrated up through the pavement: a deep pulse that settled into her ribs like a second heartbeat. She took another drag, exhaled, and stepped forward.

A bouncer's hand shot between her legs.

Marti slapped his wrist away, lips curling back into something between a sneer and a snarl. No hesitation. No fear.

The bouncer wiped his hand on his jeans, unbothered. "Relax. Gotta check you're a guy." His gaze slid over her, slower this time, assessing in that way men did when they weren't sure what box to shove you into yet. "You look kinda femme."

Marti kept her mouth shut tight, couldn't risk speaking, and just nodded once.

The second bouncer laughed, sharp and mean and ran his hands along her chest and hips. "Nice," he said, his smirk curling satisfied around his teeth. "You're good."

Guess he had a latex fetish.

She stepped inside, crossing from cold rain into thick heat in an instant. The world shifted around her: bass rattled her bones and turned her blood electric. Flashing lights shattered everything into color-sharp fragments. Bodies writhed together under layers of neon haze. Sweat-slick skin caught glints of violet and red as hands found hips found mouths found something worth losing themselves in.

Marti inhaled deep, cigarette smoke fading into something heavier now. She surveyed the room through half-lidded eyes.

Time to find him.

The air hung thick: sweat, musk, cum, and something sour and synthetic beneath it all. Bodies tangled against walls. Some grinding, some kneeling, some just standing around. Overhead, screens flickered in stuttering loops, porn scenes bleeding light over bare shoulders, parted lips, the slow drag of fingers down spines.

Marti pushed through the crowd, gaze cutting through the swarm. The man with the birthmark was here somewhere. Or would be soon.

Heat pressed in from every side. A couple blocked her path, lips locked, oblivious to anything beyond each other. She sidestepped them, her boots dragging for just a second as if the floor itself wanted to trap her.

Ahead, a hand skimmed low, slipping past the waistband of another man's jeans, fingers disappearing with ease. No rush. No hesitation. Just the certainty that came with knowing how this night would end.

At the bar, she flicked a crumpled twenty onto the counter. "Whiskey. Double."

The liquor burned down hard and fast, clawing its way into her chest before settling behind her ribs. Some of the tension unraveled, just enough for another shot. Then another. A beer for pacing.

She moved slower now, scanning faces, thighs where shorts rode high or pants slung low. A hand brushed against hers. Then lower. Fingers curled around the hard length beneath her jeans.

This time, she didn't snarl. The heat of the whiskey settled low in her stomach, and something sharp and electric flickered through her. His grip was firm, confident; no hesitation.

And no clue.

He would never make her hard.

A smirk tugged at the corner of her mouth as she let it linger a second too long before shifting her hips back, just enough to break contact. He wouldn't think twice about it: just another body moving in the crush of sweat and bass.

She took a slow pull from her beer, swallowing down the rush of adrenaline. Deception had its own kind of thrill.

Focus. The birthmark.

Two hours and too many drinks later, there it was: a slip of a birthmark on a pale thigh under loose-hanging fabric that deserved to be called shorts. Her breath caught. That was the dick.

She raised her head to see his face.

Fuck.

Colin Bonner. The name hit her like a slap. The city official who'd been on Marcus Thornfield's payroll when Marti investigated the gangster's murder. She'd interviewed him back then. If she recognized him, he might recognize her. Every instinct screamed at her to retreat.

But Bonner's attention was elsewhere. His dick out in full display like he owned the room, one hand wrapped around a beer while his other slid smooth over a glass that wasn't his own.

A flick of his wrist. Something slipped inside like a magician's trick.

Marti moved without thinking, shoving off from her perch, cutting between bodies until she reached them just as the glass lifted toward unsuspecting lips.

She crashed into the stranger's arm. Liquor splashed across his shirt.

"Shit," she muttered, catching the guy by the waist when he swayed forward on unsteady legs.

Bonner's voice sliced through the noise: "Hey! Fuck you! He's mine!"

But he didn't follow. Didn't protest further. A dime a dozen.

Good.

Marti dragged the young man toward the bathrooms, her grip firm on his arm. Inside the dim yellow light of a stall, she pressed him against cool tile, fingers tight around his shoulders as his head lolled forward.

"Listen." Her grip tightened as his knees wobbled. "That guy? He drugged your drink."

Something cut through the slack-jawed emptiness behind his wide-blown pupils. He swallowed hard but said nothing.

"You need to get out of here." She let go when he didn't slide to the floor.

The kid blinked, face pale. "What? No, he wouldn't..."

"I saw him do it." A beat. Then, quieter: "You're not safe with him." How many others had he drugged? Did he drug Albert?

Fuck.

Something in the kid cracked; not loud, not sudden, but like wood warping under pressure. His shoulders sagged. He nodded once, like he'd known, just needed someone else to say it. "Okay. Okay, thanks."

Marti grabbed his arm, firm but careful, and steered him out of the bathroom. Across the club, Bonner was busy slamming his birthmark into some guy's face in the VIP room, oblivious in the dim haze. He never noticed when he thought he was winning.

Outside, rain slicked the pavement, pooling in neon reflections. Marti flagged down a cab with a sharp whistle and shoved damp bills at the driver. "Take him home."

The kid slumped into the backseat, mumbling an address, limbs loose like a puppet with half its strings cut. Before the door shut, his eyes caught hers: wide and lost under the washed-out glow of a passing car. Drowning with no shoreline in sight.

The cab pulled away, exhaust curling into the night like cigarette smoke. She told herself he'd be fine. Told herself she believed it.

A shoulder slammed into hers, jarring her spine. Two men crashed to the ground, fists flying wild and sloppy. A third followed, drunk and mean, eyes glassy with rage that had nothing to do with whatever started it.

They tumbled across wet pavement like meat on a butcher's block. One swung wide; another dropped with a sick crunch that promised tomorrow would hurt worse than tonight.

Idiots.

Marti lit a smoke and watched them tear at each other, amusement and disgust mingling as they bled over nothing that mattered. They stumbled into traffic. Horns blared. Drivers yelled from windows while wipers struck frantic rhythms against glass.

Someone would call the cops soon enough. Time to move.

A cab sat stalled behind the chaos, driver slack-jawed as he watched the fight. Marti yanked open the door without waiting for permission.

"Need a fare?" Her voice was all gravel and exhaustion and nicotine.

The driver blinked at her through the rearview before nodding. She slid inside and slammed the door.

"1532 Ravencrook," she muttered, slumping against worn leather that smelled like cheap cologne and too many regrets.

She wanted home. Needed it like a fix waiting just under her skin.

The city blurred past rain-streaked windows. Adrenaline bled from her veins, leaving exhaustion behind like an old lover sliding under covers she hadn't realized were cold until now.

Her apartment was dark when she pushed through the door. No lights, no ceremony. Just muscle memory guiding her hands as she peeled herself apart piece by piece. Tight clothes hit the floorboards. The hairy chest piece. The fake dick. The beard. Until only raw skin remained beneath lights too harsh for tenderness.

It would scare the shit out of her in the morning.

Hot water hit her shoulders, and she let herself breathe. Steam curled against tile while grime and cheap perfume swirled down rust-streaked drains like dissolving ghosts.

By the time she made it to bed, hair damp against sheets that carried old heat but no comfort, her body had surrendered. No more thinking tonight.

Tomorrow would come with its own ghosts, with Colin Bonner's mess trailing behind him like spilled gasoline waiting for a spark.

Tomorrow she'd chase answers through alleys and past locked doors until something broke under pressure.

But tonight?

Tonight, she was going to forget about all of it.

The apartment felt too quiet. The bottle of whiskey was half-drained on the counter, but Marti wasn't drunk. Not really. The buzz was a dull companion now, familiar as her own shadow.

She stood by the window, looking out at the city bleeding neon into the night sky. Falls City never slept, just shifted from one kind of desperation to another.

Maybe she was finally tired. Not of the work. She'd die before she gave up the cases. Not of the city. It was in her blood. But of the noise in her head that never shut up no matter how many chemicals she dumped on it.

The drugs didn't work like they used to. Tolerance was a cruel mathematics. And the price kept climbing while the payoff kept shrinking.

She rubbed her face, fingers trembling just slightly. No witnesses to this moment. No confessions to make. Just her and the facts, laid out like evidence.

"It's time," she said to her reflection in the glass. "Time to cut one loose."

Not all of them. She wasn't turning into some fucking saint. The drinking stayed. Whiskey was practically a food group. The smokes. Maybe the occasional Fentafill when wounds got too painful. She needed her edges sharp enough to cut. Needed something to keep the world at arm's length.

But Shadow? The inhalers, the dealers, the whole ritual of chasing that particular ghost? They were slipping out of her hands anyway, becoming more trouble than escape. And for the first time in years, she didn't feel like chasing after them.

"Fuck it," she said softly to the woman in the window. "Maybe I can do it if no one is watching."

That was as much of a promise as Marti Starova was ever going to make to anyone, including herself.

Chapter 32

Marti dragged herself into her office, cheap cologne still clinging to her hair despite the evening's shower. The silicone body parts had, in fact, scared the shit out of her. Her boots landed heavy on the hardwood, each step echoing last night's cautionary talk in the club's washroom.

She froze in the doorway.

Lori?

Naomi.

Naomi was already there, lounging at the desk like she owned the place, flipping through the employee manual with unearned casualness.

Before Marti could spit out a demand for explanation, Naomi's gaze flicked up: sharp, deliberate. A finger to her lips.

Marti frowned. Naomi tilted her head toward the desk and slid a scrap of paper forward with two fingers.

There's a bug in your office.

A muscle jumped in Marti's jaw. She scanned the space: same mess as always. Papers scattered across the desk, bottles overturned, whiskey ghosts clinging to the walls from yesterday's temper tantrum. No cockroaches. Not even a spider looking for rent money.

She leaned back into the doorway and scowled. "What?" she mouthed.

Naomi slipped past her with fluid grace, claiming the space whether Marti agreed or not. She crossed to the window without hesitation and pointed. "There," she mouthed.

Marti followed her line of sight to a small silver box clamped onto the ledge outside. A heavy-duty listening device. Something cold curled under her ribs.

She turned back to Naomi, the question hanging between them: Who put that there?

Instead of answering, Naomi reached toward yet another device. This one a sleek black box perched against the glass on Marti's side of the window. A green light flickered awake under her touch. "Dissonance enhancer," she murmured, fingers resting against smooth plastic. "Scrambles every listening device within twenty feet."

Marti exhaled slowly. "Oh." She leaned in closer, inspecting the box outside before cutting Naomi a glance from beneath dark lashes. "Wait! Is this a dissonance enhancer?"

"Yep."

"Shit! I just made one the other day in my garage. But mine was purple, so I threw it out."

"Jerk."

"Where'd you get it?"

Naomi shrugged as if it didn't matter, which meant it did. "Chen."

Of course it was Chen. She needed to make nice with this guy.

Marti shifted her weight to one hip, arms crossing as something unsettled twisted deep in her gut. "Appreciate you finding this little nest of eavesdropping bullshit, but why were you in my office in the first place?"

Naomi hesitated, a fraction too long, before flashing an easy smile that lit up her eyes. "Snooping." A lazy tilt of her chin toward the box outside. "Found that."

"Jesus Christ." Marti dragged a hand through her hair and let out a humorless laugh. "Boundaries exist for a reason."

"I know." Naomi pressed a hand flat against her chest in mock sincerity. "But I don't trust you, and you don't trust me, so we're even. Besides." She let the moment stretch between them. "Could've been listening for days. Weeks even. Or maybe just some perv hoping for phone sex material."

Marti snorted despite herself. Her shoulders tensed as she glanced back at the device. Someone had been listening. Watching. The thought crawled across her skin like unwanted fingers. She focused on the black box inside, its red glow steady beneath Naomi's fingertips.

"And you ran straight to Chen?"

"He's got his little network of suppliers." Naomi watched Marti too closely now, waiting for something more than irritation.

Marti shifted closer until barely a breath separated them, bending down for a better look at the enhancer beside Naomi's hand. Jasmine drifted from Naomi's skin, curling around Marti like heat rising off pavement after rain.

She ignored how it settled low in her stomach.

"So I just press this?" Her voice came out rougher than intended.

"That's it," Naomi murmured.

Marti clicked her tongue against her teeth, a smirk too sharp around the edges to be anything but trouble. "Well, fuck, what does a dissonance enhancer do? Seriously? What's it enhancing?"

Naomi rolled her eyes but shifted just enough that their shoulders brushed, a fleeting contact neither acknowledged aloud.

"A dissonance enhancer takes every noise," Naomi said smoothly, fingers tracing idle patterns over buttons she already knew by heart. "Voices, traffic noise, cat purrs: it distorts sound until nothing makes sense anymore." She tapped another button. "No one hears what they're supposed to hear."

The space between them hummed with something unspoken before Naomi added dryly: "Don't worry. Bertha won't notice."

Marti huffed out a sound between amusement and exasperation. "You think I give a shit about the cat?"

"As long as this thing is on…" Naomi moved closer, the silk of her blouse whispering against Marti's sleeve. "They can listen all they want, but they won't understand shit."

Marti leaned back against her desk, arms crossed, one eyebrow raised. "Clever. But who the hell would want to bug my office? I mean, besides you."

"Could be anyone." Naomi avoided Marti's gaze, her silk blouse shifting as she shrugged. "Devall? Some old client? You've got a talent for pissing people off."

"True," Marti admitted without apology. "But whoever planted this is keeping tabs on me specifically. Like those fucking trackers."

Naomi turned the bug over in her fingers, alert. "Trackers? Plural? This looks official."

Marti exhaled, thoughtful. "So tell me: who's so invested in my thrilling one-woman monologues?"

"Local cops, maybe?" Naomi tapped a manicured finger against her chin. "Could be keeping an eye on you after your spectacular exit from the force."

"Nah." Marti shook her head. "Too long ago. They're not that subtle or that smart. This feels bigger."

"Like... federal big?"

Marti pushed off the desk and started pacing, energy crackling through her limbs. "Bingo. Had a little run-in with the feds recently. Found a GPS tracker on my car, courtesy of our friends at the Federal Unified Crime Taskforce."

"And they just labeled it?" Naomi blinked.

"Big old sticker on the side," Marti said, deadpan. "Real professional-like."

A low whistle slipped from Naomi's lips. "Shit. You think they planted this too?"

"Wouldn't be surprising." Marti's fingers twitched toward where a cigarette should be. "They've taken a sudden interest in little old me."

Naomi gnawed her lip, worry creasing her forehead. "What's the move?"

Marti waved a hand as if she was brushing dust off her sleeve. "Let them listen in. I've got nothing to hide." She hesitated, then smirked. "Well, nothing they can prove."

"Fine, but don't mention anything about Chinese food unless the device is on."

Marti frowned. "Wait. If this enhances sound to be whatever, why can I understand you?"

"It's digital. Electronic." Naomi rolled her eyes. "It isn't like a boombox for fuck's sake, it's like a radar jammer. You can still drive around with a radar jammer, right?"

Marti blinked once. Twice. "The fuck is a boombox?"

"A portable radio."

"The fuck is a radio?" Marti teased, stepping over to the dissonance enhancer. She flipped the switch, watching the green light wink out like an extinguished star. Her tone shifted from amused to sharp purpose. "I need you to dig into someone for me."

Naomi crossed her arms. "Who's the lucky bastard?"

"Colin Bonner." Marti grabbed a pen, dragging it over an old receipt without writing anything. "City health inspector." She glanced up, eyes narrowing. "I want employment history, parents' names, anything that smells rotten."

Naomi chuckled softly, pulling out her phone to type something in rapid bursts. "Is he the birthmark guy? You find something?"

"Call it intuition," Marti said dryly, though the evidence was stacking up like bodies in a morgue.

Naomi tilted her head but didn't press further. "Fine," she said with faux exasperation before flashing a lazy grin. "You know I'm gonna bill you for this device."

Marti barked out a laugh as she dropped into her chair. "I'm not paying you. You have access to the accounts. File the receipt, repay yourself."

"Receipt? Shit," Naomi muttered, shaking her head with amusement before heading toward the door with slow, deliberate steps that made every inch of fabric cling just right.

Marti watched her go, not just because of how she walked but because of how damn useful she was proving to be. Dissonance enhancer? This woman knew about good stuff.

The door closed behind Naomi with a soft click. Marti turned toward the window and shoved it open wider than necessary. Damp air rushed against her skin: sharp, bracing, carrying rain and exhaust in its embrace.

She pulled out a cigarette and lit up just as something small and quick darted past her shoulder. Bertha landed on the couch as if she'd been invited, fixing Marti with one of those slow, imperious blinks.

"Well, well," Marti drawled, tapping ash into an empty coffee cup. "Look what the cat dragged in."

Bertha twitched an ear but otherwise didn't acknowledge the joke.

Marti reached out to scratch behind one ear; Bertha ducked away at the last second as if touching was beneath them both.

"What's wrong now, Farta? Still pissed I told you to bathe?" She watched Bertha stretch beside her like royalty on a throne. "You smelled like someone set fire to garbage. Still do."

Bertha flicked her tail once, slow and deliberate. A warning.

Marti smirked, dragging smoke deep into her lungs. "Fine. Be a little shit. Just don't come begging when the fleas start their feast."

The cat yawned wide enough to show tiny, lethal teeth, then curled into herself as if the conversation had bored her to sleep.

Marti exhaled, leaning back in her chair, looking at old water stains that bloomed like even older bruises. The case gnawed at her bones: missing boys, one found dead already. Feds nosing around and tracking but also going out for dinner. Corrupt civil servants who drug their dates. Layers of rot, peeling back one by one, but... related?

"What do you think? We cracking this one open?" she asked the cat.

Bertha flicked an ear but stayed curled up tight, done with the discussion.

"Yeah," Marti muttered, grinding out her cigarette, "that's what I thought."

A sharp knock on the doorframe pulled her attention. Naomi strolled in without waiting for an invite and flipped a thin file onto the desk. "Got Bonner's details."

Marti snatched it up, skimming fast: address at 462 Winthrop Park Road, health inspector for two decades. She snorted at a particular line. "Married a woman in 2038. Divorced 2039. That was quick."

"Significant?" Naomi tilted her head.

A grin tugged at Marti's lips as she flipped the folder shut with a slap. "It means there's an ex out there who might love nothing more than to torch his life." She leaned back, fingers steepled as possibilities unfurled. "Maybe he sent her dick pics; maybe she caught him slipping roofies to guys in bars. Either way? Bet she's got stories."

Naomi's gaze sharpened, voice dropping low. "You want me to feel her out? See if she'll talk?"

"Still too risky." Marti picked up her glass, empty, and frowned before setting it down with a dull clink. "If she tips him off, we're fucked six ways to Sunday. Have to find out if she hates him, first."

Naomi nodded, shoving her hands into her pockets. "Then we start with divorce records," she mused, almost to herself. Then louder: "Or good old surveillance."

Marti's lips curled at that. "You suggesting we stalk him?"

"Was hoping you'd ask." Naomi smirked.

Marti snorted and shook her head, stretching long and lazy against the chair back. "Not happening."

"Why not?" Naomi pouted, folding her arms across her chest. "I think stalking a civil servant should be pretty safe."

Marti shot her a flat look, counting off on her fingers: "One: you've got kids. Two: you don't have a gun."

"Right... no gun." Naomi blinked as if this was brand-new information before shrugging in resignation. The playfulness drained from her face. "Shit... you think you'll need one?"

Names flickered through Marti's mind like muzzle flashes in the dark. Thornfield first, then Ari Stirling bleeding out under too-bright fluorescents... Kane and Montgomery... Katsaros... Dunstone... Furh... ghosts lining up side by side, watching, waiting, reminding.

She reached for the whiskey bottle instead of answering right away. Amber liquid filled the glass, steady and sure. The familiar burn down her throat steadied her nerves.

"Yeah." She set the glass aside with finality. "I might need a gun."

Chapter 33

The whiskey had worn off hours ago, replaced by cold coffee and stale cigarettes as Marti watched Colin Bonner's house through smoke bleeding into the damp morning air. The cigarette burned low between her fingers, glowing ember against chipped nails. She sat in her car, engine off, hoodie pulled up, eyes locked on.

Bonner lived at the edge of the Marrow District, just east of the river. It was once a nice area of the city. Now? Boystown had formed to the north, and the sex and drugs had filtered down. A stranger hanging out in a car was nothing new for these neighbors.

Three stories of beige normalcy, fresh paint trying too hard to blend in. The lawn was manicured, the hedges trimmed with surgical precision. Nothing flashy, nothing ostentatious: just another middle-class illusion wrapped in vinyl siding. But Marti knew better. Behind that façade lived a man who'd built his life on other people's pain.

Her lips pressed tight. The first time she met Bonner, he'd played at being harmless, slipping through corruption like it was water and he was made of oil. The yacht, the watch, the pen that cost more than a year's salary: all paid for with favors and blind eyes. She'd seen it long ago, but details like that stuck. Despite Thornfield being dead, Bonner was still on someone's payroll. Had to be.

She flicked ash out the window, fingers brushing against the inhaler in her pocket. Her hand twitched, just a little, but she felt the itch curl around her spine. Shadow whispered at the edge of her thoughts, but she swallowed it down. Later.

8:47 AM. If Bonner kept banker's hours, he'd be leaving soon.

Cameras tucked into eaves caught morning light just so. A sleek alarm panel was visible through a side window. The house wanted to look unremarkable, but the tech said otherwise. Said secrets lived here.

She adjusted her CamLobes: lens on the left, shutter button on the right. She tapped it a few times, capturing the scene while nicotine threaded through adrenaline.

The garage door shuddered to life at 8:53 AM.

Marti moved fast. Door eased open without a sound, body slipping low beside her car. Inside the garage sat two cars: a sedan as forgettable as bad coffee and next to it, something sleeker, all polished chrome and arrogance. A sports car meant for someone who liked being seen.

Bonner emerged, briefcase in hand, striding past his expensive toy without so much as a glance before sliding into the driver's seat of his bland little cover story on wheels. The garage door rumbled down as he backed out, not shut yet, just enough space left if she ran now.

Marti pushed forward. Legs screaming from too long without a cane, but it was too late. The door slammed closed with heavy finality, locking her out with nothing but frustration clawing up her throat.

"Fuck." She bit down on the curse, glancing toward the cameras tracking her without blinking. At least she kept her hood up; no clean shot of her face meant no easy trail back.

She strode back to her car like this had never been more than a morning stroll through suburbia, mind buzzing hot with failure and nicotine. Circling the block once, twice, she kept pace with the neighborhood's rhythm: not slow enough to get noticed, not fast enough to seem desperate.

A few streets over, wedged between two SUVs, she cut the engine and sat for a moment. Her breath pushed out through clenched teeth as a new plan formed.

She tugged off her hoodie and tossed it onto the passenger seat before reaching for latex gloves in the glove box. The snap of rubber against skin steadied her, or maybe that was just an old habit pretending it still helped.

Stepping out into sharp morning sunlight, she squinted toward Bonner's street. Then she saw it: a package resting neat and unattended on some poor neighbor's porch two houses down.

An idea bloomed as she moved toward it. She scooped up the box and continued on, tucking it under one arm. Knocking on doors worked best when you had something worth answering for.

Three sharp raps against Colin Bonner's front door. Nothing. She knocked again, knuckles stinging this time, letting the sound hang in the damp air.

A prickle crept up her spine. Someone was watching.

She turned slowly, pasting on a smile like it belonged there. Across the street, a man stood in his yard, hose limp in his grip, water slapping at petunias drowning from the last downpour.

"Hey," she called out, voice warm like she wasn't trespassing in spirit. "Trying to drop this off for Colin Bonner, but no one's home. Think you could sign for it?"

The neighbor flicked the hose once before shaking his head. "Nah. Just leave it in the garage like everybody else does." He nodded toward the house. "Door's down, but it ain't locked."

Something sparked in Marti's chest. "Perfect," she said. "Appreciate it."

She pivoted back up the drive, throat tight with anticipation. The garage door handle turned smooth under her grip, too smooth, but she slipped inside anyway.

The package hit concrete dead center. She turned to leave when her eyes caught the empty space where the neighbor had been standing.

Perfect.

She exhaled slowly and shut the garage door behind her. Dim light slanted through narrow windows, painting shadows over racks stacked high with overpriced tools and cardboard boxes lined up with military precision. The house door loomed ahead: solid, locked. But the security panel beside it caught her attention first. Sleek and modern where everything else felt lived-in enough to be ignored.

She moved through the garage like water finding cracks, rifling through drawers until her fingers closed around cold steel. The screwdriver felt good in her palm: solid, purposeful. She was on camera; might as well make it count.

Plastic cracked under the edge of the flathead as she popped the console open. Wires spilled loose like guts: blue to copper, white to silver, three greens braided tight against red and black, thick black feeding into Z4.

Marti stared at the tangle for half a second before something settled hard in her gut. Her fist closed around a handful of exposed wiring and pulled. A sharp snap rang out, followed by silence thick as held breath. No alarm, not yet, anyway.

Her mouth twitched as she turned to the lock next. The screwdriver jammed deep into wood until something groaned and split apart. The handle twisted free; she stepped inside before doubt could catch her heels.

Chapter 34

The living room stank of wealth. Leather that had never creased, mahogany that gleamed too bright, air so still it felt staged. A coffin masquerading as a home.

A TV stretched across one wall: sleek, black, impersonal. Three different gaming consoles glowed beside it. Above sofas stiff as corpses hung expensive abstracts that meant nothing. Art meant to impress, not to feel.

On the bar cart, crystal decanters caught the light, refracting it into sharp edges. Marti's jaw tightened as memory flickered behind her eyes: Bonner at the club, easy grin and careless charm, the flick of his wrist as he slipped something into a drink while laughter drowned out warning bells.

All of this would be a glorious playground for young men.

Her fingers hovered over a framed photo on the bookshelf: Bonner with some kid, arms slung around each other. The boy couldn't have been more than eighteen. Maybe younger. Bile rose in her throat.

This wasn't just a room. It was camouflage. A predator's den dressed up in designer furniture and soft lighting, built to lull prey into believing they were safe.

Something white-hot expanded in her chest, pressing against her ribs until she thought they might crack. Her skin felt electric, hypersensitive to every soft surface, every perfect angle

You don't get to keep this, she thought, cold fury settling into her bones. You don't get to hide behind all this perfection.

Her boot connected with glass before conscious thought caught up. Shards rained down like broken promises, the sound vibrating through her ribs, sharp and unsatisfied.

Not quite pleasure. Not yet.

But close enough for now.

Paintings tore from walls, frames splintering against polished wood as color scattered across expensive surfaces. Each crash fed something hungry inside her, something that had been waiting since she'd seen him try to roofie that kid. It was a shit move, something cowards would resort.

Marti stood in the wreckage, breath measured but heavy, a smirk curling at the edges of her mouth. Let Bonner come home to this mess and wonder who was watching him now.

She adjusted her earring, angling the tiny lens before tapping the CamLobe trigger. The feed fled online, capturing evidence as she moved through the house with deliberate steps.

The kitchen gleamed with untouched perfection: stainless steel appliances, granite counters, custom cabinetry. She ran a gloved hand along the cool surface, then yanked open cabinets. Boxes of food tumbled to the floor with dull thuds. Unsatisfying. Plates and glasses followed, their shatter-song echoing through empty rooms.

Upstairs, her boots sank into plush carpet as she entered the master bedroom. A king-sized bed draped in luxury sheets dominated the space. The covers landed on the floor with a soft whoosh.

Custom closets lined one wall, their cherry wood doors hiding whatever secrets lay within. Marti flipped the mattress with a grunt. Underneath: porn magazines and a stack of crisp bills. Her eyebrow arched. She considered leaving the cash; trespassing charges were one thing, robbery another. But fuck it. What was graft ended up tucked in her pocket.

The home office sat pristine: mahogany desk polished to a high shine, leather chairs waiting for someone with power to sink in and issue commands. Click, click, click. More evidence captured by her CamLobes.

Leather-bound classics and hardcover bestsellers lined the bookshelf, spines aligned. She plucked one at random, some business strategy tome with an embossed title. The weight felt substantial in her palm.

On the desk sat Bonner's sleek laptop, silver casing reflecting destruction back at her. The tiny black eye of its camera stared, a silent witness. Marti's skin prickled with awareness.

She flipped the book open to its middle, splaying its pages like wings, and laid it tent-style over the laptop. The camera disappeared beneath words Bonner never read. A small victory, but it sent satisfaction coursing through her: one more way to blind the predator in his own den.

Marti jiggled the mouse; a login prompt flared to life. A quick flick sent the monitor crashing to the floor with a crack as satisfying as sex. Books joined the wreckage, curtains came down, papers flew free before gravity claimed them.

She stood amid chaos, shoulders rising and falling with each breath, hands flexing at her sides. Something in her chest loosened at the sight: the destruction breathing for her when she couldn't manage it herself.

Then she stilled mid-step.

One frame still stood on an untouched corner of the desk, upright amid destruction as if it hadn't gotten the memo. Her smirk faded as her gaze locked onto it, stomach twisting sharp and fast.

The faces in the photo smirked back at her: Colin Bonner, all gleaming teeth and easy arrogance, flanked by Douglas Franklin, Falls City's police chief, and his brother William, head of Internal Affairs.

What. The. Fuck.

A trifecta of men that shouldn't exist in the same frame. Not like this, not with arms around shoulders and drinks raised high like they were celebrating something no one else was invited to know about.

This wasn't just a keepsake. It was proof of something ugly.

She snapped a picture, the quiet click slicing through silence. Set the frame back with careful hands, her heart hammering so hard she was sure it would give her away.

Upstairs was done. Ground floor was done. Now, the basement.

The basement sprawled like a rich man's playground: home theater in one corner, gym equipment in another. But the wine cellar pulled her forward. Dim light glowed off rows of dark glass, air thick with pretension and cork. Upstairs had been pristine, clinical. This was indulgence without apology.

Marti reached for a bottle, fingers wrapping around smooth glass. Bordeaux, old enough to matter. She turned it once, tested its weight, then let go.

The shatter rang sharp and final. A grin crept across her face as she grabbed another bottle and pitched it hard into the rack. The crash echoed through the cellar, red pooling across tile like blood. She grabbed another, and another, each destruction feeding something primal that had been starving for too long.

She stepped through broken glass back to the stairwell, surveying her work. Not subtle, but that wasn't the point. She wanted mess, wreckage, something that screamed bad luck before Bonner could wonder why.

She tossed the mattress cash in the air, watched as bills fluttered to the floor. She placed one last bottle beside it, whole, untouched: the kind of detail that made people start guessing when they should be running scared. Was Bonner's payroll up? Did he fail to do something for his masters? Or did someone else want something more?

One last glance over her shoulder. Then she moved, up and out, slipping into sunlight with danger sinking into her bones where it belonged.

She slid into her car and pulled a cigarette from her pocket with steady hands. Lit up, inhaled deep. She liked to smoke after fucking someone over. And this was a fucking. She exhaled slowly, watching something heavier than nicotine slip into the air.

The photo on her phone screen glowed in the dim light: Colin Bonner with Douglas and William Franklin, arms around each other, smiling like they owned the world.

Her lip curled. "Bullshit."

Bonner was a sleaze with greasy palms who drugged pretty young things in bars. A health inspector with a flexible definition of "A-rated" restaurants, when drug lords needed somewhere to stash product. But why was he looking so cozy with the Chief of Police and Internal Affairs?

She dragged a hand through her hair, pieces clicking into place. Childhood friends? Blackmail? Fuck buddies?

Cops don't hang out with health inspectors for no reason.

They were protecting him. Maybe reports of sexual assault vanishing before they hit a courtroom. Complaints buried six feet deep. If Bonner ever got sloppy, if some kid ended up identifying him after one of his little tricks all it took was a phone call to make sure no one gave a shit.

Or maybe they weren't just covering for him; maybe they were using him. Bonner had access: kitchens, back rooms, places no one looked twice at an inspector walking through. Maybe he wasn't just turning a blind eye to shipments. Maybe he was moving product himself. Who'd suspect a guy checking for rat droppings?

Her stomach turned as a worse thought clawed in. Maybe they shared his perversions. Bonner liked them young, vulnerable. If Douglas or William had the same taste, keeping him close wasn't just protection: it was opportunity. Insurance. Silence. Prey.

The cigarette burned too close to her fingers. She flicked it out the window, exhaled hard. The taste of ashes clung to her tongue.

Whatever this was, it was filthy all the way down to the bones.

She flexed her fingers once before picking up her phone again, staring at their grinning faces as if she could burn holes through them with her mind.

This just got really fucked up.

Chapter 35

Marti sat at her desk, the morning light feeling as exposing as the day's discoveries. Her hand trembled as she lifted the shot glass: partly from the break-in, partly from staring at the damning photo until dawn. The taste of ashes still clung to her tongue, even after three cups of coffee.

Across from her, Naomi lounged in the chair like it wasn't a piece of shit office chair, legs crossed, eyes sharp as she watched Marti take a drag from her cigarette.

Near the sill, the green 'on' light of the dissonance enhancer glowed steady, scrambling their words for any unwanted ears.

Marti exhaled, watching the smoke curl and dissipate. "Colin Bonner's dirty," she muttered. "I know he's tied to Albert's disappearance, but his place was clean."

A smirk tugged at Naomi's lips. "That why you trashed it?"

Marti huffed out a laugh. "Kicked in the TV, stomped his laptop, smashed some wine bottles." She leaned back in her chair and stretched with satisfaction. "Almost as good as an orgasm."

Naomi arched a brow, amused. "Perv boys look so ordinary."

"Ain't that the truth?" Marti grinned, tilting her head with mock innocence. "Look at me: I look normal as hell, but we both know I'm a freak."

That got a laugh out of Naomi, low and knowing. They let it sit between them for a second, laughter laced with just enough darkness to feel real.

But then Marti's mind drifted back to the photograph she'd found at Bonner's house. She could still see it clear as day: Bonner standing shoulder-to-shoulder with Chief Douglas Franklin and his brother William. No family photos, nothing personal. Just two pictures displayed like trophies. Bonner with some teenager. Bonner with the cops.

She downed the rest of her whiskey and set the glass down with a solid clink. "Bonner's picture," she said, voice tight. "Him, Douglas, William. Together."

Naomi's smirk faded. "Yeah? So what?"

Marti's fingers tightened around the empty glass. The pieces were starting to fit together, jagged edges clicking into place. Bonner's unexplained wealth. His preference for drugged boys. His connections to Franklin.

"Fuck," Marti breathed, gripping the edge of her desk. Then again: "Fuck."

Naomi tilted her head but said nothing. Waiting.

Marti dragged a hand through her hair, her throat desert-dry. "I've been hearing whispers for over a year now." Her voice dropped low, as if the walls themselves might carry her words away. "Cops snatching kids off the street."

Naomi's expression didn't shift much. Just one blink, but she tapped two fingers against the arm of her chair before folding them under her chin. "Yeah, I've heard that too." A pause, thin as wire between them. Then: "Figured it was just some hustler bedtime story."

Marti's chair creaked as she stood, her pulse hammering against her ribs. "What if Douglas and Williams aren't just covering up?" The question hung in the air, heavy with implication. "What if they're running that shit themselves?"

Naomi exhaled sharply, unimpressed. "That's a stretch."

Marti poured another shot, watching the whiskey catch light before knocking it back. Warmth spread down her throat, settling deep in her gut like liquid resolve.

"Wouldn't be the first time men did something awful just to get off," Marti muttered, tapping the desk with her fingertips. One tap. Two. Three. The rhythm matched her racing thoughts. "If they're involved in this, there's got to be evidence somewhere."

"And you think you'll just waltz in and find it?" Naomi's voice carried a warning.

Marti leaned forward, the idea taking shape with each passing second. "I need to get inside Douglas Franklin's house."

Naomi's smirk vanished. "That is the worst idea you've ever had."

Marti tipped her head back against the chair, grinning. "You've only known me for a couple of days. Trust me, I've had much, much worse ideas."

The words sat between them, heavy as a loaded gun. The idea of getting caught sent a cold thread down Marti's spine, but that wasn't enough to stop her. Not when there were answers she needed. Not when there was something rotten at the core of it all.

And then it hit her. Sharp and electric. Marti raked a hand back through tangled hair that smelled of smoke from last night's mistakes and clenched her jaw so tight something might crack. Thunder rolled outside, matching her mood.

No Plan B for this one. Well, no clean Plan B anyway.

She looked up at Naomi, determination hardening her features despite the setback. "Looks like Franklin's house will need breaking into the old-fashioned way."

Rain spattered against the window, the first drops of what promised to be a downpour. Marti stared at Naomi's reflection in the glass. "I need you to find him. Where he lives, where he's going to be over the next couple of days. Everything. Can you do it?"

"Do the brothers live together?" Naomi asked, mental calculations already running.

"That's for you to find out," Marti said with a dismissive wave. "Soon as you can."

Naomi nodded and retreated to her desk. The weight of what she'd just agreed to settled between her shoulder blades like a knife. Four days. Just four fucking days working for Marti, and she was neck-deep in shit that could drown them both.

Chief Douglas Franklin's digital life spread across her monitor as her fingers hovered over the keyboard. Facebook. Instagram. A pathetic LinkedIn profile with that smug official department photo. The man splashed his existence across the internet like cheap graffiti on an abandoned building.

"Stupid," she muttered, clicking through vacation photos of Franklin holding up fish like trophies. "You're a goddamn cop. You should know better."

She'd spent three years learning to hide in plain sight while this idiot advertised his every move with gym selfies. The irony twisted her mouth into a bitter smile.

The city assessor's database confirmed what his pizza delivery check-ins suggested: Franklin owned a two-story at 1247 Maple Street since 2052. Belmont Heights neighborhood. Fancy. Expensive. The cached real estate listing even provided interior shots. Master bedroom upstairs, facing the street. Kitchen in back.

Her phone buzzed against the desk.

Kids are fine. Watching cartoons. You working late again?

The knot in Naomi's stomach loosened just enough to breathe.

Almost done. Thank you.

The old woman never asked why Naomi worked such strange hours, or why her accent didn't match the Japanese passport she'd flashed when they first met. Some people understood the value of selective blindness, like pretending not to notice when someone's husband never visited, never called.

Back to Franklin's digital trail. A group photo from two weeks ago at Murphy's Bar caught her eye. Franklin with arms slung around fellow officers, faces flushed with too many beers. She jotted down names and addresses. One officer lived two blocks from Franklin. Another checked into the same gym three times a week.

People were nothing but patterns if you knew how to look. Naomi's own pattern had shattered the night she'd grabbed the kids and run, leaving behind the debts and the men who collected them. Her fingertips tingled at the memory of packing in the dark, the children's sleepy questions, the rearview mirror checked every mile for headlights that might be following.

The image of a young girl flashed through her mind. Dark hair, gap-toothed smile, unicorn necklace catching neon lights. Marti had stood in the club that first night, holding that photo with hands that didn't quite steady.

"Fuck," she whispered, blinking hard to refocus on the screen and clear her memories.

Franklin's routine assembled itself piece by piece. Coffee shop check-ins at 7:15 each morning. City Hall selfies captioned with bullshit about "serving the community." Gym posts on Tuesdays and Thursdays, always with the same #NoExcuses hashtag like he deserved a medal for basic fitness.

The street view of his neighborhood revealed older homes with enough trees for cover, houses spaced just far enough apart that neighbors might miss someone slipping around back. Naomi traced his likely route to work on the map: Maple to Fifth, past that pretentious coffee place with the blue awning where he spent eight dollars on lattes three times a week.

The gym's website confirmed his schedule. Tuesday and Thursday nights, 7 PM kickboxing class. Two-hour window, empty house.

She compiled everything into a folder, maps, photos, schedules, and sent it to print. The pages emerged warm, dangerous in their completeness. As she collated them, she tallied what she'd need: four days of pay, access to company accounts, maybe another week before whatever Marti was chasing exploded in their faces.

When the feds came, and they would come, she'd need to vanish again. No forwarding address, no digital footprint. The printer hummed to silence as she stared at Franklin's photo, at that official smile that didn't reach his eyes. Whatever Marti was hunting in that house would be bad news for everyone involved, and Naomi had just built the road map that would take them there.

She rose from her desk, folder clutched against her chest like armor, and approached Marti's office. The door stood half-open. Through the gap, she could see Marti hunched at her desk, that mangy cat sprawled across her papers. Her boss's hand trembled as she raised an inhaler to her lips and drew deeply, her eyes fluttering closed for a moment.

Naomi knocked on the door frame. Marti's eyes snapped open, too bright, too dilated.

"I've got Franklin's information," Naomi said, keeping her voice steady despite the tightness in her chest. "Address, schedule, neighborhood layout." She stepped into the office. "He's like clockwork: coffee at 7:15, work by 8, gym on Tuesday and Thursday nights."

Marti straightened, pupils contracting as she focused. "That's perfect. You're good at this."

"Yeah, almost like I had a real office job when I was younger," Naomi said, then caught herself. Stupid. "I mean, I'm thorough."

"I can see that." Marti gestured for the folder. The tremor in her hand had vanished. "Anything else I should know?"

Naomi hesitated. She could warn her. About federal attention. About how investigations like this ended. About how Shadow users made mistakes.

Instead, she said, "Just be careful."

"I will." Marti's confidence seemed absolute as she flipped through the pages. "I know what I'm doing."

That's what they all said before the fall.

"Anything else tonight?" Naomi asked.

"Nah, go home to your kids. Thanks for this."

Naomi nodded and returned to her desk. She gathered her purse, fingers finding the hidden pocket where her passport waited. Not tonight, but soon. Maybe a week at most before this all went sideways.

She'd let Marti discover whatever Franklin was hiding. Then she'd do what she'd done: vanish when the spotlight got too bright, taking her children somewhere new, somewhere safe.

It wasn't betrayal. It was survival. And in this world, you couldn't have both loyalty and survival. She'd learned that lesson through blood and tears.

Her children were all that mattered now.

Chapter 36

Rain hammered the roof of the rented sedan, the sky's steady pulse against the quiet tension inside. Marti slouched in the driver's seat, one hand curled around the steering wheel, the other flicking Mike's knife open, shut, open again. The rhythm steadied something in her, or at least pretended to. She exhaled, watching water snake down the windshield, distorting the neat little neighborhood beyond. Picture-perfect homes, manicured lawns, picket-fence dreams.

Douglas Franklin's house sat among them like an old predator pretending to sleep: stone walls slick with rain, shutters tight against the world. Window boxes overflowed with bright flowers that should've softened things but didn't. They just looked like they were hiding something.

Marti had followed a photograph here: a singular photo hiding in plain sight in Colin Bonner's pristine home. Bonner, last man in contact with one of the missing. Bonner with reddish hair that could be blond in the right light. Gringo with a beard, smiling in that picture beside the Franklin brothers as if they were old friends. That alone made her stomach knot.

Her fingers drummed against the wheel. Open-close-click. The knife glinted in the low light before snapping shut again. Her hand fell absently to the Pro-Grip, a beautiful little lock picking system that would get her arrested for carrying it. How ironic.

Forty-eight hours tracking Franklin's movements between his office and home, his routine buttoned-up and predictable as Naomi had said. He wasn't a beat cop anymore; he clocked in at headquarters, shuffled paper, kept his hands clean while dirt pooled around his feet. She hoped Bonner had had his heart attack already.

Right on time, Franklin stepped out onto his porch. Umbrella up, suit crisp despite the rain, always polished, always careful. He slid into his car and pulled away without a glance back. One vehicle remained: a second car tucked in the driveway. His wife's.

Marti frowned and waited. An hour crawled by, rain drumming a patient rhythm until that car backed out of the driveway and disappeared down the street.

That was her cue. She drove around the corner and into the alley, killed the engine, and slipped into the downpour. Naomi's research had proved itself invaluable. The rain soaked through her hoodie as she kept close to fences and overgrown hedges until she reached his backyard gate. A quick pull-up-and-over landed her on wet grass, crouched low amid private greenery.

The yard was small but closed-off: high fencing on all sides, a patio set pushed under an awning to keep dry. In another corner, a vegetable garden thrived despite the drowning weather. Tomatoes clung to their vines like red warning lights flashing stop-stop-stop. Flower beds ran along the fence line, too neat for comfort, petals drooping under sheets of water.

And at the back of it all stood a shed: plain wood construction, locked up tight but humming with potential secrets beneath its unassuming frame. She'd spotted it yesterday while scoping the place. Something about it nagged at her.

Marti tilted her head, rolled her shoulders back against tension creeping up her spine. "Alright then. Let's see what you're hiding, Dougie."

She pulled on her gloves, working the leather tight over her fingers. No prints. No evidence. No mistakes. Latex was for amateurs, fragile, unreliable. This wasn't a Colin Bonner job. No message here.

The shed first. Maybe she'd find gold or bodies stacked like cordwood. Rain pattered against her hood as she crossed the yard, each step careful on the slick grass. The window was smudged with dust, the glass warping the daylight, but inside, nothing sinister. Just rust-speckled tools, a lawnmower, the faint scent of old gasoline seeping through the cracks. A letdown.

The house. That must be where the real rot would be hiding. Her gaze swept the exterior, tracing along weathered stone and shuttered windows. No cameras that she could see. Either Franklin was overconfident or he had something better in place.

Hunching deeper into her hoodie, she slinked along the fence line toward the back door. Tried the handle. Locked. Of course.

A cool breeze rustled nearby bushes, carrying the scent of someone's late breakfast from a neighboring house. Marti pulled the ProGrip FlexPick from her jacket pocket. The titanium device warmed against her palm, its weight reassuring. Three crisp well spent. Again.

"Don't fail me now," she whispered, powering it on. The micro-display flickered to life with a soft blue glow that illuminated the lines of her face.

The fiber-optic probe extended with a barely audible whisper. Thin as a pencil lead but flexible as a snake. Birds chirped as she slid it into the keyway, angling the tip upward toward the pin tumblers. The camera feed revealed the lock's guts: five pins, standard residential setup. Nothing fancy for the chief of police. Typical.

Her fingers found the tension controls, muscle memory taking over. The auto-tension kicked in, a subtle vibration against her skin as it applied just enough rotational pressure to the cylinder. Too much pressure and the pins would bind; too little and they'd drop back into place. She'd learned that lesson the hard way.

The first pin clicked home. The ProGrip pulsed against her palm. A quick, satisfied throb. Success. Sweat beaded along her hairline.

A dog barked somewhere in the distance, sharp and sudden. Marti froze, heart hammering against her ribs. She held her breath, listening as the sound faded, replaced by the hum of early morning traffic blocks away. Fifteen seconds wasted. She returned to the lock, jaw tight.

Third pin. Fourth. Each one accompanied by that subtle haptic feedback, like the device was whispering secrets only she could understand. On the display, shadows and light revealed exactly where to position the probe. What used to be an art was now closer to surgery. Clinical, precise.

The fifth pin resisted. Stubborn bastard. On the screen, she could see it catching slightly, refusing to settle into the shear line. Marti adjusted the probe angle, applying gentle pressure while memories of her last failed job flashed through her mind. Not this time. The pin shifted, found its place, and the ProGrip delivered its final pulse of satisfaction.

The cylinder turned with a soft click that sounded thunderous in the quiet night.

Marti retracted the probe and pocketed the device, her hand already reaching for the door handle. Forty-three seconds. Not her best time, but good enough to avoid detection. All that mattered was what was in that house.

Inside, she slipped off her boots, setting them beside the door. Boot prints were for amateurs. The sudden warmth of the house prickled against her rain-chilled skin as she let her socked feet slink along hardwood, each creak of the floorboards tightening around her ribs like wire.

The kitchen smelled of coffee and something citrusy-clean, too clean for a man like Franklin. His wife's touch, had to be. White cabinets, marble countertops, appliances that were functional, not fancy. A tidy little bistro table sat near the window, quaint if she ignored what lurked beneath this picture of normalcy. The lace curtains stirred in a whisper against some unseen draft, as if they knew something she didn't yet.

She moved through the living room next, softer here, quieter still. A well-worn couch with a crocheted throw draped over its back, armchairs angled for conversation no one wanted to have. Framed photos lined the walls: happy smiles frozen in time, a grinning family man playing pretend for whoever cared enough to look. A painting of some pastoral scene tried to lend warmth to a space that felt cold beneath its surface.

The fireplace stood against one wall: a sturdy brick facade. Above the mantel sat a wooden clock and stupid little knick-knacks that had been dusted by some dutiful housekeeper or an angry wife who still cared too much about aesthetics.

She crouched near the hearth, using the poker to sift through cold ashes on instinct alone, but nothing stood out except for how ordinary it all seemed.

That's how she knew there was something rotten here. Franklin wouldn't be this obvious about hiding his shit.

Upstairs then. The carpeted steps muffled her weight as she climbed, heart quickening with each step higher.

Three doors waited at the top of the hall like choices in some twisted game show: pick right or die trying.

The first opened into Franklin's bedroom, cozy enough to fool someone who didn't know better. Queen-sized bed buried under a patchwork quilt most definitely his wife's choice; dresser and bedside tables mismatched as if they'd been thrown together in an afterthought of domesticity; closet doors cracked just enough to hint at pressed shirts and shoes lined up with military precision.

The dresser gave her more of the same: socks, folded shirts, pressed slacks. She sifted through them anyway, disturbing their careful arrangement just enough to look, but not enough to leave a mark. Nothing hidden between cotton folds or tucked beneath pressed collars.

The closet doors slid open with a whisper. A burst of color: dresses, skirts, silk blouses hanging in neat rows. Franklin's wife? Or Franklin's? Marti smirked at the thought and pushed them aside, running her hands along the back paneling, searching for anything that didn't fit.

Nothing but cedar and stale perfume. She arranged the clothing back in place, disguising her intrusion.

Next, the bathroom. Cool air brushed her face as she pushed open the door. Clean lines and white tile greeted her as if they had nothing to hide. His and her sinks both tidy, just a few flecks of makeup on hers and a shaving kit on his.

And then the stain.

Dark against stark white porcelain tile. On his side.

Blood.

Her heart kicked up once before settling into something slow. She crouched closer, gloved fingers ghosting over dried edges. This wasn't today's shaving accident: the brown-black edges had settled into the grout, days old at least.

Snap. She took one photo, the flash illuminating the crimson-turned-rust. Stepped back. Took another from a different angle.

Evidence now, maybe. Not just suspicion, but something he had missed. If he missed this, what else had he overlooked?

The air felt heavier as she backed out of the bathroom. The house's silence pressed against her eardrums, each creak and settling noise amplified in her heightened awareness. She moved toward bedroom number two, the door hinges whispering as she pushed it open.

Not quite an office, not quite a guest room, either. Single bed tucked into one corner; desk set flush against another wall as if it had been placed without thought for comfort or convenience; books stacked on shelves alongside papers and office supplies.

This was his space, not theirs. A place he could let his guard down. She could feel it in the staleness of the air, the lingering scent of aftershave and paper.

Marti moved through the office with quiet determination, fingers skimming the edges of drawers before pulling them open. Bills, receipts, paperwork: mundane, meaningless. She flipped through folders, checked beneath staplers and file organizers. Nothing.

What the hell was she expecting to find under a fucking stapler? Marti shook her head. Only drugs would be there, and she didn't give a shit about that.

She turned to the smaller built-in closet beside the desk. Her fingers wrapped around the handle, cool metal against leather as she eased it open. The shift in scent hit first: polished leather, starch, faint traces of cologne gone sour with time. This was Franklin's space. The suits stood stiffly at attention, their owner absent but omnipresent.

Suits hung in perfect alignment, like soldiers waiting for orders; ties coiled over a rack; shoes lined up with military precision along the floorboards. Above them, shelves held a few hats and...

Her breath caught.

A shoebox sat on the highest shelf, pristine against the dustless wood. Her gloved fingers hesitated only for a second before pulling it down. The lid lifted without resistance.

Her stomach dropped.

A dozen ID cards spilled across the box's interior like discarded playing cards, each a photo frozen in time: young men staring back at her with eyes they no longer had use for. The air left her lungs in a slow exhale as ice bloomed along her spine.

Trophies. Serial killer's trophies

"Fuck me," she murmured, the words audible even to herself. "Fuuuuck me."

The IDs fanned out before her like an accusation. She'd taken orders from Franklin, believed in him when he'd stood in front of their precinct talking about justice and duty. Her mouth went dry. The badge he wore wasn't protection: it was camouflage.

Her hands trembled as she spread the cards out. One by one, she sifted through them:

Luis Baez: the grainy photo showed a teenager with a half-smile, uncertain in front of the camera.

Antonio Molina: dark eyes that had seen too much before they closed forever.

Carlos Hernandez: jaw set in defiance even in his ID photo.

She pulled out her phone and snapped photos fast and steady, checking each shot before moving on to the next card in line: Albert Alvarez... César López.

Her fingers clenched around that last one as recognition hit like a sucker punch to the ribs. Nat was going to fucking die.

She swallowed hard, throat tight against something that wasn't quite a sob. Her fingers moved, continuing to document each face, each name. Faces she knew, faces she didn't. Seventeen goddamned ID cards. Evidence of men Franklin had...what? Arrested? Fucked? Killed?

Not enough. The weight of it pressed against her chest, making each breath shallow.

When every card had been photographed, she arranged them as she'd found them: the box on the shelf, IDs nestled inside as if they hadn't just shifted something irreparable inside her. The closet door closed with a soft click that echoed in her ears like a gunshot.

The house felt different now, charged with an absence so thick it seemed to cling to her skin. She moved through it, each floorboard's creak a warning, each shadow a potential witness. The staircase felt steeper going down. Rain still drummed against the windows, a soundtrack to her retreat.

Chapter 37

Marti stood frozen at the kitchen sink, her reflection a pale smear in the window. Just three steps to the back door.

Freedom. Safety. Sanity.

But that nagging certainty had followed her down the stairs, materializing now as the basement door that crouched in the corner of her vision, patient as a predator. Each passing second, she felt it more acutely: a cold, insistent tug at the base of her skull.

"Fuck." The word escaped through gritted teeth, barely a whisper. She hoped for a gym, a home theater, a wine room. Something that said this was not possible.

But the names materialized unbidden in her mind, a grim roll call of monsters who'd once seemed ordinary to their neighbors: Holmes. Deeming. Gacy. The Wests.

Corll. Penzel. Killers who'd built tombs in their houses. Killers who'd turned basements and garages into dumping grounds.

Her stomach clenched as she crossed the kitchen. Her fingers hovered over the knob, trembling. The brass felt cold against her skin. One slow turn and the latch released with a soft click that seemed to reverberate through the empty house: a sound like bones settling.

The hinges whispered as the door swung inward, revealing nothing but darkness. Marti switched on her phone's flashlight, its harsh beam cutting a stark path down wooden steps that disappeared into black air thick enough to touch. The smell hit her then: damp earth and something else underneath, something her brain recognized before she could name it.

No wine cellar down here.

She descended, each step groaning under her weight. The air thickened with each step, damp and sour, seeping into her skin like rot sinking into wood.

At the bottom, she halted. The floor wasn't concrete. No tile, no foundation. Just earth, raw and unsettled. She shifted her foot, and the dirt gave beneath her heel as though something beneath had stirred.

She swept her light forward. Shadows swallowed the weak beam until it landed on shallow depressions pockmarking the ground. Graves. Hasty, uneven. Not dug with care. Clawed open just enough to take a body and keep it.

Her throat constricted. She stepped closer, skirting the edges of the disturbed soil. Then she saw it: a shape jutting from the dirt ahead, barely breaking the surface.

Fingers. Four, and part of a thumb, curled stiff as if grasping for something just out of reach. Bloated flesh peeled in places, nails lifting from soft beds, everything tinged with a sickly gray-green that spoke of time and neglect. The hand looked desperate even in death.

"Jesus fuck." The words caught in her throat, barely making it past her lips.

She aimed her phone with steady hands and started snapping pictures, unsure if the CamLobes would work in dim light. The flash detonated in the dark, throwing light in sharp bursts that revealed more with each explosion of brightness: layers of shadow shifting back to expose what they'd concealed.

It cast jittery shadows across raw earth. No furniture. No signs of life. Just shallow graves, the dirt uneven where bodies had settled. The air pressed against her ribs like it wanted to keep her down there with them.

The graves stretched in every direction. Sunken pits, some with edges still raw from recent digging, others smoothed over by time. Her pulse pounded in her ears as she counted the mounds. One for each of the ID cards. How many? She hadn't taken the time to count. How long had Franklin been feeding this place? Another thought sliced through her: How long before the next one?

Her legs tensed, ready to bolt up the stairs and hit dial before Franklin came home and turned her into another buried secret. Instead, she forced herself still, phone shaking in her grip as she captured photo after photo. Details. Evidence. Proof.

When she turned toward the stairs, she risked one last glance back. The hand in the dirt remained outstretched, reaching. Not for salvation anymore, but for someone to remember it was there at all.

A final snap of the camera, then Marti turned. Time to go.

She moved backward, slow and deliberate, eyes locked on the ground as she brushed away her own footprints. Each motion precise. Ritualistic. At the base of the stairs, she peeled off one sock, then the other, silent, methodical, and stuffed them in her pocket before climbing.

Step by step, her ribs tightened around her lungs. Even after years as a homicide detective, after bodies sprawled in gutters and hooked on river rocks, this was different. This was buried. Hidden under layers of dirt and lies.

Chief Franklin.

Her teeth clenched at his name. She'd trusted him once, looked up to him as a fresh-faced rookie buying into the myth that good cops stayed good. Now the badge she'd once respected gleamed like a warning sign: a predator's lure.

She hit the top step and stopped, bracing against the wall as her stomach rolled. A deep breath, then another. The bile stayed down, but just barely.

"Get it together, Starova." She straightened up, pushing past it. Proof would matter now. Hard evidence that could hold up in court.

Then—Bam! Bam!

A knock. Loud enough to shake through her bones.

Her heart slammed against her ribs before she dropped fast, pressing flat against the kitchen cabinets.

BAM! BAM! BAM!

Another knock came harder this time.

Fuck.

Her pulse pounded in her ears as she scanned for an exit. She moved low, crawling across the kitchen floor with slow precision, keeping her body close to the ground. Her breath stayed shallow, a controlled whisper against the silence, as she edged toward the back door.

Rain tapped soft against glass and wood like a second heartbeat. She hesitated at the doorframe, listening, waiting, but no voices followed from the front of the house.

She snatched up her boots but didn't put them on; bare feet left less to notice. One glance over her shoulder, then she twisted the knob and slipped out into cold air and darkened skies before easing the door shut behind her without a sound.

Outside, rain hit harder: sharp drops stinging against bare skin. Marti crouched low in the yard, scanning for movement between flashes of lightning. Her hands shook with fury curling deep in her gut.

How could he do something so fucking evil?

The wet grass sucked at her soles, cold and slick, but she kept moving, swallowing the urge to shiver. One last look at the house. Then she ran.

The fence loomed ahead. She launched herself over it, landing hard in the alley beyond. Asphalt scraped against raw skin, but she didn't stop. Couldn't.

Rain had soaked the ground, turned every step into a splash, every movement too loud in the hush of the backstreets. Her car was close. Too far. Close enough.

Keys slipped through damp fingers, rattled against metal before catching in the lock. She yanked the door open, threw herself inside, and slammed it shut behind her.

For a moment, nothing but the pounding in her chest filled the car. She wrestled her boots on with stiff fingers. The engine roared to life, tires shrieking as she tore out of the alley and into the street.

Falls City blurred past in streaks of neon and rain-slick reflections. Her grip was iron on the wheel, knuckles white. She drove faster, needing space between herself and that basement, between herself and that hand crawling out of dirt like the kid had one last prayer left in him.

The image flashed behind her eyes: those fingers, reaching. She swerved, corrected, focused on the road instead of ghosts clawing at her memory.

It took almost no time to drive through Belmont Heights to Ironwood. Turned out, both neighborhoods were rotten to the fucking core. She pulled into Sally's Super Sales, the flickering neon sign cast sickly light onto wet pavement. She sat for a moment, hands still gripping the wheel. Those fingers in the dirt kept reaching for her. She closed her eyes, opened them. They were still there.

Inside the rental office, fluorescent lights buzzed like insects trapped in glass. The clerk pushed a payment terminal toward her without looking up from his phone. Marti's pen hovered over the signature line, her hand steady. The steadiness felt wrong, obscene. How could anything be steady after what she'd seen?

She scrawled her name and pushed the terminal back, then walked out without waiting for a receipt. The rain had softened to a drizzle that seemed to suspend time between each drop.

Back in her own car, she sat with both hands on the wheel, not moving. The leather felt different under her palms: familiar in a way that hurt. When she turned the key, the engine's rumble seemed to shake something loose inside her chest.

The streets passed in a blur, buildings bleeding into one another like watercolors left in the rain. By the time she pulled up outside her office building, exhaustion had settled into her bones like an old friend.

She climbed the stairs slowly, water tracking behind her in small, betraying puddles. When she pushed open the door, Naomi looked up from the couch, a smile forming that faded.

"You look like hell," Naomi said, the lightness in her voice not quite reaching kindness.

Marti dropped into the chair opposite and reached for her cigarettes. Her hands still steady, still wrong. She lit up, took a drag, exhaled slowly.

Naomi studied her face. "Rough gig?"

Marti didn't answer. She just pulled out her whiskey and drank straight from the bottle. The burn wasn't enough, not for what she'd seen. Her fingers found the small pill bottle in her jacket pocket, shook out two Fentafill tablets. Not Shadow. That was still off limits. But these... these were different. Medical. For pain.

Yeah, that worked.

She dry-swallowed them, chased them down with another pull of whiskey. The combination hit her bloodstream like warm honey mixed with broken glass. Everything slowed just enough.

The silence stretched between them, filled with smoke and unasked questions. Naomi waited, watching as Marti stared past her at nothing, trying to blink away the image of bloated fingers reaching for the light.

"Naomi." Her voice came out raw, scraped over gravel. "I found something."

Naomi's posture shifted, subtle but immediate. "Where?"

Marti slid a phone from her pocket, thumbed through a few screens, then handed it over. "Franklin's basement." A beat. "Pictures. I'll transfer them to you. Put them in the case file under the missing men."

Naomi took the phone, but didn't look right away. "You want me to see this?"

"Only if you can handle it." Marti's voice was flat, but her eyes said more.

Naomi clicked open the images. Her breath caught, the color draining from her face as she scrolled.

"Jesus," she whispered. "Is that a hand?"

"Yeah." Marti watched Naomi's face contort. "And those are shallow graves."

Naomi shook her head, handing the phone back with fingers that trembled. She retreated to her desk, but the photos followed her there, gaping and rotten in the glow of her monitor.

"This is fucked," Naomi said, her voice barely audible over the hum of electronics.

Marti took another drag, let the smoke curl between them. The pills were kicking in now, wrapping the edges of everything in soft gauze. Not Shadow's electric buzz, but close enough. "And it'll never see trial."

Naomi's head snapped up. "What do you mean?"

"Franklin is chief of police," Marti said, stretching out like exhaustion lived in her bones now. "His brother runs Internal Affairs." She met Naomi's stare. "No Falls City cop is touching this."

Naomi rubbed at her temples. "So what do you do?"

Marti crushed what was left of her cigarette into the ashtray and moved to Naomi's desk. She leaned forward, elbows on her knees, eyes steady despite everything screaming inside her head.

"The first thing we do," she said, "is meet with the mothers."

Naomi flinched. Not much, but enough.

"I'll call them," she said, voice tight. "But I can't go with you when you tell them." A pause. "It's too fucked up."

Marti nodded once. No judgment, just understanding wrapped in exhaustion.

"Tell them to meet me at Diego's Dive at five-thirty," she said quietly. "Say I've got an update, but don't tell them what kind."

Naomi swallowed hard and looked down at her screen. "What if they ask?"

"Say you don't know. You're new. I didn't tell you." Marti watched the weight of it settle on Naomi's shoulders. "Lie."

A slow inhale from Naomi. Then an even slower exhale as she nodded. "Lie," she repeated, testing the word. "Okay."

Marti stood without another word and made for her office, shutting the door behind her. The couch welcomed her like an old confession booth. She sank into it, bones heavy with what she'd seen.

Warm sand spilled from her pocket as she pulled out balled-up socks. She let the dirt sift onto the floor like evidence of where she'd been.

"When you get a chance," she called through the doorway, "vacuum my office."

A muffled reply from Naomi filtered through, but Marti wasn't listening anymore. Her fingers found the Shadow inhaler in her other pocket, smooth and familiar as a lover's skin. She gripped it tight enough to leave marks, then shoved it back down. "Fuck you," she whispered to it. "I need something that actually works."

Because tonight was coming fast.

And shit was about to get worse before it got better.

The phone in her pocket pressed against her ribs: evidence that would shatter more than just Franklin's reputation. Evidence she'd have to show those mothers. Their sons' IDs, one after the other, in a place they should never have been.

Chapter 38

Three hours crawled by.

Diego's Dive reeked of stale beer and the sorrow of women who knew in their bones. The Fentafill high had faded to a dull throb behind Marti's eyes as she hunched over a scarred table, watching smoke curl from the cigarette between her fingers. Outside, neon flickered against boarded-up windows, casting sickly colors across the warped wood floor.

A shot of whiskey waited in front of her, untouched. She needed clarity tonight. The manila envelope lay beside it like a silent accusation.

Marti felt Angel before she saw her, that heat lingering at the edges of her awareness. No need to look up.

"Hey, Marti."

She reached for her lighter instead of answering. Flame flared, orange and hungry.

Angel slid in close. "Not now," Marti muttered, exhaling smoke through her teeth.

"How about in five minutes?" Angel's finger traced the curve of Marti's ear, leaving goosebumps in its wake.

Marti drummed her fingers against the table, slow and deliberate. Her shoulders stiffened, a wall going up brick by brick. "I'm here on business." A pause. "No time for pussy pleasures."

Angel didn't flinch. She leaned closer, her lips brushing Marti's ear as she whispered something low and dangerous. Her fingers wandered, trailing heat up Marti's thigh until resistance thinned into something else.

For half a second, Marti let herself feel it: that pulse of want coiled tight in her chest. Then her gaze caught on the envelope again. She grabbed Angel's wrist, firm but not rough. "No, just fuck off," she said, voice flat as dead air on a wiretap line.

Angel held her gaze a beat before pulling back with a smirk that said this wasn't over. Then she slipped behind the swinging kitchen door with the ease of someone who knew every dark corner of this place by heart.

But it was over.

It was over then, and it was over now.

Marti tossed back the whiskey, letting it burn its way down to something rawer.

The door groaned open. They arrived within minutes of each other but walked in one by one, a procession of worry and exhaustion wrapped in coats too thin for the cold outside. Adriana Hernandez first, shoulders squared as if she was bracing for impact. Ana Córdova next, eyes red-rimmed and distant. Susanna Alvarez followed, stifling a sob when she saw the others. Not loud enough to turn heads, but enough to bleed into the air between them.

Carmen Molina and Nat López entered last, swallowed in a black coat that made her look like ghosts slipping through the doorframe. They settled into cracked vinyl seats around Marti as if gravity had pulled them there against their will.

The bar buzzed around them: muted conversation, clinking glassware, someone sniffing deep before taking another hit off something illegal. But inside their little island, everything went quiet except for the weight pressing down on Marti's chest.

Their eyes found hers, wide and glassy with unspoken fears, and she had nothing to give them but silence and truth sharpened to a knife-edge.

Marti's fingers traced the edge of the manila envelope. "I won't waste your time," she said. "I found bad news."

Nat's jaw tightened. The other women barely breathed.

Marti flipped the envelope open and pulled out the printed photos. ID cards, faces staring back like ghosts caught on plastic. She placed them on the table one by one, carefully, deliberately.

Silence thickened. Then Nat slammed a palm against the table hard enough to rattle the drinks. "I know that face," she said through gritted teeth, finger jabbing toward Marti. "Goddamn you, Starova, I know that face." Her breath hitched. "They're dead, aren't they?"

Marti held her gaze and nodded once.

Nat sucked in a sharp breath, pressing a fist against her mouth. Adriana straightened, eyes blazing. "Kept them like trophies? Sick bastard." She turned to Marti. "And you're surprised it's connected to authority? This is exactly what I've been saying. The whole system's corrupt."

Susanna sat with her spine straight, fingers curled into fists so tight they shook. "No," she whispered, then louder, "No, this can't be right. What about the blue car? Did you check the blue car connection? There has to be more evidence."

Ana slammed her fists against the table. Once, twice. "Enough crying," she said harshly. "We knew this was coming. Question is—where are the bodies and what's the plan?"

Carmen stared at her hands, guilt clouding her eyes. She had her son's body. All they had were photographs of plastic IDs with smiling faces. "At least I can still hold Antonio," she whispered. "I can still pray over him."

Marti inhaled the scent of sweat and spilled whiskey, letting it out slowly. "I wish I had something else to tell you, but every lead points to one thing: your sons were murdered."

The words landed like steel on bone. Falls City didn't leave room for redemption. It took and took until there was nothing left but ghosts and regrets carved into brick walls no one bothered to look at twice.

Marti tapped a finger against one of the photos. "These ID cards were boxed up in a house I've been investigating. Not dumped, not destroyed. Kept."

Nat's hands trembled as she traced her son's smiling face. "Kept?" The word barely rose above the noise of the bar.

Marti watched them holding those small scraps of paper as if they could bring their boys back. As if love alone could undo Falls City's rot.

She wished it could, too.

But wishing never got anyone shit in this city but dead.

"A way for the killer to remember." The cigarette burned between her fingers, smoke mingling with the cheap whiskey that kept appearing in her glass. "It means the man who's doing this has been hunting young men in Falls City for years." She tossed the last stack of photographs onto the table. Proof. Cold, undeniable.

Strangers to the women. Victims to the killer.

Susanna turned away, arms locked tight across her chest, then spun back. "Where exactly are they buried? How many feet down? What kind of soil conditions? We need specifics—"

The first sob cracked the silence, small and brittle, then shattered into something raw.

"I know this is hard," Marti murmured, her hand finding Nat's shoulder.

The bar swallowed their grief, soaked it into every scarred surface. Ana gripped the table edge, knuckles white. "Cut the details, Susanna. Where's my kid and who do we make pay?"

Marti exhaled smoke before answering. "I think some of them are buried in a basement. Maybe all of them." She hesitated. "I saw hollows in the dirt down there. And I saw part of a hand sticking out of the ground."

Carmen reeled back as if struck, crossing herself. "Dear God... how many mothers has he hurt? How many families?" Quiet mourning filled the space around her words.

"I'm sorry," Marti said, voice rough. She pressed her palms flat on the table. "With luck, maybe the cops or the Feds will do something soon."

Her fingers twisted together beneath the table where no one could see them shake. An arrest wasn't coming, not really, and hope felt about as real as God right now.

The women barely registered her words; they weren't what they needed. Nothing would be enough now. Their boys were gone, and nothing Marti said could fill that absence.

Nat's fingers drummed against the table before she pushed up from her chair, the legs scraping against the floorboards. "Where are they? What the fuck happened?"

Questions flew at Marti like bullets.

"Where exactly in the basement?" Susanna demanded. "We need documentation. Evidence. A paper trail. How do we prove this?"

"Was it the Robber Riders?" Adriana asked, though her tone suggested she already knew better.

"Did they... did they hurt him before...?" Carmen's voice barely rose above a whisper.

Ana cut through them all: "Cut the questions. Where's my boy and what's our move?"

Marti tensed, inhaled slowly. "No," she said, shaking her head. "Not a gang." She leaned forward, voice lowering.

"But I believe one man, or maybe more than one, is responsible for all of this." She paused. "I found all your sons' IDs together. He kept them."

The silence stretched razor-thin as Marti finished: "There were seventeen in total."

All young men. All dead.

"The police must be notified!" Carmen's voice cut through the murmur, her knuckles white. "They have to do something."

Marti ran a hand through her hair. "Quiet," she said, voice steady. "There's more."

She let the silence build. "The house where I found those IDs? It's owned by Police Chief Douglas Franklin."

The room went still. Then chaos erupted: gasps, curses, choked sobs.

"Of course it's a cop," Ana said flatly. "System's rigged top to bottom. Question is, what do we do about it?"

"We need proper procedures," Susanna said, voice shaking. "Chain of evidence. Documentation. But how do we—"

"Procedures didn't help my son when they were chasing him for stealing milk," Adriana cut in. "See? This is what I've been telling you people. Who investigates when it's the police?"

Marti met each woman's gaze. "That's up to you. You hired me. Do we go to federal agents? Try local? State?"

Ana spoke before anyone else could. "Not local cops. Cops protect cops. That's the bottom line."

Heavy silence settled between them. Marti leaned forward. "If we go to Falls City PD now, Franklin gets a heads-up. He'll move evidence, bodies, everything, before they even pretend to look."

They all knew how it worked. Or didn't.

"I can't lose my son again," Nat whispered, face buried in her hands, voice cracking.

Marti sat back, running her tongue along her teeth. "I know a fed who might take this on. She's a straight arrow." She paused. "Heather Blair. Works with the Federal Unified Crime Taskforce."

Ana narrowed her eyes. "And you trust her?"

"As much as I trust anyone with a badge," Marti admitted. "If anyone will go after Franklin, it's Heather." Even that felt like a promise she couldn't keep.

"Federal agents?" Adriana shook her head. "Right. Like they don't protect their own too. But what choice do we have?"

Susanna rubbed at her temples. "Talk to her," she said, exhaustion and resolve mixing in her voice. "See if she'll take it. But we need guarantees. Procedures. Some kind of oversight."

Marti nodded and pushed up from her chair, grabbing her jacket. The women folded into each other as she headed for the door, their quiet mourning filling the space she left behind.

Rain had started falling when she stepped outside, the pavement slick and shining under streetlights. She was halfway to her car when footsteps approached from behind. A light touch at her shoulder.

Nat stood there, face blotchy from crying, rain slicking curls against her cheeks. "Wait," she said quietly.

Marti turned, waiting.

"Thank you." The words came raw but sure.

Marti dipped her chin, saying nothing.

Nat swallowed hard before speaking again. "I need to see where he is." Her voice trembled but held.

Marti chewed on that request, weighing the risk against the need in Nat's eyes.

"I just... I need to sit there," Nat pressed, fingers twisting together.

Every survival instinct screamed against it, but Marti nodded once. "Tomorrow night. We won't approach; just sit near the house."

Nat blinked fast against fresh tears and nodded.

She turned and disappeared into the rain like a ghost surfacing just long enough for one last look at life before fading again.

Marti watched the empty space where Nat had stood, then climbed into her car and drove off into a darkness that could make anything disappear.

Even grief if you let it linger long enough.

Chapter 39

Rain slid in tired streaks down the window, just like it had last night when Nat disappeared into it.

Marti sat at her desk, one hand absently running through Bertha's fur, the other curled around an unlit cigarette. She hadn't been able to steady her hands enough to light one since watching that mother's face crumple. The office smelled like stale coffee and last night's pain.

She should've felt relief. The mothers of the lost boys finally knew the truth. But all it left her with was a raw, aching emptiness, like she'd ripped out a tumor only to find rot underneath.

The main door creaked open. Low voices filtered through: Naomi's sharp and unimpressed, the other clipped, professional. Cop energy changed the air in a room. Marti exhaled, flicked on the dissonance enhancer with a lazy tap. The green light glowed steadily. Whatever came next, nobody outside this room was going to hear it.

"Marti," Naomi called from the doorway, bored but amused. "Your favorite cop's here."

"Send her in." Marti pushed Bertha off her lap, the cat landing with an indignant thump.

Heather Blair stepped inside, red hair vivid against the gray light leaking through the blinds. Usually, her green eyes were all focus and fire. Today they held something else. Something wary and considering, like she'd already calculated half the consequences of whatever this conversation might bring.

"Starova." Heather shut the door behind her with a soft click. "You rang? Demanded my attendance?"

Marti nodded toward the chair across from her desk. "Yeah. Have a seat."

Heather studied Marti a moment, waiting for a punchline that never came, then sank into the chair slowly, testing its stability before committing her full weight.

"I need you to be straight with me," Marti said, voice even but edged in steel. "Did you put a tracker on my car?"

Heather blinked once. "No." Her tone was firm, a practiced cop response, but something sharp flickered across her face. "Why? You find one?"

Marti reached into her desk drawer and pulled it out: a small GPS chip with an ugly little sticker slapped onto its casing: Federal United Crime Taskforce. She turned it between two fingers before tossing it onto the desk like a bad poker hand.

Heather leaned forward, gaze narrowing as she took in the device's details. "That's not mine."

"But it's from your unit." Marti watched Heather's reaction more than the tracker itself.

Heather exhaled sharply and dragged a hand through her hair before sitting back, arms crossed tight over her chest. "I swear to you. I didn't put that there." A muscle jumped in her jaw. "And I didn't know someone else had."

Marti let silence fill the space between them for a beat before setting the tracker aside with two fingers, like it might burn her. "FUCT is following me," she said plainly, then tilted her head. "And maybe they're following you too."

Heather scoffed, not dismissive exactly, but halfway there, and shook her head. "Why? What would they get out of tracking either of us?"

Marti shrugged before leaning forward onto her elbows. "Don't know. Don't care."

Heather stared back, shifting slightly in her seat, just enough to signal that maybe the question wasn't as absurd as it should have been.

Marti tapped two fingers against the edge of the dissonance enhancer. "This conversation can't leave this room. Noise jammer."

Heather quirked an eyebrow. "A noise jammer?"

"Scrambles any bugs or microphones nearby." Marti nodded toward the glowing device. "FUCT has this place wired six ways to Sunday. I'm not taking chances."

Something unreadable crossed Heather's face, but whatever thought had been forming there vanished when Marti reached into another drawer and pulled out a worn folder. It landed on the desk with an unceremonious slap.

"Here."

Heather hesitated before reaching for it, flipping open its cover with cautious fingers.

The first photos made her nostrils flare: ID cards arranged like gravestones. The second made something in her expression harden: a group shot featuring Falls City Police Chief Douglas Franklin standing exactly where he shouldn't have been. The last one, the dead hand half-buried beneath damp basement dirt, made every muscle in Heather's body go wire-tight.

For a long moment, neither of them spoke.

"What the fuck," Heather muttered, the words escaping like they'd been trapped behind her teeth.

Marti crushed out her cigarette with pressure against the overflowing ashtray. Across from her, Heather held the photos like they might detonate, shadows carved deep beneath her eyes.

"This is Falls City Police Chief Douglas Franklin's place," Marti said. "ID cards. A body. Proof."

"Of?"

"Multiple murders over years."

Heather's fingers twitched against the paper. "And let me guess; you got these while committing a crime."

A lazy, sharp smirk spread across Marti's face. "Trespassing, technically." She leaned back, stretching like a cat with all the time in the world.

"It's inadmissible," Heather snapped, grip tightening on the photos. "Fruit of the poisoned tree."

Marti rolled a shoulder. "Shouldn't apply because I'm a private citizen, but you know they'll make it stick if they can." Smoke curled up between them before fading into nothing. "I don't want to give them a chance at all to fight." She fixed Heather with a pointed look. "That's where you come in."

Heather ran a hand through her hair, steadying its tremor before dropping it back to the table. "You want me to build a case from scratch."

Marti grinned around her cigarette, all teeth and trouble.

"You hate me, don't you?" The question escaped Heather in a breath that might've been a laugh under different circumstances.

That pulled Marti up short. She blinked once before laughing, low and amused. "What?"

Heather met her eyes, voice flat as glass: "This could cost me my job."

Marti flicked ash without looking away. "This could cost you your life, if you take it."

The words hung between them, heavy and undeniable, before Heather shook her head and leaned in. The scent of whiskey heat brushed across the space between them. "Jesus, Marti: what's your endgame? You're always after something. Info, sex, burning everything down just to watch the flames." Her lips pressed thin. "What is it this time?"

Marti let the silence stretch, let it settle deep behind her ribs before answering.

"I gave you Andreas Katsaros's killer," she said, voice honed to something knife-sharp. "All tied up with a bow on top." She tapped ash with two fingers, smirking just enough to make Heather shift in her seat. "I don't always take. Sometimes I give."

"You gave me Cliff?"

Marti nodded. Heather studied her too long before shaking her head with that little half-laugh that wasn't one at all. "You're something else."

Marti tilted her head, considering that before offering a noncommittal shrug.

"You act tough," Heather murmured, her voice rougher now. "But deep down?" A dry chuckle escaped her throat. "You care about Falls City."

That got a snort from Marti: smoke and disbelief and something close to bitterness.

"The fuck kind of Hallmark bullshit is that?" She stubbed out her cigarette hard enough that burned tobacco scattered across glass. "What? You think tossing one fucked-up serial killer behind bars makes me some kinda hero? I don't want anybody to know about this. Not my involvement."

Silence stretched between them, heavier than empty, weighted with things neither of them wanted to name.

"Okay," Heather said, softer now as she gathered up the folder like armor.

Marti watched her straighten, expression blank.

"This is dangerous," Marti muttered. "It will cost you. Friends, colleagues."

Heather narrowed her gaze before shaking her head, slower but somehow firmer.

"FUCT isn't covering for Franklin," she said.

Marti arched an eyebrow but didn't fill the silence this time. She let it stretch thin until Heather shifted under its weight.

"Look," Marti continued, "just... keep your eyes open and your head down." Her voice dipped low, not quite affectionate but not detached either. "I don't wanna see you get hurt."

"Hurt again," Heather corrected with a ghost of a smile.

Marti exhaled, like pushing out more than just air.

"Take care," she said instead: clipped words wrapped in more than they said outright.

Heather stood, like maybe this should've ended differently. She leaned down and pressed her lips against Marti's mouth, brief but firm, like punctuation at the end of some unfinished sentence.

Then she pulled back without examining whatever flickered across Marti's face.

"You too," she murmured, turning toward the door and walking out without looking back.

Chapter 40

Marti shifted in her chair, reaching toward where Heather had been before catching herself and redirecting the motion to grab another cigarette instead.

The door swung inward moments later. Naomi stepped through casual as anything, leaning against the frame with an eyebrow raised.

"So?" she asked, amusement curling at the corners of her mouth. "What's the verdict?"

"Heather's on it." Marti exhaled smoke, watching it spiral toward the ceiling.

Naomi lounged against the doorframe, arms crossed. "As long as I'm not involved. I got kids." Relief crept into her voice.

Marti glanced at the clock: past 5 p.m. "Go home, Naomi."

Naomi hesitated before stepping out. "Be careful, Marti," she murmured, the door clicking shut behind her.

Alone again, Marti stared at the empty chair where Heather had sat. The silence pressed in until she couldn't stand it anymore. She reached for the inhaler, thumb running over the cool metal before she took threw it into the corner.

Nothing would help her forget the faces that formed in the darkness: the lost boys, their mothers, Nat's desperate eyes. Franklin's smug smile twisted into something monstrous in the corner of her vision.

She gasped, stumbling to the window and shoving it open. The city air was thick with pollution and regret, but she gulped it in like salvation, letting the cold rain spatter against her face until the hallucinations receded.

Her thoughts cleared, sharp as broken glass. She dropped back into her chair, lit a cigarette, let the ember burn low as she smoked through the comedown, watching the minutes drag until they hit 8:00 p.m.

Time to get Nat.

Neon shimmered as she cut through Falls City's maze of streets, sharper as daylight fought a losing battle. She kept one hand steady on the wheel; the other drummed against her thigh, nerves crawling beneath her skin. This wasn't just another job. It never had been. But tonight felt heavier somehow, like the night itself carried extra weight.

Nat's apartment complex loomed ahead. Marti pulled up and grabbed her phone. One ring, two. Then movement through the growing darkness. Nat emerged from the building like a fragment of some old ghost story, coat clutched tight against the night's encroachment.

She slid into the passenger seat, turning eyes on Marti that held gratitude deep enough to drown in. "Thank you," she breathed. "I can't tell you what this means."

Marti kept her gaze forward, jaw tight. "We don't know for sure if César is there." The words hung between them like fog. "Not yet."

Nat shook her head, lips tugging into something too sad to be a smile. "I know he is. A mother knows." Her voice wavered but held firm. "I have to see that house. I have to pray."

The rest of the drive passed in silence save for radio static: a metronome counting down to something neither of them wanted to face. When they reached Franklin's home, Marti killed the engine and nodded toward the dark structure.

"That's it," she said softly. "That's where I think your son is buried."

Nat crossed herself, lips moving without sound as she whispered something holy into the space between worlds. Marti let her have the moment but kept her eyes moving, scanning dark streets and quiet doorways for trouble.

Then, movement down the block.

A car parked too neatly in the shadows.

Heather.

Cold dread pooled in Marti's gut.

"Stay here," she muttered to Nat before stepping out into the night.

The tension clung to her like smoke as she approached Heather's car, shadows warping across her face under the flicker of a dying streetlamp. She rapped twice on the window. Heather glanced up, hesitated, then unlocked the door. Marti slid inside, the scent of asphalt and sweat trailing in behind her.

"Starova, Starova, Starova." Heather's voice carried a weariness that hadn't been there hours ago. "What are you doing here? You gave me the case."

"You took up my case fast." Marti lit up a cigarette, smoke rising like a curtain between them.

Heather didn't smile, but something heavy lurked behind her eyes. "Higher-ups weren't happy about it." She lowered her voice. "I told them I needed to clear Franklin... in case my source went public."

The wrongness of it all gnawed at Marti's insides.

"You think he knows?" she asked with a head nod toward the house.

Heather shook her head once, firm but with uncertainty underneath. "Not from me. And FUCT? They don't rat. We've taken down bigger."

Marti snorted and pushed open the door without another word.

Back in the cool night, she crouched near Heather's car, pain shooting through her leg and hip as she ran her fingers along its underside. Wheel rim after wheel rim until she found exactly what she expected: a tracking device small enough to miss if you weren't looking for it.

She ripped it free and climbed back inside. Held up between them, the small device blinked accusations in the dim light.

Heather exhaled sharply. "Shit."

Marti smirked and tossed it onto Heather's lap. "Yeah. Shit."

Heather's stomach twisted as she turned the tracker over, the FUCT logo gleaming mockingly. "They're tracking me. Their own agent." Her voice tightened with disbelief. "And they were dumb enough to stamp their name on it?"

Marti plucked it from her hand, slipping it into her pocket. "Just like mine." Her voice dropped low, conspiratorial. "Maybe it's a con, someone different tracking us both. But if you're still planning to sniff around Franklin, you need to watch your back. Someone's eyes are on you."

"Maybe they're tracking me after the shooting. Want to keep me safe?"

"Trackers don't stop bullets. But they might help find the body." The words hung between them, heavy with implication. Marti took it gently from Heather's hand.

Heather exhaled. "I don't even know if this qualifies as an investigation anymore." She dragged a hand through her hair, frustration etched in every line of her face. "Right now, I'm just watching the house. But what if Franklin brings someone home while I'm here? What if he kills another man while I look away?" Her throat tightened visibly. "I have to track him, at least as much as I can without getting myself killed."

Marti studied her, then gave a slow nod. Something unspoken settled between them, and for the first time in days, Marti felt like she could breathe.

Heather met her gaze, those green eyes burning sharp even in the dim light. Marti smirked because of course Heather looked beautiful even now, wound tight with tension but somehow radiant.

She leaned in and kissed her.

For one perfect second, Heather didn't pull away. Then she did, breath unsteady, eyes flicking past Marti's shoulder toward something outside.

"Who is that?" Heather's voice sharpened, and the intimate moment shattered like glass.

Chapter 41

Marti stared through the grime-streaked windshield, the ghost of that something-kiss still burning on her lips. Dim lighting visibility to a murky blur, but there was no mistaking Nat.

"Shit," Marti muttered when Heather's hand shot out, pointing hard.

Nat Lopez slipped beneath the streetlight, hunched and quick, like a mouse darting up the cat's back. Desperation disguised as boldness.

Heather shifted in her seat. "Who is she? Marti?" Her voice cut sharp.

Marti didn't move. Didn't blink. Just felt the weight settle in her chest. "I brought her." The words sat thick in her throat. "One of the mothers. She wanted to pray for her son." Her fingers twitched against her thigh. "Wanted peace. Wanted to pray over his body."

Heather exhaled, jaw flexing as she stared at the woman standing motionless in the storm. "A mother's love doesn't know when to quit, huh?" The softness in her voice contradicted the tension in her shoulders.

Nat's back suddenly straightened, her head higher as she moved toward Franklin's front steps.

Heather's hands clamped tight on the steering wheel. "Oh no," she breathed. "No, no, no; what is she doing?"

Marti shoved the door open and hit pavement with a thud, pain needling up her leg as she sprinted forward. Slo-mo.

Nat knocked once, twice, on Franklin's door with calm, never looking back.

The knob turned, slowly like bad luck rolling in. Franklin squinted out into the dark, and Nat moved with speed, hand ripping out of her pocket as metal glinted under streetlights.

Marti's pulse slammed hard enough to crack bone.

Gunfire split the night. Franklin jerked back inside before toppling like a puppet with snapped strings. Nat followed him through with finality, three more shots ringing out before silence swallowed everything whole.

"Fuck." Marti pivoted and ran back to Heather's car: he was done, time to help herself. Heather was halfway out, gun raised and ready for a fight she hadn't planned for.

Marti caught her arm rising up, gunmetal meeting nothing but air as she yanked Heather against her. "Get in your damn car." Her voice sliced through the night, steady where the world wasn't. "Don't be first on scene."

Heather's face crumpled, features gone suddenly young with shock. "What? I can't just—"

"You aren't even supposed to be here. I can fuck with the tracker, but you can't be on scene when he dies." Marti tightened her grip, feeling Heather's pulse hammer against her fingers. "And you can't be seen leaving the scene. For fuck's sake, Heather." She pushed, punctuating her desperation. "Leave!"

Heather pushed back.

Marti pressed closer, her lips nearly brushing Heather's ear, voice dropping to something feral and urgent. "Five minutes. No less."

A beat.

"Go! He's beyond saving. Get lost."

"No, I—" Heather's fingers flexed around the gun, knuckles white.

"Franklin's dead." Marti had to shout as the downpour intensified, drumming against dumpsters and concrete.

"His people are already moving. You stay, and Nat dies in some filthy alley tonight instead of living long enough for a courtroom."

Heather's hesitation lasted three rapid heartbeats. Marti seized the moment and pushed, palm flat against the fabric of Heather's jacket.

"You aren't supposed to be here, and you can't bring her to justice by destroying your career!" She steered Heather backward toward the sedan.

"So I just leave her?" The crack in Heather's voice mirrored the lightning splitting the sky above them. "She just shot—"

"I'll keep her alive." Marti maneuvered her another step back, feeling resistance crumbling with each inch. "Long enough for you to arrive on scene to make sure she gets arrested and not murdered. Clean and proper."

Pain streamed down Heather's face like cold fingers tracing her jaw, but Marti didn't relent.

"I stay, keep her here, keep her breathing when the dirty cops show up thirsting for blood. But you?" She gave one final push, Heather's back now pressed against cold metal. "Your clean badge is the only shield she's got. Without it, they'll make her death look like a botched arrest, and the whole fucking mess dies with her."

Something flickered across Heather's face. Shock dissolving into grim understanding. She nodded once, sharp and decisive, then spun toward the driver's side.

The engine protested with a wet cough before roaring to life. Tires carved twin arcs through standing water as Heather disappeared down the block, taillights smearing crimson through the darkness like fresh wounds against the night.

Marti dug into her pocket for the FUCT tracker: the tiny blinking bastard that made sure they weren't alone out here tonight. She hurled it into a gaping storm drain with enough force to banish every damn mistake tied to it.

"The sewer brought it here. Plausible deniability," she muttered before turning back toward Franklin's house: the scene of something waiting just beyond an open door swaying on its hinges.

Inside stood Nat Lopez, gun slack at her side, knuckles white around it as if letting go wasn't an option.

Behind her lay Franklin, eyes vacant under ribbons of red pooling beneath his skull.

Marti stepped forward, hands up. "Nat," she said, voice low, steady. "Put the gun down. It's over."

Nat stood over Franklin's body, her breath jagged. Tears cut through the pain on her face as she looked at Marti.

"It is over," Nat murmured, audible beneath the storm. Her fingers flexed around the grip of the gun before loosening. "That bastard will never hurt anyone again." She inhaled. "This is the only justice that meant anything."

Marti swallowed hard. She could argue it wasn't justice, but what would be the point? Instead, she lifted her chin toward the door. "Come sit with me. Cops will be here soon."

She looked around quickly. No sign of Franklin's wife. Thank God for small mercies.

For a long moment, Nat didn't move. Then her whole body seemed to deflate. The gun dangled in her hand before she pocketed it and stepped away, heavy-footed, as if gravity had tripled just for her.

Outside, Nat sank onto the front porch steps, elbows on her knees, eyes fixed on some point beyond the night. Marti sat beside her, close enough for warmth but not touching.

"You know what happens now," Marti said after a beat, watching Nat's profile. "They'll arrest you." She paused. "You might never walk free again."

Nat nodded once: sharp, resigned. "I know." She exhaled. "But it was worth it." Her mouth twisted into something too bitter to be called a smile. "For César. For all of them. He won't get away with it."

Lights snapped on in kitchens and bedrooms, neighbors peeking out curtained windows. lighting up sin in thin dirty trails.

"I set things up before I did this," Nat continued. "Gave my sister access to my bank account so she can send me money inside. Wrote some letters. Wrote my will." A chuckle escaped her throat. "You learn a lot when your kid gets murdered: about how to survive after they take everything from you."

Marti listened in silence as Nat tipped her head back, tears sliding down her cheeks.

"When Severo died," Nat continued, voice thinning, "it was like someone carved out part of my soul and left me bleeding." Her fingers curled against her knee: a hard grip that turned knuckles white beneath rain-slicked skin. "And when I lost César..." She trailed off, staring into the darkness.

She turned, locking eyes with Marti for the first time since pulling the trigger. "If I let Franklin go to trial? Let him manipulate his way out of it? Walk free after taking my son and all those other boys?" Her jaw tightened until Marti could hear her teeth click together. "I couldn't risk it."

Marti nodded because what else was there to say?

A ghost of a smirk played at Nat's lips: gentle if there weren't so much devastation behind it.

"I'm okay," Nat murmured; not quite a lie, not quite the truth. "I had nothing left but revenge." She inhaled, a finality settling into each syllable. "Now? My future is clear. The state can deal with me."

Marti watched her for a long moment. "Justice isn't supposed to feel this empty, is it?"

Nat hummed low in response; not agreement or denial, but something impossible to name after everything they'd witnessed.

"My heart was dead," Nat whispered into the storm-dark air. "Can't kill what's gone."

Her eyes became unreachable.

Sirens howled in the distance, wolves scenting blood in the air. "Maybe now I'll find peace."

Nat's breath hitched, then evened out, as if she'd surfaced after drowning. She squeezed her eyes shut, exhaling. "Marti, it's okay. I can breathe again." She laughed. "I can fucking breathe again."

Marti watched her a beat, then nodded. She laid a hand on Nat's shoulder, steady, tender. "I'll stay with you until they get here." Her voice almost disappeared beneath the approaching sirens. "Then they'll separate us. It's going to be rough, but you'll be okay. You'll have a guardian angel."

The wail of cop cars swelled, pressing against her ribs like a warning. Lights flickered off siding: red and blue dancing in the night.

Doors cracked open just enough for faces to peer out: neighbors emboldened with the wail of police cars.

Marti leaned in close. "Nat, put the gun down beside you before they see it in your hand."

Understanding clicked into place behind Nat's eyes. She sucked in a breath and set the gun on the step beside her: slowly. Then she reached for Marti's hand and held on as if it was the only thing keeping her from slipping under.

Tires screamed against pavement as patrol cars skidded to a stop out front. Doors flew open; boots hit the ground hard and fast.

"Hands where we can see them!" The barked order cut through rain and sirens alike. "Put your fucking hands in the air!"

They obeyed: fingers splayed, movements careful as they rose to their feet.

"Down! Now! Motherfucking bitches!"

Marti lay flat against the cold concrete, cheek pressed to cold stone as calm pooled in her limbs. She turned her head just enough to meet Nat's gaze and mouthed it without sound: You'll be okay.

The cops moved in rough: knees on backs, hands yanking arms, metal cuffs biting skin. Marti registered the pain, focused instead on Nat's face as they dragged her toward a separate cruiser.

An ambulance wheeled around the corner, lights flooding the street. Paramedics rushed inside: boots pounding up wooden steps. But Marti had seen Franklin's eyes, blood, brains.

The fucker was dead.

Marti slid into the vinyl back seat as the rear door slammed shut around her.

Through the filthy window of her cruiser, Marti caught sight of another car approaching the scene. A familiar car. Heather's wide eyes locked onto hers for just a moment: a pledge passing between them before distance swallowed the connection.

As the police car pulled away, carrying Marti into uncertainty, the image of Heather's face burned in her mind. Some endings were just fucked-up beginnings wearing different clothes.

Chapter 42

The rain traced lazy patterns down the floor-to-ceiling windows of Lori's eighteenth-floor apartment. Falls City spread below like a watercolor left in the rain, all the hard edges bleeding into gray. She curled deeper into her oversized armchair, ceramic mug gone cold in her hands, Pride and Prejudice splayed open across her lap. Elizabeth Bennet was tearing Mr. Darcy a new one when Lori's phone buzzed against the glass coffee table.

Caldwell Property Management. Her stomach knew what was coming before her brain caught up.

"Lori Harring."

"Miss Harring? Bob Caldwell here. I manage the building where you work for Miss Starova?"

Where you work.

The error stung like antiseptic on a fresh cut. "I don't work there anymore, Mr. Caldwell."

"Oh. Well, shit. Sorry to bother you then. It's just… Miss Starova's two weeks behind on rent, and that new girl, Naomi? She's gone. Vanished. I thought maybe you'd—"

"How much?"

"Five thousand. Due tomorrow or I gotta start eviction."

Five thousand dollars. The exact amount Marti would blow on a three-day bender, chasing oblivion through Shadow inhalers and bottom-shelf whiskey. Lori's banking app was already open, her thumb hovering over the transfer button.

This is how it starts, she thought. This is how you slide back into her orbit.

But someone had to keep the lights on. Someone always had to clean up after Marti's spectacular messes. And who better than Lori, who'd catalogued every dealer's number, memorized every bar's closing time, learned to read the subtle shifts in Marti's posture that meant the difference between a bad night and a catastrophic one?

"You should have it now, Mr. Caldwell."

"You're an angel, Lori. Thanks."

Now, where the fuck was Marti?

The question triggered something – a flash of limestone walls, the smell of sage and her own sweat. Christ. The retreat.

Three days after quitting, her therapist had worn her down. "Just try it," she'd said, sliding the brochure across her desk like it was evidence in a case. "Sacred Mountain Meditation Retreat. My other clients have found it transformative."

Your other clients probably haven't had to dig glass out of a beautiful disaster's scalp at 4 AM.

But she'd gone. A plane, a train and then a rental car up mountain roads that made her calculate rollover velocities with every curve.

The yogi – Bramesh or Brahesh or some shit – had taken one look at her and known. That was the worst part. The knowing in his eyes as she'd stood there in her tactical pants, scanning exits while the other retreatants hugged and shared their "intentions."

"Welcome, Lori," he'd said. "You're safe here."

Like safety was something you could just declare. Like it wasn't earned through constant vigilance, through memorizing license plates and keeping your back to walls and knowing exactly how many seconds it took to get from any room to your car.

In the first meditation session, he had told them to close their eyes.

She had lasted thirty seconds.

The second session, he'd suggested she could keep them open, "just soften your gaze."

Her gaze didn't fucking soften. Her gaze was what kept people alive.

By day three, she'd mapped every sound in the cave. Water dripping at 4.7 second intervals. Someone's deviated septum whistling on inhales. The woman from Vancouver who cried during every session, soft little sobs she probably thought were spiritual but sounded like luxury to Lori.

Crying because you were "releasing trauma," not because someone had just put a knife to your throat.

The morning of day four, Bramesh had pulled her aside after sunrise yoga.

"Your body is very loud," he'd said gently. "It's trying to protect you from dangers that aren't here."

"You don't know what dangers are or aren't here," she'd snapped, then caught herself. Even her anger was tactical: controlled, measured, ready to escalate or de-escalate as needed.

He'd smiled like she'd proven his point. "This hypervigilance, it's served you, yes? Kept you alive?"

She'd said nothing.

"But here, now, in this moment, what if you could rest? Just for an hour?"

"People who rest end up dead." The words were out before she could stop them.

"Ah." He'd nodded like she'd given him a gift. "And people who never rest?"

That night, she'd lain on the thin mat in her cell-like room, listening to the mountain breathe around her. Every sound was wrong. Too quiet. Too safe. Her body screamed for sirens, breaking glass, Marti's voice cutting through 3 AM darkness with some new crisis.

She'd made it to noon on day five before inventing a work emergency.

"I understand," Bramesh had said as she loaded her rental car, hands shaking with relief at the weight of car keys, the promise of motion. "Sometimes healing looks like leaving."

She'd wanted to tell him to fuck off with his fortune cookie wisdom. Instead, she drove down the mountain at exactly the speed limit, windows down, drowning in exhaust fumes and purpose.

Now, staring at her phone, Lori touched the place on her wrist where Bramesh had placed two fingers during that final goodbye.

"Your pulse," he'd said. "Is still preparing for war."

Someone has to, she thought.

Chapter 43

Lori put the phone down and picked up her holo-tab, the translucent screen casting blue shadows across her face. Weeks of self-imposed exile. Weeks of chamomile tea and Victorian novels and pretending she didn't wake up at 3 AM wondering if Marti had finally pushed the wrong person too far.

Her fingers typed before her brain could stop them: "Martina Starova."

The headlines hit like a sucker punch:

FALLS CITY POLICE CHIEF SHOT DEAD

DISGRACED EX-COP ARRESTED AT MURDER SCENE

CHIEF SERIAL KILLER: 18 BODIES FOUND

"Jesus Christ, Marti."

She scrolled through article after article, the story assembling itself like crime scene photos spread across a desk. Marti and Natalie Lopez arrested at Chief Franklin's house. Nat putting bullets in Franklin's chest, convinced her son was there. Then the basement. Eighteen young men, their faces staring out from missing persons posters that had papered the city for years.

The same young men whose mothers had sat in Marti's office three weeks ago, clutching faded photographs and begging for help. The meeting where Marti had ordered that drink, that fucking drink, and Lori had knocked it back in frustration, not knowing it was spiked with Bright until the world went sideways and her heart tried to punch through her ribs.

Asshole.

Franklin was the Falls City Monster. The press was painting Nat as a vigilante hero. And Marti? Radio silence, which meant she was rotting in a cell while her life fell apart.

Good, Lori tried to tell herself. Let her rot. Not your problem anymore.

But her hands were already reaching for her car keys.

The office building looked like it had aged a decade in three weeks. Rain-streaked concrete, broken neon, the kind of place where hope went to die. Bob Caldwell met her in the lobby, his paunch straining against a shirt that had seen better presidents.

"Appreciate this, Miss Harring. Know it's not your circus anymore."

"Just need to assess the damage." She pocketed the spare key, already dreading what waited upstairs.

The elevator wheezed its way to the fifth floor, each ding marking another level of her descent back into Marti's chaos. When Caldwell unlocked suite 502, the smell hit first. Stale cigarettes, rotting coffee, and something else. Desperation, maybe. Or just the lingering ghost of too many bad decisions.

Her office—former office—looked like someone had performed an autopsy on it. Papers hemorrhaging from filing cabinets, coffee rings overlapping like Venn diagrams of neglect. But it was Marti's inner sanctum that made her chest tight.

Desk drawers yanked out like pulled teeth. Client files scattered across the floor, their secrets spilled for anyone to read. Empty bottles standing sentinel, their contents long since converted to liquid courage or liquid amnesia.

Movement outside caught her eye. Bertha, that mangy survivor, pressed against the fire escape window. The cat took one look at Lori and vanished into the labyrinth of rust and rain. Wrong human, wrong savior.

"Even the cat knows I'm not supposed to be here," Lori muttered, settling at her old desk.

The computer welcomed her like an old enabler. No password change. Of course not. Marti probably still used her birthday for her ATM pin too.

5,793 unread emails.

Lori cracked her knuckles and dove in, sorting chaos into categories with the efficiency of someone who'd learned that organization was armor against disorder. Interview requests from vultures masquerading as journalists. Love letters from prison groupies who found danger to be an aphrodisiac. Death threats from citizens who preferred their monsters to angels.

Then she found it. Sent from Marti's own account, a digital knife twisted between the ribs:

Marti,

Thanks for believing in me. Stupid, but thanks. By the time you read this, I'll be long gone. I took everything from the business accounts. I have to get the fuck out and find my husband. You know why.

Don't bother looking for me. You've got bigger problems.

-Naomi

P.S. Thanks for the freedom. Hope yours comes soon.

"Unbelievable." But wasn't it entirely believable? Marti collected broken people like stray cats, never learning that wounded things bite.

The last transaction was only $25,000. That's all that Naomi took, but it was everything. Lori found a transaction for $150,000 transferred to an anonymous account at 3:24 AM. What the fuck did Marti buy?

Lori kept sorting, fingers flying across the keyboard. Delete, forward, flag. Each click a small rebellion against entropy. This was what she did, what she'd always done. Imposed order on Marti's chaos, built levees against the flood of her self-destruction.

She needs you, her brain whispered. Who else knows which bartenders will cut her off and which will keep pouring? Who else can spot the telltale tremor that means she's forty-eight hours without Shadow?

By the time she finished, afternoon light slanted through the windows like an accusation. She'd deleted 4,384 messages, salvaged what mattered, created a roadmap back to functionality that Marti would probably ignore.

Time to find the idiot herself.

"Falls City Jail, how may I direct your call?"

"I need information about an inmate. Martina Starova."

"Still here. That's all I can confirm, ma'am."

Next call. "Agent Blair, please. It's Lori Harring."

Heather's voice came through tight as piano wire. "Lori. I was not expecting to hear from you. How are you?"

"When's Marti getting out?"

"I'm fine, thank you. Marti gets out tomorrow, noon. All charges dropped." A pause heavy with unspoken warnings. "You planning to pick her up?"

"Someone has to."

"Does someone, though?" Heather's laugh had edges. "Look, I can't... there are things I can't say. But Marti was at the center of the biggest clusterfuck this city's seen since the Water Riots. Some people think she's a hero. Others..."

"Others think she should have seen it coming. That she worked with Franklin for years and never noticed he was collecting boys like butterflies."

"I didn't say that."

"You didn't have to."

After Heather hung up, Lori sat in the gathering dusk, watching the city lights flicker on like neurons firing in a damaged brain. She found herself moving through the offices again, this time with purpose. Marti's car keys in the desk drawer, nestled between empty Shadow inhalers and sex toys that would make a dominatrix blush. Cleaning supplies exactly where she'd left them, patient as priests.

She cleaned because she couldn't not clean. Because leaving disorder felt like leaving an open wound. Each swept pile of debris, each organized file was a small "fuck you" to chaos. She wasn't coming back. That bridge was charred beyond recognition. But she could restore some dignity to the ruins.

This is what you do, she thought, scrubbing at a coffee stain shaped like a question mark. You clean up. You organize. You make the unbearable bearable.

The office gleamed by the time she finished, sterile as a morgue. Ready for Marti to stumble back in and destroy it all over again. The cycle eternal as rain in Falls City.

Morning came like a hangover: slow and inevitable. Lori stood in the jail parking lot, leaning against her car in the red dress Marti had once called "a cardiac event waiting to happen." The fabric clung in all the right places, which seemed important somehow. Like armor. Like a flag to a bull.

She checked her watch. Any second now, those institutional doors would vomit Marti back into the world. She would emerge blinking and disoriented, expecting Naomi, finding Lori. There'd be questions. Accusations maybe. That suspicious squint Marti got when people did nice things without apparent motive.

Why are you here? Marti would ask.

And Lori would lie. Say something about the rent, about basic human decency, about tying up loose ends. She wouldn't mention the dreams where Marti didn't make it out. Wouldn't admit that three weeks of safety had felt like suffocation. Wouldn't confess that somewhere between organizing files and scrubbing floors, she'd accepted a truth both terrible and necessary:

She wasn't built for safety anymore. The hypervigilance that once kept her alive had evolved, adapted, found its purpose in tracking Marti's chaos instead of avoiding it. She was a trauma specialist now, and Marti Starova was her patient, her purpose, her perfectly dysfunctional ecosystem.

Lori smoothed her dress and prepared to pretend this was just a ride home, nothing more. Just one recovered addict helping another, navigating the wreckage of Falls City's latest catastrophe.

She could quit again tomorrow.

She always could quit tomorrow.

Chapter 44

Marti was held for three weeks, until the idiots realized she had nothing to do with the shooting. All the neighborhood witnesses agreed: Marti showed up after the gunfire.

Three fucking weeks of concrete and steel had a way of grinding down moments into dust. That blood-soaked night when everything went to hell? Just another ghost in Marti's collection now.

The property clerk barely glanced up as he shoved the plastic bin across the counter. "Sign."

Marti scratched her name on the form without reading it. Three weeks inside, and this place had seeped into her fuckin' marrow: stale air, buzzing fluorescents, the slow rot of time. Only the bad jailhouse sex had kept her from losing what was left of her mind.

She clawed through the bin like a raccoon in a trash can. Phone first, probably dead, naturally. Wallet, keys, crumpled pack of cigarettes with one last soldier standing. She shoved everything into her jacket pocket and thumbed the power button on her phone.

Not dead.

The screen lit up. 5,793 unread emails.

Her teeth ground together. That number had Naomi stamped all over it. She could hear her now, all lazy amusement and faux innocence: *What, you expected me to answer them all?*

Marti muttered a curse and scrolled as she walked toward the exit, barely skimming subject lines. Legal notices. Late bills. A handful of names she'd tried to bury six feet deep. Somewhere in this catastrophe, something important was lurking, waiting to bite her on the ass.

The final set of doors swung open. Cold air slapped her face, traffic noise flooded her ears, and the stink of wet pavement and diesel fumes filled her lungs. But something else had her by the throat.

First came scent, subtle to start, teasing at the edges of recognition before slamming into her brain like a freight train: warm skin, expensive perfume with just enough sharpness to bite back. Then, sensation: fingers tingling like they wanted to grab something soft and unwise.

Her eyes followed instinct before reason caught up. Red heels first, then smooth legs leading up to that tight red dress clinging like a second skin. Heat snapped through her so violently she nearly swayed on her feet.

Shit. Shit.

"Uh…" The sound scraped from her throat, barely recognizable as language.

Lori Harring leaned against a sleek black car, arms crossed, eyebrow raised: the very picture of collected amusement while Marti stood there with her brain short-circuiting.

"Well," Lori said, shielding her eyes from the sun with one hand. Her lips curved into a knowing smile. "Look at that."

Marti blinked hard, forcing her thoughts into some semblance of order. "Not that it's not nice to see you…" Her fingers fumbled with the cigarette pack. "…but where the fuck is Naomi?"

Lori tilted her chin toward Marti's phone. "Maybe she sent an email. Maybe."

"I've got thousands of those fuckers." Marti lit her cigarette, the flame trembling before steadying.

She stepped closer, inhaling deep. She regretted it. Lori smelled like clean warmth and fresh linen-sweet skin, everything that wasn't three weeks of prison filth soaked into Marti's pores.

"Did you just sniff me?" Lori bit back a laugh that curled at the edge of her lips. "Like a dog?"

"If I was a dog," Marti said smoothly, "I'd have sniffed your ass." She took a slow drag instead of elaborating further.

Lori's smirk deepened. "Barely restrained."

"Why are you here? Are you picking me up?"

Lori tilted her head, considering Marti with that look that always meant trouble. "You really don't know?"

Marti squinted, rolling her hand in a "get on with it" gesture.

Lori reached out, brushing an errant strand of hair from Marti's face with unexpected gentleness. "Mr. Caldwell called me. Your landlord? He thought I still worked for you."

"And?"

"Said you missed rent."

"That's paid automatically," Marti muttered around her cigarette.

Lori's smile turned indulgent, the kind reserved for someone about to learn a painful lesson. "Yeah," she said slowly. "Naomi took everything."

The cigarette froze halfway to Marti's lips. Her eyes narrowed to slits.

"She sent an email to the general account. I read it," Lori added, leaning back against the car. "Cleaned you out completely, though there wasn't much there. Packed up, took off with her kids." She stretched lazily before delivering the final blow. "To Shanghai. With everything except Bertha. Gone to look for her husband."

Marti closed her eyes. Breathed in deep. Exhaled one long, muttered curse: "Fuck. The least she could have done was taken that fucking little monster. Fuck!"

"You trusted her with the goddamn bank passwords, didn't you?" Lori shoved Marti's shoulder firmly enough to make her point.

Marti took a slow drag and blew smoke into Lori's face. "No, I didn't."

Lori coughed, waving her hand through the cloud. "But you let her read the binder? The one I left for you?"

Marti's lips twitched despite herself. "Cosmic joke. Give it ten minutes, I'll probably get hit by lightning."

"Or arrested again," Lori said, laughing. She jerked her head toward the car. "Get in, loser."

The sky darkened as they pulled onto the road. Within minutes, rain battered the windshield, wipers slashing against the sudden downpour. Marti stretched out in the passenger seat, boots on the dash, cigarette dangling between two fingers like she owned the car. Which she did.

"How were your three and a half weeks in the slammer?" Lori asked, eyes fixed on the road ahead.

"Oh, you know: the usual." Marti flicked ash into the cupholder. "Shit food and even shittier sex."

Lori shot her a sideways glance. "You? Shitty sex?"

"Even shitty sex is still sex."

Lori's laugh filled the car. "You're impossible."

"At least those trespassing charges were dropped. No proof I went past the front door," Marti said, watching raindrops race down the window. "Now if I can get Heather Blair to just drop that bullshit drug charge, I'd be golden."

"Yeah, like that's happening."

Their laughter mingled with the drumming rain. Marti found her gaze drifting to Lori's hands on the steering wheel: steady grip, fingers tapping absently. Then further down, to where her dress stretched across her thighs. The car suddenly felt too warm. She coughed into her fist and stared out at the rain-slicked streets instead.

"I know you got more tangled up in this than the official record shows," Lori said. "What happened?"

Marti shook her head slowly. "Guess I just don't understand praying."

Chapter 45

By the time they reached Marti's office building, the downpour had intensified. They dashed from the car to the entrance, but those few seconds were enough to leave them both soaked.

"Shit," Lori muttered, shaking water from her hair as they stepped into the dimly lit hallway. "This dress wasn't made for swimming."

Marti tried not to notice how the wet fabric clung even tighter now. She failed.

Lori flicked on the office lights and switched to business mode. "Police searched Franklin's house," she said, wringing water from her hair. "Found eighteen bodies buried between the basement and backyard."

The words hit Marti like ice water. "Eighteen?" She exhaled sharply, her mind struggling to process the number. "Jesus fucking Christ. I only found seventeen."

That got Lori's attention and earned her a brief, mostly true explanation.

"Franklin's wife bolted straight into hiding, smartest thing she's ever done." Lori moved toward the desk, leaving wet footprints on the floor. "But get this: William Franklin's still on TV swearing his brother's innocent."

"How the hell is he even trying to spin that?" Marti peeled off her damp jacket, tossing it over a chair.

"No clue," Lori said flatly. "The mothers from the file, all of them except Ana, donated DNA samples. Police are matching remains now and notifying families." Her voice dropped. "And other families have been notified. They found ID cards."

"This is gonna get worse before it gets better." Marti rubbed her temples. "What about Colin Bonner?"

Lori frowned, running her fingers through her damp hair. "Who? That health inspector from the Thornfield case? What's he got to do with this?"

"Guess I forgot to mention him. He led me from Albert Alverez to Douglas Franklin," Marti said, moving closer to where Lori stood by the desk.

"I don't know if he's been publicly named yet." Lori tapped at her phone screen, searching. "What did he do, exactly?"

"Not sure. They arrest him?"

Lori scrolled, tapped and sighed.

"Found him. 'Colin Bonner, 42, a city health inspector for the past eight years, was found deceased in his locked downtown apartment Tuesday morning after failing to report to work. Police confirmed there are no suspects being sought in connection with his death and that the investigation has been closed.' That was from two weeks ago."

Lori looked at Marti. "No tie to Franklin as far as I can see."

Marti nodded. "It'll come. I'll make sure. Anything about Nat?"

"Nat's lawyer won't shut up, telling the press she was just a grieving mother avenging her son. Calls Franklin 'The Monster of Falls City.'"

"Bunch of fuckers," Marti muttered. She moved to the window, watching rain lash against the glass. "I used to get pissed off about dirty cops. Now I'll just assume they're all corrupt shitbags until proven otherwise." She'd had three weeks of nothing to do but think about it. About it all.

When she turned back, Lori was sitting at the desk, her old desk, golden hair catching what little light filtered through the blinds. Marti's pulse quickened.

"Well, would you look at that?" A crooked smile touched Marti's lips. "It's good to have you back."

"I'm not back," Lori said firmly.

"And yet here you are." Marti gestured toward the office like it proved something.

"I'm not staying." Lori shifted in her seat, crossing her legs. "And stop looking at me like that, perv."

Marti smirked and pushed past her into her private office. "Nice to have you back. I missed you."

"I said I'm not back."

The air inside Marti's office was thick with old whiskey and stale smoke. Same as always. Unhealthy? Sure. But it smelled like home. Stacks of unopened mail teetered on her desk like some depressing monument to irresponsibility. She slumped into her chair and poured herself a drink, watching amber light catch as her non-salvation gurgled into the glass.

Lori stood in the doorway, arms crossed, watching.

Marti struck a match and brought it to her cigarette. The flame illuminated her face for a brief moment before darkness reclaimed the corners of the room. She exhaled slowly, letting smoke curl upward in lazy spirals.

"I'm not working for you again," Lori said finally, her posture rigid despite the damp clothes clinging to her frame.

Marti let her gaze linger a moment too long before shrugging. "Good news: I've been robbed blind and can't pay you. Thanks for volunteering."

Lori rolled her eyes, but something else flickered across her face. A softening around the edges, there and gone in an instant.

"You look like shit," she said, stepping further into the room despite her protests.

"I feel like shit." Marti took another pull from her cigarette. "You look amazing. Figures."

"Do you even realize Naomi took every penny?" Lori's voice sharpened. "You're in debt to me and whoever else is coming for their cut."

"Whomever?" Marti echoed, swirling the whiskey in her glass.

"Whoever," Lori shot back without missing a beat.

"Lori."

"Marti."

Marti huffed out a laugh, low and bitter, and lifted her glass in mock salute before draining it in one go. The whiskey burned all the way down, a perfect fucking nightcap for the middle of the day. She coughed hard.

"Why the fuck are you still here?" she asked, pouring another finger.

"Why the fuck do you think you still have an office?" Lori dropped into the chair across from her, the wooden legs scraping against the floor. "I paid the damn rent, asshole. You owe me."

Marti snorted.

"I'm not coming back because I forgive you or because I'm a pushover." Lori's voice was steady, controlled. "I'm coming back because I choose to. With conditions."

Marti folded her arms on the desk and rested her head, every movement betraying exhaustion. "Conditions? That something you and your therapist worked out?"

"Maybe." Lori moved toward the window, the city spreading before her in rain-slicked neon. "Bailing you out puts me in control for once. I'm tired of being the one who gets hurt and runs away."

She pressed her palm against the glass, leaving a brief print that faded as quickly as it appeared. "My therapist has a term for what I do. 'Attraction to familiar dysfunction.' I keep choosing people who need fixing because that's what I learned growing up."

"Your old man." Marti shifted her head without raising it from the desk.

"My alcoholic detective father, yeah. Angry, destructive, impossible to please." Lori's reflection wavered in the window. "But sometimes he'd have good days, and I'd think maybe if I just tried harder, stayed loyal enough. My therapist calls it trauma bonding, forming attachments to people who hurt you."

"So you like a little bondage with your trauma?" Marti settled back in the chair with a grunt.

"Trauma bonding." Despite herself, Lori's mouth twitched.

"I know what I said."

"Jerk." But there was warmth in it now, familiar territory they could navigate.

The moment hung between them. Not forgiveness exactly, but something like recognition. Marti rolled whiskey in her glass, watching light fracture through amber. "I should probably be crying about the money. But I've been fucked over worse. I'm just unlucky with secretaries."

"Secretaries?" Lori turned from the window. "You are one of luckiest unlucky bastards on the face of the earth."

Lori studied her for a long moment, that penetrating look that always made Marti feel too exposed. Finally, she sighed and tapped her fingernails against the desk. "Tell me you at least have a case."

"Probably in those five thousand bajillion emails." Marti blew smoke toward the ceiling where it gathered like storm clouds.

Rain rattled against the windows. A siren wailed in the distance, swallowed by the city's endless noise. The office clock ticked steadily, marking seconds neither of them was counting.

Lori yanked Marti's laptop toward her and muttered, "Fine. I'll deal with your goddamn emails. And all this paper mail. Who sends paper mail? I'll figure out who else you owe and how you're planning to pay them."

Marti couldn't help the smirk that spread across her face. No case. No plan. Not even enough cash for a new drug.

But she had leftover whiskey. A partial pack of smokes. Fentafill in the medical cabinet at work. And maybe she had Lori.

She leaned back in her chair, letting her eyes make their way slowly up Lori's body.

"The fuck are you staring at?" Lori asked without looking up.

"My new secretary," Marti said, tapping ash into an empty coffee cup. "I hope."

Lori snorted, shoved the laptop back across the desk, and turned her back toward Marti.

Beautiful.

"New secretary. We'll see," she said before disappearing into the outer office, her office again, apparently.

The door didn't quite close behind her.

Marti exhaled slowly, watching smoke twist and fade like ghosts. The city had a way of twisting quiet moments into something darker if you let it, if you weren't careful enough to hold on when things were still unsteady under your feet.

Through the partially open door, she could hear Lori at work: papers shuffling, drawers opening and closing, soft muttering that sounded like curses directed at Marti's filing system.

Lori might be back, but that didn't mean shit was safe now. Marti could see it in her, a sharp edge underneath that no-nonsense tone, fire in her eyes like she'd decided to play along even knowing how bad it could get.

Marti looked at the listening device still perched outside her window, at the dissonance enhancer Naomi had purchased, at the possibility that someone, maybe Heather, maybe not, was out to get her.

The question wasn't whether Lori could handle the mess; she could handle damn near anything. But whether Marti was ready to pull her back into it all over again.

She knocked back another drink, let it sear away anything soft still clinging to her thoughts. Tomorrow would be another wreck waiting to happen.

But maybe this time she wouldn't have to wade through it alone.

More Marti Starova

Catch up on the complete Marti Starova series:
Drowning in Broad Daylight (available now)
Shadow Work (available now)
Rain-Soaked (available now)
Almost (available now)
New to the series? Start from the beginning!

Looking for more Marti? Try ***Beyond the Scent of Sugar: A Memoir by Billie River***

www.ingramcontent.com/pod-product-compliance
Lightning Source LLC
LaVergne TN
LVHW040035080526
838202LV00045B/3354